L. MARIE ADELINE

S·E·C·R·E·T
SHARED

❧

a
S·E·C·R·E·T
novel

B\D\W\Y
BROADWAY BOOKS   NEW YORK

Published in the United States by Broadway Books,
an imprint of the Crown Publishing Group,
a division of Random House LLC,
. a Penguin Random House Company, New York.
www.crownpublishing.com

Broadway Books and its logo, B\D\W\Y,
are trademarks of Random House LLC.

Simultaneously published in Canada by Doubleday Canada,
a division of Random House of Canada Limited, Toronto.

Library of Congress Cataloging-in-Publication Data
Adeline, L. Marie.
S.E.C.R.E.T. shared : a S.E.C.R.E.T. novel / L. Marie Adeline.—First edition.
pages cm
I. Women—Fiction. 2. Secret societies—Fiction. I. Title. II. Title: Secret shared.
PR9199.4.A34S37 2013
813'.6   2013026488

ISBN 978-0-8041-3686-0
eISBN 978-0-8041-3687-7

Printed in the United States of America

Book design by CS Richardson
Cover photograph: © stphillips

I0 9 8 7 6 5 4 3 2 I

First Edition

To Cathie James, for your wise words, always . . .

TEN STEPS

Step One: Surrender

Step Two: Courage

Step Three: Trust

Step Four: Generosity

Step Five: Fearlessness

Step Six: Confidence

Step Seven: Curiosity

Step Eight: Bravery

Step Nine: Exuberance

Step Ten: Liberation

DAUPHINE

I laughed. What else was there to do? This was really happening. He was really here. And it seemed like the most natural request in the world, for a handsome man to be standing knee-deep in the warm Abita River, summoning me to get naked for him. The rolled-up cuffs of his jeans were darkened by the water lapping at his muscled calves, his lean torso naked in the hot sun.

He extended a tanned forearm to me.

"Dauphine, will you accept the Step?"

Instead of giving him an immediate yes and splashing towards him like I wanted to, I froze on the grassy bank in my vintage green sundress, which I had shortened to just above my knees. And now I was regretting it. It was sexy, not like something I'd usually wear. *Do I look terrible in this? What if he isn't attracted to me? What if we get caught? What if I'm no good at this? What if I drown? I am not a good swimmer. In fact, I've always been afraid of water.* We were well hidden behind the swamp roses and pink mallow that sloped towards the riverbank, yet fear surrounded me. *Control and trust, trust and control. My two competing demons.* Why now? Hadn't I put myself through school? Started a successful vintage clothing business, even before graduating college? Hadn't I made it through recessions and hurricanes, pulling my little store behind me with the ferocity of a war hero rescuing a wounded comrade? I had done all those things—and more—but they required discipline and control and a steady hand on the rudder.

Accepting this compelling stranger's invitation to join him in the rushing water meant inviting my life's current to change directions. It meant allowing myself to enter a new world, one filled with spontaneity and risk, desire and possibly disappointment. It meant giving up control, learning to trust. Still, for all my bravado that day at the Coach House, I was suddenly unwilling to let things unfold as I had been told they would, as I had sworn to myself I'd finally allow.

But goddamn, this man was fine—and much taller than me. Then again, at five foot three, I was shorter than most men. He had smiling eyes, a rakish build, with messy, brown hair that the sun had coated with a copper sheen. I couldn't tell if his eyes were green or blue, but he didn't take them off me. The sun grew hotter on us, making my own hair feel like a long, heavy veil. I slowly slipped off my sandals. The grass felt cool on my feet. Maybe I could wade in. Start slow.

"Will you accept the Step? I can ask only one more time," he said, without a note of impatience.

Now. Go to him. You must. I felt my hands drift up to my shoulders, following the lines of the halter on my dress. My fingers paused at the knot behind my neck. Then my hands worked of their own accord and the straps suddenly fell limp. I peeled down my top and bared my breasts to him. I quickly averted my gaze. I had to move fast before my mind caught up to my terror. *What if my body disappointed? What if I wasn't his type? Stop thinking. Act.* I unzipped the back of the dress and let it drop to the grass. Then I rolled my panties down my legs, and straightened again, standing naked save for the gold chain circling my left wrist.

"I'll take that as a 'yes,'" he said. "Get in, beautiful. The water's warm."

My heart started pounding. As calmly as possible, I made my way towards him, towards the water. As I moved, I strategically covered myself. I dipped a toe into the edge of the river. It was warmer than I had expected. I placed the rest of my foot into the gentle current, then navigated the path of flat, moss-covered rocks leading to him. And I could see the bottom. I'd be fine.

As I stepped closer, our height difference became nearly hilarious enough to change the mood from sexy to funny; he must have been six-four! But before I burst out laughing, before I even reached him, his hands moved to the button of his jeans, causing me to stop and go quiet. *Do I watch him? Do I not watch him?* My Southern upbringing made me turn around to hide how red I knew I was becoming. I fixed my eyes on a distant oak shading the plantation beyond.

"You don't need to turn away."

"I'm nervous."

"Dauphine, you're safe. It's just us."

My back still to him, I heard a slight splashing and the sound of cloth against skin. Then he tossed his jeans over my head, where they landed on the riverbank next to his well-worn boots, my sandals and my green dress.

"There. Now I'm naked too," he said. I heard him moving slowly through the water towards me, until his warm skin pressed hard against my back.

I could feel his chin resting on the top of my head, then his face nuzzling my hair and down the side of my neck. *Jesus.* I closed my eyes, took a deep breath and tilted my head to give him my neck and the skin there. I could feel how much he wanted this, and me. My senses were electrified. My skin, warmed by the water, cooled by the air, soothed by his touch, came tingling alive. The wind carried the smells of the South— cut grass, the river, magnolias. *I want this. I want this. I want him! What's the hesitation? Why can't I just turn around and face him? This man is here solely to please me. My only obstacle is my inability to let him.*

Then, as he placed his hands on my hips, I heard that inner voice again, loud, insistent, with my mother's Tennessee timber. *He thinks you're too flabby. Too curvy. Too short. He probably doesn't like redheads.*

I squeezed my eyes shut against the voice. Then I heard a low groan, the kind I recognized as deep male approval. *Okay, he likes what he's touching.* He placed his mouth by my ear, his hands tugging my hips backwards, pulling both of us into a deeper current.

"Your skin is incredible," he murmured, as he walked me farther backwards until I was waist-deep with him. "Like alabaster."

He's lying. They told him to say this. I begged my own critical voice to get lost.

"Turn around, Dauphine. I want to look at you."

My arms slowly fell to my sides, my fingers touching the water. I opened my eyes and turned around to face the expanse of his chest and the unmistakable evidence of his desire for me. *This is happening! Let it!* I tilted my head back to look up at his calm, handsome face. Then *whoosh!* He scooped me right off my feet, so swiftly and deftly that I screamed out of joy, even as my stomach fluttered. By the time I secured an arm around his muscled neck, he was cradling me in the sparkling river, teasing, slowly dipping me in.

"It's cold!" I gasped, clutching him harder.

"You'll soon warm up," he whispered, lowering me all the way into the water. His arms beneath me, I let my body give in to him and to the river. I stretched out, floating, dipping my head back, letting my hair drift inch by inch into the river. *Okay here we go . . .*

"That's right, just relax into it. I've got you."

I felt marvelously buoyant. The water wasn't scary at all. I closed my eyes and let my hair spiral out, and for the first time in a long time I knew a real smile was spreading across my face.

"Look at you, Ophelia," he said.

With one arm holding me up in the middle of my back, he moved the other arm out from beneath me and traced a firm hand up my leg, past my thigh, pausing at the crest, then moving to my stomach where he stooped to kiss the water in the pool my belly button created.

"That tickles." My eyes were still closed. *You're weightless and divine. You're body is beautiful, Dauphine.*

"Does this?" he whispered, letting his hand travel across my curves, cupping a hand beneath me, his fingers exploring my cleft. *Oh god.*

"A little," I said. My body opened like a starfish, my waving arms keeping me afloat. I loved what the water was doing to me. The chill firmed my skin. My nipples were ripe and hard. I opened my eyes and found his face, and I could see desire there. I watched him stoop to kiss my breasts while his hand below nudged my thighs open.

"How about this?" he asked, slowly sliding one, then two fingers inside me.

"Nope," I gasped, "that doesn't tickle." I felt pulses of hot pleasure course through me. *This could happen so fast,* I thought as his firm fingers warmed my insides. I clenched around him, as he gently teased my opening with this fingers, tentative at first, and then more insistent, deeper. I felt the water ripple across my skin—a combination that quickened my breath. Right then and there, I wanted to come, I could have . . . but I pushed it back to savor the floating feeling. I arched slightly to urge his fingers deeper still, my hair fully submerged so that it spooled around my head. I imagined it looking like a fiery corona.

"You're something to behold, Dauphine," he murmured, the fingers of one hand gently moving in and out, his other hand keeping me afloat. Then he expertly maneuvered my floating body a quarter-turn, positioning himself between my legs. But before I could wrap around him to pull him into me, he bent down, his mouth meeting the water trickling over the inside of my thighs, now glistening in the sun, his other hand still beneath me. The heat of his lips married with the rushing water and his urgent fingers created a feeling so intense I slapped at the current to gain purchase. Then he slung my knees, one, then the other, over his shoulders, his strong arms underneath me, supporting my back, keeping me afloat. Both hands now beneath me, he brought his tongue to my soft groove, where my thigh curved into my short, red curls, and I watched as he nuzzled, the water like a million fingers across my body. For a second, I couldn't tell the difference between the river lapping at my skin and his eager mouth, until his tongue, warm and insistent, found my perfect place, isolating it with a few talented strokes of his fingers. *Ahh* . . . I lifted my pelvis, my thighs opening wider, instinctively, hungrily, keeping my face above the gentle flow, my ears below the water. The rush of the current intensified the build as he drew circles on me, around and around, thrusting a finger in and out and . . . *oh god.* I felt his other hand, his wide palm spread across the middle of my back while his mouth and fingers did their dance. Then he reached up to tease my nipples. His mouth was liquid and warm, his tongue fluttering, lapping at me, drinking the whole of me in. I think he felt it before I did, the tension seizing my body, my knees clenching, my arms extending out at my sides, palms to the sun. *Yes . . .*

The first wave was warm and familiar. *Ah this,* I thought, *I remember this.* Then it intensified to something more, something deeper, with an urgency that made me cry out loud into the vivid sky. His fingers explored me deeper as his tongue traced faster and faster circles, and I was laughing when it happened, when I finally came, once, twice, in wave after wave of pleasure. I writhed, the backs of my knees clasping his shoulders, and we were, for a moment, one body. Then, after this blissful, floating moment, my breasts heaving in the sun, my own fingers on my cool skin, I came back to myself.

"So, so good," he whispered. He moved me gently on the surface of the water like a paper boat, as I subsided.

"But . . . it's not over, is it?" I asked, my thighs quivering, my legs now straddling his waist.

Nearer to the shore, I slid my legs off him, my feet finding stones to stabilize me in the shallower part of the river. I stood waist-deep as the water fell down my breasts in rivulets, my nipples still hard. I pushed the hair off my face, feeling dizzy, exhausted, satisfied.

"This is as far as I get to take you on this step, Dauphine. I don't want to, but I have to give you back."

He walked towards the pebbly beach where we had entered the river. Near our clothes was a pile of bright white towels. He released my hand and climbed the bank, the water shining off his back. Then he turned to pull me onto the grass. I shivered as he plucked a towel from the pile and swaddled me, pressing me to him, squeezing warmth back into my body, rubbing my arms hard.

"I feel so . . . I don't know what to say."

"You don't have to say anything. The pleasure was all mine." He turned to dry himself off.

I pulled the towel tightly around me, watching as he tugged his jeans over his muscled thighs and pulled on a crisp white T-shirt, which clung to his damp torso. He stepped towards me again, this time placing his big hands on either side of my face, pulling me into a lingering kiss.

When he pulled away, he said, "I mean it. The pleasure was mine, Dauphine."

After planting a final kiss in the middle of my forehead, he walked backwards for a few steps. Then he turned to head towards the plantation, finally disappearing around an ivy-covered corner.

I wanted to scream a thank you for leaving me so beautifully shipwrecked. But the words were still underwater with parts of the old me, the parts that were afraid of surrendering, of wanting this, of simply receiving pleasure and trusting it was possible. Instead, I laughed out loud again, this time thinking, *I did it. Something happened and I let it!*

I turned to my dress and pulled it up over my damp, quivering legs. Smoothing it down over my hips, I felt something in my pocket and took it out. A small purple box. Inside, nestled in a cotton cloud, was a gold charm, pale and rough-edged. I picked it up. It had a Roman numeral on one side—*I*— and the word *Surrender* engraved on the other side. My heart leapt as I took the charm out of its nest, squeezing it tight in my palm. It felt like a warm, flat stone. It was mine. I secured it to my chain, the one I'd been wearing for three weeks.

I made my way slowly up the sloping hill towards the waiting car. As I passed a high stone wall covered with bougainvillea, I caressed the tiny pink petals. *You did it. You gave up control. Now it's time to take the rest of the Steps, however tentative, towards your new life—and away from those voices, away from that heartbreak, away from your sad past.*

CASSIE

Three thoughts occurred to me that morning while stretching awake across my bed in Marigny.

One, it had been six weeks since that incredible night with Will.

Two, I had fallen asleep with my S.E.C.R.E.T. bracelet on again, which hadn't been a problem when it had only one or two charms on it. But there were ten now, so the gold pressed into the tender flesh of my wrists, leaving marks.

And three, it was my birthday. My cat, Dixie, blinked at me from the foot of the bed. I reached down and pulled her into an embrace, where she purred herself back to sleep, a skill I wish I had.

"I am thirty-six years old today, Dixie," I said, scratching her ears.

Another year had snuck up on me like a bratty prankster. I hadn't been paying attention to time passing until after my night with Will. Time had begun to slow. Some days ached past, work at the Café Rose being both a major comfort and the salt in the very wound I needed to heal. How could I get over Will when I saw him every day? How could I continue acting like nothing had happened between us the night I'd danced in Les Filles de Frenchmen Revue and we'd kissed our way back to the Café, up the stairs to that dusty room, where he tore off my burlesque outfit and tossed me backwards on a mattress lit by moonlight? Though he didn't know it, I had chosen him that night as my final fantasy. He knew only how badly I wanted him.

For me the lines between fact and fantasy had dissolved and he became real to me. His skin felt like home. We kissed like we'd been doing it for decades. We fit, our bodies perfectly molded for the things we did to each other naturally, wordlessly. It was beyond fantasy. And to think that all this time he had been right under my nose and I hadn't seen him, couldn't see him. But after a year of S.E.C.R.E.T., after a year of pushing myself past self-imposed boundaries, I had unleashed something very real inside of myself. And when Will told me he and Tracina had broken up, I felt the universe finally aligning in my favor. The morning after our magical night, I thought Will was my reward for coming back to life.

I was wrong.

More than any other memory from that night, it's Tracina's face that haunts me—ashen yet hopeful, her steady voice delivering the kind of hard facts that kill fantasies. She told me she was pregnant with Will's baby, and that he was thrilled when he found out.

What do you do with that very real information just when you think you've found the love of your life? You feel the final bubble burst around your fantasy and you walk away. That's what I did. All the way across the city to the Coach House, where Matilda dried my tears. There she reminded me that embedded in every fantasy is reality.

"People love the fantasy," she said. "But they ignore the facts to their detriment. And there's a price to pay when you do that. Always."

Fact number one: Will and I were finally together.

Fact number two: I was quite possibly in love with him.

Fact number three: His ex-girlfriend was pregnant.

Fact number four: When she told him, they got back together.

Fact number five: Will and I cannot be together.

Because Will was my boss, I had planned to quit my job right away, but Matilda urged me never to let heartbreak get in the way of very practical concerns, like work, paying rent, being responsible and fulfilling obligations.

"Don't give men that much power, Cassie. Get on with the task of living. You've had a lot of practice this past year."

I was such a tear-stained mess that morning. I wasn't certain whether joining S.E.C.R.E.T. was the right decision. But at least I was making *a* decision. That was new for me. Prior to S.E.C.R.E.T., I always went with the most powerful force governing my life at any given time, usually my late husband Scott's. He had brought us to New Orleans almost eight years ago, but his drinking erased any notion that we'd made a fresh start. We were separated when he died in a car wreck; he was sober at the time, but still a broken man. I was broken as well. And for five years after, I worked hard and slept fitfully, falling into a pattern of isolation and self-pity, until one day I found a diary detailing one woman's journey through a mysterious set of steps that seemed to have a lot to do with sex—a journey that was transformative, to say the least.

Then I met Matilda Greene, the woman who became my Guide. She said she had come to the Café Rose for the diary her friend had dropped, but really she came for me, to introduce me to S.E.C.R.E.T., an underground group dedicated to helping women liberate themselves sexually, by granting them sexual fantasies of their choice. Joining the group, letting these women arrange fantasies for me, and finding the courage to go through with them, she said, would pull me out of my malaise. She told me she'd help me, guide me and support me. Finally, after a week of turning the idea over in my head, I said yes. It was a reluctant yes, but it was a yes nonetheless. After which my life changed completely.

Over the course of a year, I had done fantastical things with unbelievably attractive men, things I would never have thought possible. I let a gorgeous masseur pleasure me without asking for a thing in return. I met a sexy British man in a dark bar who secretly brought me to orgasm in the middle of a boisterous jazz show. I was taken by surprise, in many ways, by a tattooed bad-boy chef, who stole a bit of my heart while ravaging me on a prep table in the Café's kitchen. I learned to give the most mind-blowing orgasm to a famous hip hop artist, who enthusiastically returned the favor, the memory of which still makes me tingle when I hear his songs on the radio. I took a helicopter to a yacht, then went overboard in a storm with the most handsome man I had ever laid eyes on. Not only did he rescue me, but his whole (incredible) body restored my faith in mine. Then the Bayou Billionaire himself, Pierre Castille, took me in the back of a limousine, after making me feel like the most beautiful girl at the ball. I skied the risky black diamond runs with Theo, the adorable Frenchman who pushed my sexual limits further than anyone had before. Then I went into sensory overload with a man I could only feel, not see, during a night that was blindingly sexy in more ways than one.

Then came my final fantasy, when I chose my beloved Will. I chose Will over S.E.C.R.E.T. and couldn't have had a happier night, or a more glorious morning after.

Now, six weeks later, there was no Will waking me up on my birthday with a thousand kisses. Instead, he was probably sleeping soundly next to Tracina, maybe even spooning her, his arms wrapped around her growing belly. She was just shy of three months pregnant, but yesterday afternoon she suddenly began lumbering around the Café like she was about to give birth at any moment. She kept one hand in the middle of her back while pouring refills, groaning and stretching between serving tables. She hadn't cut down on her shifts yet; she wasn't at the point of asking for help.

Still, I wasn't the only one rolling my eyes at her exaggerated discomfort. Dell wiped down tables while I refilled the salt and pepper shakers. When Tracina made a show of bending down to pick up a dishrag, Dell let out a long, slow whistle.

"That girl's making an Academy Award–winning performance out of a regular baby growing in her. I had overdue twins and it wasn't such a burden."

We watched Tracina meander from the kitchen to her customers to the cash register, making everyone around her look like they were in fast-forward. She even made Dell—at age sixty—look spry. During a lull, she lumbered over to where Dell and I were clearing a large table. Her belly barely protruded through her tight T-shirt.

"Oh, let me help, Dell," Tracina said, waving her away from a tray of half-filled ketchup bottles. "My legs are sore. You take the next tables. I don't mind losing the tips. I just don't want to push things while I can still work. 'Cause soon I'll be all 'feet up watching TV,' right?"

"Why *thank* you, Tracina," Dell said, hoisting herself off the chair. "Nothing like the pregnant one giving the old one more to do."

"I'm just saying . . ." Tracina began, but Dell threw up a hand and followed the bell to the kitchen to fetch ready plates.

After the lunch rush, almost on cue, the hammering began. Will needed to make more money from the Café and the only way to do that was to expand to fine dining upstairs.

After finally securing the proper permits and a business improvement loan, Will had started renovating. And now, with the baby on the way, the work was more urgent. The loan covered materials, but not much extra labor, so Will was doing the renovations himself, one wall, one window, one beam at a time.

In those six weeks since Will and I had been together, I had done everything in my power to avoid small talk with Tracina, because it felt littered with landmines of truth. So I avoided Will and work topics as best I could, switching to Dell, or the baby, or gossip on the street. I still couldn't tell how much she knew about what had happened that night between Will and me. Everyone at the Blue Nile saw us leave together, and half of Frenchmen Street saw us kiss, so she knew something had occurred. And even though she hadn't participated in the burlesque show on account of the pregnancy, she had hung out afterwards with Angela and Kit, both of whom were S.E.C.R.E.T. members, and both of whom danced in the Revue. Now, sitting side by side at the big round table, we gave each other matching high-eyebrowed, tight-lipped smiles.

"So, uh, things are good then? With the baby and everything? You seem good," I said, nodding like an idiot.

"Yeah, I'm, like, sooo good. Amaaaazing really. Doctor says the baby's suuuuper healthy, though Will and I both agreed we don't want to know the sex. But I swear I'm carrying a boy. Probably a linebacker. Will wants a little girl," she cooed, her hand circling her belly.

The sound of Will's band saw coming from upstairs caused her to jump, nearly sending her off her chair. I grabbed her arm to steady her.

"Oh my god! Has he been upstairs all morning?" she asked, trying to hide the real question buried beneath. *Have you been alone with him today?* Since reconciling over the baby, Tracina had moved back in with Will, so I assumed she knew where he was all day.

"I have no idea," I said, lying. I had seen him that morning. We had said our awkward hellos to each other when he walked by me in the dining room and bounded up the stairs, wearing his stiff leather construction belt, shiny new tools hanging off it.

"He brought some big spools of wire upstairs yesterday. But at least he's saving the loud work until the breakfast and lunch crowds die down."

Tracina slapped her hand on the table to brace herself, then, without another word, headed up the stairs.

If avoiding small talk with Tracina was a hobby, avoiding alone time with Will was becoming an art form. The last few words he'd spoken to me in six weeks, or the last few words I'd given him the opportunity to speak to me, were "We need to talk, Cassie." It was a harsh whisper delivered in the corridor between his office and the staff washroom.

"There's nothing to say," I replied. Our eyes darted around, making sure Dell and Tracina weren't nearby.

"You realize that right now, I can't—"

"I realize more than you know, Will," I said. We heard the trill of Tracina's voice as she cashed out a customer.

"I'm sorry." He couldn't even look me in the eye as he said it, and the agonizing moment made it all the more clear that I couldn't stay.

"Maybe we shouldn't work together, Will. Actually, it's probably best if I quit."

"NO!" he said, a little too loudly, then, more quietly, "No. Don't quit. Please. I need you. I mean, as an employee. Dell is . . . mature, and Tracina's not going to be much help soon. If you leave, I'm sunk. Please."

He clasped his hands into a fist beneath his chin, begging me. How could I leave this man in a bind, when his hiring me so many years ago had plucked me out of mine?

"Okay, but there have to be boundaries. We can't be whispering in the halls like this," I said.

Hands on hips, he waited a beat to contemplate the condition, then nodded at his shoes. The chemicals were still coursing through my system, ones awakened by the sex we'd had. We needed rules until they subsided.

Maybe Will wasn't happy about the baby at first, maybe it had come as a complete surprise and he was as gutted about our truncated relationship as I was, but over the past six weeks, you'd never have known it. I watched him go from pinched attentiveness towards Tracina to textbook superpartner, never missing a doctor's appointment, reading the books that only pregnant women seemed to dogear, and helping Tracina in and out of his truck, though she still hardly showed. This seemed to bring out a new sweetness in Tracina as well, even if it was in service of making her life easier and the lives of others a little harder.

Just before the end of my shift, I made a last-minute assist, helping Dell deliver food for a party of six. I was already cashed out, refilling my condiments and wiping down the counters. I had plans to go for a run and to have an early night, when Tracina came bounding back down the stairs, rubbing her neck. She did look pale, so when she told us she was leaving early, Dell wasn't surprised.

"I'm just so sick. I feel like I'm going to throw up. Will told me to go home. Sorry, guys. It's going to be like this for a little bit, I guess. Second trimester is supposed to get easier."

There was no way Dell could handle dinner on her own. I pretended to stifle my exasperation, but truth be told I wanted to stay. I needed the money and I had nothing better to do. Plus, there was that awful, painful, marvelous chance I'd accidentally be alone with Will, something I longed for despite all my genuine attempts to avoid it. And sure enough, an hour later, after business died down and a few minutes into the post-dinner hammering, his plaintive voice called from upstairs.

"Can someone come up here, please? I need a hand. Cassie? You there?"

Instead of heading up, I waited for Dell to garnish the final platters for our last customers.

"Please! It won't take long!"

"Are you hearing that man? Or is it just me hearing that man?" Dell muttered, handing me the hot turkey specials.

"I hear him."

"Good, 'cause he's not talking to me."

"I'm coming!" I yelled over my shoulder, thinking to myself, *No pun intended.* I'd preserved an internal sense of humor even while nursing my wounds.

I dropped off the plates and headed towards the stairs. I had a flashback to the fake tumble Kit DeMarco had taken on the floor, the one that secured my spot next to Angela Rejean in the burlesque show six weeks earlier. I had had no idea they belonged to S.E.C.R.E.T. too. As I stood now looking up the stairs, more flashbacks played out in my mind's eye: Will's face contorted in ecstasy above me, the light from the street illuminating his features. *I've wanted this since the day we met,* he whispered, while I lay beneath him. *I wanted you too, Will. I just didn't know how much.*

When does this stop? When do memories quit hurting so much?

If he were to say, *We need to talk, Cassie,* one more time, I would say, *No, we don't, Will.* I would add, *I told you we should not be alone,* and I would say this while lifting my shirt over my head, tossing it into the corner along with all the unwanted memories stored in that room up there. Will would say, *You're right, Cassie, we shouldn't be alone.* Stepping towards him, I would place my hand on his bare chest, letting him reach behind me and undo my bra. *This is such a bad idea,* I would say, pressing my skin to his, kissing his mouth, pushing him back until the window ledge stopped us. There, with his thighs straddling mine, his hands on my body, unsure where to touch first, his fingers finally traveling up to entwine my hair, his hands pulling my head back, opening my neck to his hungry mouth, I'd say, *See? We don't need to talk. We need this. We need to make each other moan and sweat. We need to fuck each other again, well, and often. And then, I need to decide what I'm going to do, because I can't be alone with you, because look what we're doing to each other, because everything pointed to me and you and now there is no me and you.*

And then the words would stop and we'd be just hands and mouths and breath and skin . . . and awful consequences.

As I took the steps up to the second floor, that delicious, piercing pain went through me again, the one that caused me to throb in places that had once been dormant but now came awake every time I was near him. At the top of the stairs, I stepped around a sawhorse and over an empty roll of cables. The hallway was lined with the detritus of recent renovations—empty pails of plaster, stray nails, remnants of two-by-fours. Behind a roughed-out wall where the new bathrooms extended, Will stood atop a stepladder, framed against the exposed brick between two windows. He was shirtless and covered in white dust. There was no furniture in the room, no evidence of the night a dozen giggly women got ready for an amateur burlesque show—no chair, no storm-tossed bed. He was holding the end of an iron curtain rod with one hand, a screw gun with the other, his T-shirt tucked into his belt.

"Thanks for coming up here. Can you eyeball this for me, Cass?"

Cass. When had he ever called me that? It made me sound like a pal.

"How's this?" he asked, balancing the rod.

"A little higher."

He jerked the rod a few inches too high.

"Nope, lower . . . lower."

He had it nearly perfectly positioned, and then he brattily dropped the rod way below the window line, at an awkward angle.

"How's this? Is this good?" he asked, throwing a goofy smile over his shoulder at me.

"I don't have time for this. I have customers."

He brought the rod even. When I gave him the go ahead, he quickly drilled a screw to hold it in place and stomped down the ladder.

"Okay. Are you going to stay mad at me forever?" he asked, stepping towards me. "I'm just trying to do the right thing, Cassie. But I'm at a loss when it comes to you."

"*You're* at a loss?" I hissed. "Let's talk about loss, shall we? You lost nothing. Me? I lost everything."

Matilda would have slapped my mouth shut. *Have you learned nothing?* she'd have said. *Why do you paint yourself as the loser?*

"You didn't *lose* anything," Will whispered. His eyes met mine, and my heart stopped beating for three whole seconds. *I picked you and you picked me.* "I am still here. We are still *us*."

"There is no *us*, Will."

"Cassie, we were friends for years. I miss that so much."

"Me too, but . . . I'm just your employee now. That's how it's got to be. I will come to work and I will do my job and I will go home," I said, avoiding his eyes. "I can't be your friend, Will. And I can't be *that* girl either, the one who . . . who hovers on the sidelines, waiting like some buzzard circling overhead, to see if your relationship with Tracina dies and turns cold."

"Wow. Is that what you think I'm asking you to do?"

He brought the back of hand to his forehead and wiped his brow with it. His face was lined with sadness, exhaustion and maybe even resignation. A tense silence fell between us, one that made me question whether I could continue to work at the Café while my heart's pain still existed. But I also knew this was my problem, not his.

"Cassie. I'm sorry for everything."

Our eyes met, seemingly for the first time in weeks.

"For everything?" I asked.

"No. Not everything," he said, quietly placing the hammer on the sawhorse and tugging his T-shirt from his belt to wipe his whole face. The sun began setting over Frenchman Street, urging me to get back downstairs and close up shop.

"Okay. You're busy. So am I. Curtain rod looks good. My job here is done," I said. "I'll be downstairs cashing out if you need anything from me."

"It's not a matter of *if* I need you. You know I do."

I'll never know what my face looked like in that exact

moment, but I imagine the flash of hope was impossible to conceal.

I went home and made a solid set of promises to myself. No more pining. No more pouting. That was yesterday.

Today was my birthday. I was meeting Matilda to talk about my new role in S.E.C.R.E.T. When you're fresh off your own fantasies, it's a tricky year. You're not on the Committee. Not yet. You have to earn your spot. But you're given a choice of three roles, and I was eager to plunge in, to have something else to do, someplace else to be, someone to think about other than Will or myself.

One of the roles was Fantasy Facilitator, a S.E.C.R.E.T. member who helped make fantasies happen, by booking travel, acting as a background player or participating in scenarios like Kit and Angela had the night of the burlesque show. Without Kit faking her injury, I wouldn't have danced on that stage. And without Angela's help with the sexy choreography, I would have made a complete fool of myself up there. This year they were becoming full Committee members, so those two slots were open.

I could also be a Recruiter like Pauline, the woman whose misplaced diary had originally led me to S.E.C.R.E.T. She was married, but her husband wasn't threatened by her role as a recruiter of the men who'd participate in the fantasies, because, well, he'd once been one of them. Recruiting men for S.E.C.R.E.T. was different from training them; Pauline merely enticed them into the fold. Full-on training, or fine-tuning a recruit's sexual skills, *that* was reserved for full Committee members, as was participating sexually in the fantasies—not that I was ready for that anyway. The third role was Guide, providing encouragement and support to a new S.E.C.R.E.T. candidate. There was no way I could have navigated the strange terrain of my crazy, sexy year without my Guide, Matilda. So I chose Guide, the least daunting of the three roles, though Matilda's advice was to keep an open mind. "The most surprising opportunities could come up," she said. Last thing left was to sign my S.E.C.R.E.T. pledge and bring it to our lunch.

> *I, Cassie Robichaud, pledge to serve S.E.C.R.E.T as a*
> *Guide for one term, doing whatever is within my power*
> *to ensure that all sexual fantasies are:*
> *Safe*
> *Erotic*
> *Compelling*
> *Romantic*
> *Ecstatic*
> *Transformative*
> *I vow to uphold the anonymity of all members and*
> *participants of S.E.C.R.E.T., and to uphold the principles*
> *of "No Judgment, No Limits and No Shame" during my*
> *term, and forever after.*
>
> _____ *Cassie Robichaud*

I signed it with a little flourish, while Dixie pawed at the reflections cast across the bedspread from the charms on my bracelet. It was time. Time to take a whole new set of steps—away from Will and my past and towards a new future, whatever it held.

DAUPHINE

That morning, I stood across the street from my store on Magazine at Ninth, watching my employee, Elizabeth, put together another one of her brash window displays. I had hired her away from our chief vintage clothing rival down the street because she had a unique eye, the kind you couldn't train. But ever the control freak, I wasn't quite sure I liked the direction Elizabeth was heading with this display. I saw bras and baskets and lots of yellows strips of crinkled paper. She hated when I did this—hovered, managed, tweaked—always doing myself what I don't trust others to do. But it was the way I ran my business and it had worked so far, hadn't it?

When my best friend Charlotte and I first bought the Funky Monkey more than ten years ago, I argued for keeping the store's original name as well as most of its inventory, cataloging much of what we couldn't sell. I didn't like change. Like most Southerners, I was superstitious of anything new or novel. Then she insisted that we sell vinyl records and custom DJ bags to attract men as well as women, and I reluctantly agreed. When Charlotte insisted we also add other specialties—the Mardi Gras costumes, the wigs and formal wear, for people who really wanted to stand out—I balked. But I had to admit those were all good ideas, the sales of which got us through the leaner times. So I let her run the merchandising while I remained in the background, an area of life to which I had always been partial. Luckily, I had a talent for making other people shine, and now, with this store, I had a treasure trove to work with.

My ex-boyfriend, Luke, was from New Orleans proper, born and raised in the Garden District. He told me the building that housed the Funky Monkey had been a shoe store, a paint store, before that a bike repair shop, then an on-site dry cleaner's. What dawned on me while watching Elizabeth slide into the empty window box, now holding a basket of pastel-colored bras (*Okay, I see where you're going with this*), was that while this building had continued to recreate itself, I hadn't. Change—that was Charlotte's forte. That's what made her a great business partner. Until, all in a day, one selfish action led her to destroy the business and our friendship.

But it was Luke's betrayal I couldn't recover from.

I met him in music class in college, and he had asked me out at the end of our junior year. I was studying Fine Arts, majoring in Design and minoring in Jazz Theory. I never played an instrument or sang. Never wanted to. But I loved to listen and learn about it, all of it—jazz, classical, alternative, you name it. Luke was tepid on music, only taking the course for easy credit. His passion was literature. When as a sophomore he precociously published his first novel, a coming-of-age story about growing up in New Orleans, I was so proud of him. He started to attract literary groupies, but they were of the earnest and respectful variety, so I rarely felt threatened. Naive of me, I realized looking back. But when he began receiving invitations to book events and festivals, that's when the rift began. I'd go with him to readings and appearances provided they were local, but I couldn't get on a plane. When I was eight, I had an uncle who died when his plane crashed into the ocean. We weren't terribly close, but I was young and it was a formative time for me; at age eight you develop intricate theories to keep nightmares at bay. After that dramatic intrusion on my childhood, my terror of flying extended to anything I couldn't understand and couldn't control. I tried to keep fear from affecting the rest of my life, but it didn't always work. I preferred sleeping in pajamas in case of emergencies, and having sex with the lights off in case someone walked in. This last habit had nothing to do with shame about the weight I'd gained in college or with the time my mother called me *zaftig*, a word I had to look up in private.

"You called me fat?" I screamed to her.

She protested dramatically. "No, honey! It means curvaceous. Why, it's a *lovely* thing to be."

Don't get me wrong, Luke constantly told me how beautiful I was, how desirable, and I believed him. I wasn't afraid of my curves. I wasn't prim. I was adventurous. I *liked* sex. I just preferred it on *my* terms, *my* way, in flattering positions, in the dark, and showering directly after.

After graduation, Luke, Charlotte and I shared the second-floor, two-bedroom apartment on Philip near Coliseum, which is where I still live, one of those old clapboard Victorians painted yellow with white trim. The apartment had original windows and faced the street corner. Luke set up his desk and began to write what he called his "Southern Opus." Our bedroom was drafty in the winter, but I didn't mind because Luke kept me warm most nights and paid his share of the rent when he could hold down a part-time job. I hired him for a brief stint in the store, but I blanched when he tried to make suggestions to improve the business, or moved stock around on the floor so it would sell faster. "Be careful," my mother warned. "Men don't like criticism or self-sufficiency in women. They need to feel needed." Dad disagreed. "Men just want to be wanted," he said.

And the way Charlotte teased Luke or threw an arm around him, I always assumed was sisterly and benign. Luke was a nerdy writer, insular like me. Charlotte just wasn't his type. He once called her flaky, whereas I was solid, layered. Charlotte was "Rocky Road" to my "Vanilla," not an insult he explained, since I was his favorite flavor.

But tastes change. Working in fashion, I ought to have known that.

It was my day off, so I wasn't supposed to walk in on them in the office at the back of the store, Charlotte atop a pile of sturdy suitcases we were refurbishing, her white skinny thighs straddling Luke, his stupid black jeans bunched at his dumb ankles, his ass clenched, mid-thrust.

"My goodness, I am so sorry," I mumbled, backing up and closing the door behind me. You know your Southern upbringing has grown twisted when your first instinct is to be polite when intruding upon your boyfriend fucking your best friend.

My back resting against the door jamb of a change room, I kept my hand over my mouth for the time it took for them to dress and assemble in front of me in a state of disarray and shame.

Luke, the writer, offered a bunch of words.

I'm so sorry . . .

We didn't mean to . . .

It just kinda happened . . .

It wasn't planned . . .

We tried to end it, but . . .

These words assembled themselves into the only answers that were pertinent. One: This had been going on for a while. Two: They were in love.

They moved out that night.

I bought Charlotte out of the business for enough money to move to New York, where Luke wanted to relocate before his second novel was published. Six months later, *Big Red* came out to more great fanfare. A "morbidly honest tale about the corrosive effects of the South on an *overweight, sensitive* young woman trying to break from the past." When I read his description of his protagonist, Sandrine, a "tense, controlling redhead" with a "sylph" of a sister and a "ballsy" best friend, I was in a state of shock for days, weeks, months . . . years. When it hit the bestseller lists, young girls ducked into the store (in the book it was called "Fancy Pansty") shyly inquiring as to whether it was true: was I really the model for the famously tragic Sandrine from *Big Red*?

Elizabeth used to get so mad at those girls. "Do you see a fat redhead in this store?" she'd yell. And here's the worst part: I never thought I was fat until the book was published. I'd always rather liked my curves. I wore only well-made vintage dresses, the kind constructed before the "era of the super model," after which clothing suddenly became unflattering sausage casings for all but the very thin. And I never doubted Luke's attraction to me, until I read his descriptions of Sandrine's thighs and the "white expanse of her upper arms," which sent me spiraling into a near-decade of self-doubt and insecurity.

People told me to take a trip, get out of town, *go* somewhere. But I couldn't, maddeningly mirroring Luke's phobic Sandrine, who atrophied in one spot her whole life. I even stopped taking short drives to the beach, afraid now to be seen in a bathing suit. On my sister Bree's advice, I took up yoga; on my mother's, online dating. Both very bad ideas, it turned out. The only thing going for me was work, so I clung to it, making my store the center of my life and my chief excuse for staying put.

Then Bree would accidentally let it be known that Charlotte was pregnant again, or that Luke's "cool indy" screenplay sold for "millions," or that their Williamsburg loft was featured in *Elle* magazine, where Charlotte also worked as a freelance stylist. Information like that would send me reeling backwards in time, undoing progress made by a few tepid dates with some guy I'd half-heartedly had sex with. That my sister remained friends with Charlotte was the least surprising betrayal of all.

"Just 'cause y'all had a falling-out doesn't mean I have to give her up, Dauphine. I was friends with her too, you know. That's unjust."

"Falling-out? She was *my* best friend. He was *my* boyfriend. They killed my whole world."

"Eight years ago! Most of your major organs have completely replenished themselves in that time! When are you gonna move on? You need a man!"

What if you don't need a man but you still want one? I wanted a man, just not all the mess—that murky pond of feelings the worst of them sometimes leave you sitting in.

Men, however, were about the only subject to which I always deferred to my mother. She was from Tennessee pageant stock and believed she knew a lot about men and their motives. She also believed she knew a lot about me. She disapproved of the way I dressed. Her face said it all one day when she and Dad came down from Baton Rouge to take me to my thirtieth birthday brunch, where I wore a gorgeous 1940s tea dress with a pillbox hat and little black veil.

"I understand there is probably a very moving story behind that hat, but you're puttin' out a message that says

'Stay away from me, for I am peculiar, stuck in the past,'" she said. *Peculiar* was the worst thing you could say about a Southern woman of a certain age.

I shook my head at this brief bout of nostalgia and watched Elizabeth lay down a yellow nest of crimped paper strips. Mardi Gras had ended, and now we were gearing up for Easter. Yesterday I scouted around for ideas for a theme and today I could see that Elizabeth had seized upon quite an interesting one. When she finished tying up the back of a pale blue corset, I knocked on the window, giving her my best *what the hell?* face.

"What are you doing here so early, Dauphine? You're on afternoons!" she yelled through the glass.

"I promised to style you. For your date tonight."

Her eyes flew open. "Right!"

"What's your plan here?" I asked, my finger circling the pile of mannequin legs and arms.

"Corsets!" Elizabeth held up a fistful of lace and ribbons.

"Right. When I think of Easter, I think: lingerie."

People strolling past the store stopped to stare at the nearly naked mannequin and the two women yelling at each other over bras through glass. She plucked vintage white Playboy rabbit ears out of a bag, pairing them next to a pale pink teddy. "Look how cute!"

If you want to keep good people close, you have to let them loose every once in a while, my dad used to say. So I just had to trust that Elizabeth would put together another traffic-stopping display. *Let her do this; let someone else take the lead.*

I gave her a weak thumbs-up and headed inside.

My stomach rumbled. I had skipped breakfast, but we had a big shipment in from a hard-won estate sale and I wanted to go through those boxes myself before we opened. So I left Elizabeth to work her magic in the window box and unlocked the store, taking in my outfit in the full-length mirror by the front counter: a dark blue, A-line dress that buttoned up the front, circa late '60s, the kind with a built-in bra, matching belt and slip lining; three-quarter-length sleeves and kitten heels. My red hair was pulled back in a chignon, now loose and fuzzy-edged from the humidity. I had on big, dark sunglasses, à la Jackie O. I had to admit it was a little warm for this dress, but they just didn't make them like this anymore, something my mother celebrated and I, of course, lamented. But when did my collars become so high, the hems this long, my sunglasses so large? *Who takes eight years to get over a guy?*

With Elizabeth busy in the window and the store still quiet, I dug into my purse for my lunch, then realized I had left it on my kitchen counter. Customers weren't allowed food or drinks in my store, but I ate all my meals perched on the stepladder behind the cash register. Screw it, I'd skip lunch too, and have a big dinner.

I dragged the smallest estate-sale boxes to the front counter. The first was filled with accessories, Elizabeth's specialty, so I kicked it aside. The second box was all girly sundresses, straw hats (vile) and ballet flats. I admired a

dark green halter dress from the '70s. It was stunning material, crepe, beautifully lined and floor-length. I noticed the
hem was fraying. I could shorten it to knee-length and get a
good price. Or I could keep it for myself. And show off my
arms? Not a chance. Still, it was so pretty, the green, and
with my red hair . . .

I set it aside for the "keeper" pile, which was getting
bigger than the "for sale" pile. Why did I do this? Save
things for some imaginary future or for some imaginary
customer who would *really* appreciate it if given the chance.

"Our back room office could be a whole other store,"
Elizabeth once said. "A better one than what's out front."

The third box was filled with men's clothes: tweed jackets,
several T-shirts, a pair of tuxedo pants (satin stripe down the
side) and a matching tuxedo jacket with stylishly slim lapels.
I put my nose to the thick fabric and inhaled. It was clean
and smelled like men's cologne. That manly-man smell was
so intoxicating. It reminded me of a late night out, of cigars
and aftershave, the back of a cab, desire. I felt a pang behind
my belly button. I imagined getting this tuxedoed man home,
unzipping my long velvet gown, surrendering it to the floor.
Underneath it I would be wearing a silk slip. He'd lie back on
my gypsy bedspread, smiling, putting aside his scotch. I
could feel his hands on my shoulders as he pulled me down
onto him, gathering a fist of my long, red hair, pulling my
head back to reveal my tender throat. I would cry out his
name loud enough to clear the cobwebs from the hallways of
the abandoned house my body had become, and—

"Dauphine!"

I nearly fell off my stepladder. "What in the *hell*, Elizabeth," I said, dropping the jacket I'd been clutching.

"I called your name, like, ten million times!"

My stomach growled so loud we both heard it. Then I saw stars in my peripheral vision and grabbed the glass case to steady myself.

"Are you okay?"

"Yes, I just tuned out for a second."

"Your stomach sounds like two wolves fighting in it. Go get some food. Sit outside in the sun. You don't officially start until two," she scolded with the adorable authority of the very young. She plucked my purse from below the glass case, grabbed my arm and shoved me towards the door.

"Return when you are well fortified, missy. And take your damn time."

"Fine," I said, still seeing stars.

Next door I nabbed the last empty patio table at Ignatius's and ordered a hot bowl of gumbo. The Sunday shoppers seemed frantic, or maybe it just felt like that because this was spring and the first time in a long time that I'd been outside, around people, instead of holed up in my store dealing with inventory. I had also been skipping breakfast, skipping mornings altogether. Maybe that's why I was losing weight, something I was contemplating when I noticed him—*him* him—Mark Drury—the lead singer of the Careless Ones.

I'd never seen him with a beard before; I liked it. His band had a regular, early-evening slot on Saturdays at Three Muses. And Mark's voice was a husky, alt-country dream. Every once in a while, he'd sing a cover of an old Hank Williams song that would make me swoon. He was all limbs and black hair and pale blue eyes. His stooped shoulders were those of a man with an instrument perpetually strapped to his back. And there he was strutting by my patio table and heading inside. He and some of his band mates would hit up the Funky Monkey for T-shirts, jeans and even outlandish wigs if they were doing a show during Mardi Gras. But I always shoved Elizabeth in front of them, too shy to help them myself. The Careless Ones was the only local band I'd go see alone, time spent listening to music being the only time I could really let go and be in my body. Music was the opposite of me. That's why I was mesmerized by performers like Mark, who could stand on stage in front of everybody and give himself permission to let go.

Talk to him, I thought to myself. *Just go up to him after the show and tap him on the shoulder and say, Hey Mark, when I feel like drinking alone, I watch you.*

Smack. I'd sound like a crazy person.

I love watching you in the dark when I'm by myself.

Ew.

I like to watch you move.

Wrong. All wrong. I truly was turning peculiar.

I tried not to stare through the glass too long as Mark Drury took a seat at the bar inside. I cursed Elizabeth for telling me to leave the store. I cursed myself for wearing a dark blue dress on a hot spring day. But my gumbo had · arrived, so I was committed. Plus, what if he had a girlfriend? *You're just talking to him. You're just saying, Hey, love your work.*

A few minutes later, the bartender handed him a takeout coffee and a wrapped sandwich. Bag pinned between his lips, newspaper held in his armpit, he pulled several napkins from a stainless steel dispenser near the door and headed straight for me. In my head, I was screaming, *Here! Sit with me!* But my eyes were shaded by my giant sunglasses. I was like a fish, mouth opening and closing, pressed up against the silencing aquarium glass.

Then, before I knew it, he was sitting at the table *next to me*, joining some dark-haired woman who had an empty seat at her table. They introduced themselves and fell into an easy banter as they ate. Watching him grin at her, making her laugh, hurt my stomach. I regarded my imaginary rival as discreetly as I could. She was pretty and fit, but I bet she didn't know that Mark had chosen the band name the Careless Ones from *The Great Gatsby*, a book she'd probably never read, having cribbed notes in junior high from people like me. Bet she wouldn't even like Mark's music. Minutes later I watched him say goodbye to her by punching his number into her phone, imagining that he was giving it to me.

What happened to me? Where did I go?

"Are you okay?"

Had I said that out loud? I *had* said it out loud . . . directly to the dark-haired woman who'd been talking to Mark Drury and was now sitting alone. She stood, picked up a glass of water from her table and moved in slow motion towards me. She placed the glass in front of me, a concerned look on her face.

"Are you okay?" she asked again.

To this day, I have no idea why I said yes when she asked if she could join me; I so rarely spoke to strangers. But as my mother would say, "Some things are fatefully divine and some are just divinely fated."

CASSIE

I t was inevitable. Will and I both tried to avoid being alone, but the Café Rose was small with narrow hallways and dark corners.

"Thanks for staying late, Cassie," Will said, the night the drywall got delivered. He'd asked me to watch for the truck.

"I wanted to."

"Wonder if you could do me one more favor."

"Sure," I said. "What is it?"

"You know what it is," he answered, his voice barely above a whisper. Crossing his arms, he leaned back on the cool glass door of the fridge.

"Is it this?" I asked, loosening the clasp on my apron and letting it fall to the floor.

"Yes. That's it. Can you do me another favor?"

"I can," I said, my voice so choked with longing I sounded underwater. I slowly lifted my shirt over my head, my hair cascading through the neck hole. I threw it down to the tiles. I wasn't wearing a bra.

"Is it this?"

"Yes . . . you are . . . so beautiful," he murmured. My skin had that effect on him and I knew it.

"Your turn," I whispered.

Without hesitating, he whipped off his shirt and threw it near mine, his hair shocked upwards. Then he shoved off his jeans, leaving his white boxers on. This was our game.

"I won't touch you. I promise," he said. "I just want to look at you. That's not wrong."

I undid my jeans and stepped out of them, hooking my thumbs in the strings of my bikini underwear. He nodded slightly, aching for me to take those off too. I hesitated, looking out at the pitch-black street. What time was it? How long had we been alone in here like this? I inched my underwear down around my thighs and brought them to the floor. I was now naked.

"Come closer, Cassie. I want to smell your skin."

"No touching."

"I know."

I took a few steps towards him. Six inches from his bare chest, I stopped. At that distance I could feel our body heat mingling, his hot breath on my skin.

I let my hand travel up to my breast, cupping it for him, letting my thumb circle my nipple. A moan escaped his throat as he extended a hand. I stepped back.

"You promised," I whispered.

"I won't touch you. But you can touch yourself, Cassie. That's not against the rules."

True. I let my other hand travel down across my stomach, the muscle in my forearm flinching as I tentatively felt myself, how wet he was making me, relishing how insanely excited this was making him.

"This is too much, I can't," he said.

He was crazed. That's the only way to explain why, with one deft forearm, he swept the condiment table next to us clean of the bowls and utensils, the trays of salt and pepper shakers, the ashtrays that hold sugar packets, the napkin holders—it all went crashing to the floor. Any other time I would have been pissed. But that night I was thrilled by his impatience, his *ferocity*. He spun me around and urged me down onto the table, my arms stretched to hold the edges.

"You said you weren't going to touch me, Will."

"I'm not going to touch you. I'm going to fuck you," he groaned, pulling my knees apart and standing naked between my spread thighs. He now held his heavy erection in his hand, stroking it, his fierce eyes on me as he prodded into my wetness, a hesitant inch, then another one, teasing, making me yearn and reach, asking, *begging* for him to fuck me, to fuck me hard, *Oh, Will*, my quivering thighs bracketing his narrow hips, my nails digging into his forearms as he—

"Excuse me. Is this seat taken?"

Oh shit, my fantasy broke like a bubble. A man—a *real* one—now stood looming over my metal patio table at Ignatius's, his face shadowed from behind by the high, hot sun.

"Sorry. I didn't mean to scare you," he said. "The patio's full and I noticed you have a table for four all to yourself. Very selfish."

"Oh. I'm so sorry. Yes, of course," I said, plucking my purse from one of the chairs at my table. I must have looked like a dozy ape, chomping on an ice cube and staring into the middle distance, fantasizing about Will—again. This bad habit had to stop or I would drive myself crazy.

"I'll just eat my sandwich and drink my coffee and read my paper," he said. "And we can pretend we're not sharing a table for lunch."

"Good plan."

He had mischievous blue eyes, and though normally I didn't like beards, even short, groomed ones, his was sexy.

"We wouldn't want to speak or make eye contact over food. That would be weird."

"And awkward," I continued. "Not to mention rude."

"Disgusting."

"The way people eat together and talk to each other. Over meals!" I added with a shudder.

There was a beat, and then we both broke character, laughing.

"I'm Cassie," I said, extending my hand. The thought occurred to me that I never would have been capable of such banter just a few months earlier, before I'd been introduced to S.E.C.R.E.T. I had changed.

"Mark. Mark Drury."

Flaky hipsters have never been my type. But this one had a nice smile and a great Cajun accent. Add those blue eyes and strong, lean hands . . .

"Lunch break?" he asked, folding his long legs under the table.

"Kind of. You?"

"Breakfast time for me."

"Late night?"

"Occupational hazard. I'm a musician."

"Get *out*! In New Orleans?"

"Strange, I know. And you?"

"I'm a waitress."

"What are the odds?"

There was that smile again.

Naturally, easily, we carried on the conversation, about the instruments he played (he was a singer, played bass, taught a little piano on the side) and the Café, where I worked (he knew it, hadn't been in a while). The next stage when talking to someone who relies on tourism in this town was to discuss the awful necessity of the awful tourists, before exchanging information about the places these awful tourists don't really know about. We accomplished that in about twenty minutes, enough time for Mark, who looked a little younger than me, maybe thirty on account of his messy brown hair and his beige leather Vans and his fitted jeans and his faded red T-shirt with the name and number of an auto body shop, to eat his sandwich and drink half his coffee, then wipe his hands on his napkin and get up to leave. Musicians do have the nicest hands. I've heard it said that the hand is part of the instrument . . .

"Wait," I said, "do you want to try having lunch together sometime? We can do like today, no talking, no eye contact, just two strangers not eating a meal together." *Holy shit. Did I say those words?*

"Um. Sure," he said, laughing. "You seem harmless enough."

Yes, harmless, unless you count the fact that almost two months ago I danced nearly naked on a stage for strangers, had sex with my boss, was gut-checked in the morning by his pregnant girlfriend, then joined a secret organization dedicated to helping women realize their sex fantasies with total strangers. Yes. Harmless.

"Okay, well . . . give me your number," I said, digging in my purse for my phone. He took it from me and punched in his number.

"Okay. Nice not really meeting you, Cassie, and not eating lunch with you or talking to or knowing anything about you," he said, extending a hand towards me.

I laughed as he turned to leave, glancing at me over his shoulder once. Wow. That was so . . . easy. *Is this what recruiting is like?* I basked for a moment in my newfound courage. *I did that. I actually asked a man out for the first time in my life, a cute one at that.* But why was that almost as hard as half the things I did last year, naked, in front of men I'd never met before? This is the sort of thing—men, dating, sex—that required practice. My year of fantasies had helped me understand that, though it might also have been the fantasy I was having when Mark sat down that prompted me to do what I did.

I was leaning back in my chair feeling proud, when I heard murmuring next to me. I looked around to see a red-haired young woman, wearing giant bug-eyed sunglasses, staring at me from the next table.

"What happened to me? Where did I go?" she mumbled, looking completely stunned.

"Are you okay?" I asked.

Maybe she was having a stroke, I thought, picking up a glass of water and making a motion to join her. She nodded, rubbing the back of her neck. She couldn't have been more than thirty, but she was wearing a heavy blue dress, despite the heat, and it made her look older.

"Here," I said, placing the glass in front of her.

She gulped the water back and wiped her mouth, regaining her composure.

"I'm sorry," she said. "That's never happened to me before. Maybe it's the heat."

"It is quite hot for early April," I said.

"Maybe." She took another gulp of water. "Sorry, I don't mean to intrude, but that thing you did with that guy—asking him out? Very impressive."

"You saw that?"

"I swear I am never this nosy. But that was hard to ignore."

A strange compliment from a strange . . . stranger, but I'd take it.

"It *was* impressive, wasn't it?" I said, sounding surprisingly pleased with myself.

"Well . . . thank you for the water and for your concern. But I'm feeling better. So I'll just head back to work."

She pushed up her sunglasses, grabbed her purse, and just at the moment she stood to leave, Matilda arrived. They awkwardly engaged in the "you first, no, you first" dance around the crowded patio table. The woman smashed into Matilda's left shoulder, then her right. Finally free, it seemed she couldn't get away from us fast enough.

Matilda and I watched her as she headed into the Funky Monkey next door. Matilda lowered herself into her chair, patting down her hair as though she'd just survived a small tornado.

"Who was that? Or *what* was that?"

My eyes stayed glued to the door of the store.

"I don't know. Just a woman . . . I thought she was ill, so I checked on her," I said. "But guess what?" I changed the subject with a grin. "*I* just asked a guy out. And the best part? He said yes!"

"Well, Happy Birthday to you, indeed!"

"Yeah, and *that* woman, she treated me like I was some kind of celebrity just for asking a guy for his number. It was weird. She looks nothing like me, yet she reminded me a little of me last year. Kind of timid. Kind of sad. Anyway, I feel like my confidence is really growing. I think I am ready to be a Guide. Here," I said, reaching in my bag for my pledge. "Signed, sealed and delivered."

"Thank you for this," she said, putting away my pledge. Her expression was suddenly thoughtful. "I wonder if perhaps we're looking at a possible S.E.C.R.E.T. candidate."

"You mean that woman?"

Matilda nodded.

"I don't even know if she's single."

"That's easy to find out."

I felt my nerves fire up. "You think I should approach her? What if she thinks I'm crazy?"

"Everyone's entitled to their opinion. You look great, by the way."

I looked down at my outfit, nothing too "out there"— slim jeans that rested on my hips and a grey tank top under a cream corduroy jacket. I was never going to be one of those dolled-up babes who crammed Frenchmen on a Thursday night, drunkenly navigating the pocked street in treacherous heels. And I couldn't for the life of me understand why I should put on mascara to go grocery shopping. But a year of being told I was beautiful and desirable by some of the best-looking men I'd ever laid eyes on made me want to put my best face forward.

"After lunch let's go next door, talk a bit with that woman."

"Today? Now?—" It was happening so fast. Why was I so nervous?

"Don't worry, Cassie, I'll take the lead, you follow," Matilda said, scanning the menu.

Oh dear. Here we go.

DAUPHINE

could not get away from Ignatius's fast enough. Back at the store, I darted past Elizabeth to my office and slammed the door behind me, lifting my sunglasses to peer into the makeup mirror on my desk. My cheeks were red from my encounter with that dark-haired woman on the patio. For the first time, I spotted tiny wrinkles forming around my eyes, my mother's frown lines etching into my cheeks. Was I fading? Was my desirability leaving me for good? Mark had sat with her, not me. He had flirted with her, given his number to her, not me.

"You merely have the 'sads,' darling. They're from your father's side of the family," I could hear my mother drawl. This was a particularly Southern take on depression, one that felt more like the burden of inheritance than anything to do with serotonin levels.

I fell into my chair and looked around my office. I had too much stuff, I knew that. But I told myself that because I was obsessively neat and obsessively organized I couldn't be a hoarder. Everything was in its place, everything had a label, right down to the paper punch. And yet I couldn't let go of a thing. What if I lost weight and finally fit into that one-of-a-kind purple pantsuit? What if I put together the perfect outfit for a customer but didn't have that owl pendant that would pull it together? What if I absolutely needed something and it was longer there? Hence the six filing cabinets and wall-length closets, all filled with "marvelous finds" I could neither bring myself to wear nor bear to sell.

Shake it off, Dauphine. Shake it off.

Elizabeth stuck her head into the office.

"Okay. Store's empty. I quickly threw it on. Be honest," she said, walking into the frame to reveal her long body in a black jumpsuit and white go-go boots that I had set aside for her anniversary date. "So?"

She was a teenager when I hired her part-time on weekends. She was twenty-four now, studying psychology part-time at Tulane, practicing some of her theories on me. She told me I was fear-based and rigid. I told her, while picking up five sugar grains on the glass countertop with the very tip of my index finger, that she sounded a lot like my mother.

She stood now in front of the mirror looking absolutely lovely, head to toe.

"Amazing," I said.

"You think?"

"I do. You need a Pucci scarf. And pale lipstick," I said,

fetching both. And I was right. We moved towards the full-length mirror behind the door. I stood behind her, my chin on her shoulder. "Yes. A home run."

"Are you sure I don't look like a go-go dancer?"

"No! You're breathtaking."

"You should be the one wearing this, Dauphine," she said, squirming. "You put it away for so long, and you have the curves for it. You keep talking about getting back out there. When is that going to happen?"

"I'm fine. And *you* are almost set," I said, pulling out a lint brush from a drawer labeled "Lint Brushes."

"I'll wear it for the rest of the day, if that's okay," she said, while I finished rolling over her legs.

"Yes. Now go. I'll be out front in a minute."

As I watched her trip back to the front of the store I felt a maternal flush of pride. In the years I'd known her, I had helped her polish no less than ten online dating profiles, styling her for most of the pictures and some of the dates. Her current boyfriend, Edward, was no dreamboat, but they were clearly smitten with each other. Elizabeth had a vitality about her that she attributed to incredible sex. She and Edward were celebrating one year together with dinner at Coop's that night, followed by live music on the patio at Commander's Palace. Elizabeth, with her short blond hair, too-close eyes and gangly limbs, was not traditionally beautiful, yet she was never single for long. Eight-year gaps between serious boyfriends would be unthinkable for her. Life was too short for that kind of nonsense.

I looked at myself in the mirror, loosening the belt of my blue dress. Maybe I should change too. I could try on that green sundress now hanging from a coat rack, waiting to be labeled and stored. I could have Elizabeth pin the hem. Nah, too much trouble, and I'd never wear it anyway. Then why was I keeping it? I forced myself back out to the floor, passing an overstuffed rolling rack of outfits, some to be sorted, some priced. It was a quiet Sunday afternoon, but Elizabeth was occupied with a couple of customers near the display case. As I approached them, I realized she was helping the two women who had been sitting next to me at Ignatius's, the one who stole Mark Drury from me, and the attractive older woman with red hair a shade or two lighter than mine—the one I had smashed into. The redhead dressed crisply and professionally, like my mother, and didn't look like the type that scoured second-hand racks. The dark-haired woman dressed a little too plainly to be a Funky Monkey shopper, let alone a musical genius's future girlfriend.

"There you are!" said Elizabeth, making it difficult for me to duck into the men's side of the store to avoid them. "These two ladies were gushing about my outfit and I told them you picked it out for my date tonight. They were very impressed."

"Hi," said the redhead, her hand jutting towards me. "Great taste. Love the boots. I'm Matilda."

"Hi. Dauphine," I said, smiling stiffly.

"And I'm Cassie," the dark-haired woman said, seeming

a lot shier than the woman who had snagged Mark Drury's attention half an hour ago. She could barely meet my eye.

"It's a charming store," Matilda said, looking around. She was definitely the chatty one. "Nicely curated. Second-hand stores can be such a hodge-podge."

"Thank you. I like to think we know what we're doing," I said.

"And your name. Is it like the street?"

"My parents came to New Orleans for their honeymoon and named me after the street."

"Oh? Where are your people from?" she asked, using the word *people* as in "tribe," tilting her accent to signal that she was not only Southern but knew Southerners were obsessed with geography and lineage.

"Baton Rouge. Mostly Louisiana, with some Tennessee stock thrown in."

"Ah. A bit of 'cotton in the roux,' as they say. Cassie's from the north," she added. "She has no idea what we're talking about."

Matilda yanked out a sparkly blue, floor-length, strapless number and a yellow, more diaphanous gown from the formal rack.

"I'm going to try these on," she said, looking directly at Cassie. "Cassie, I believe you are looking for something special too. Perhaps Dauphine can help you?"

"I'll take you back there," Elizabeth said, gathering up the dresses.

After they left, I stood awkwardly for a few seconds with Cassie, feeling like we were two school kids forced to play together.

"So you're from the north," I said.

"Michigan. Yeah. But I've been here almost eight years, so I feel more and more like a local."

Her eyes landed on the glittery tower of clip-on rhinestone earrings on the display case.

"*Those* are what I'm looking for!" she said. "I have this *thing* to go to."

She removed a heavy pair of clip-on clusters, almost tipping over the whole tower.

"Oh, sorry. I'm so clutzy."

I could not picture this woman being invited to the kind of event that would require these earrings. She was too casual, too down-to-earth.

"This is a really nice store," she said, struggling to center the earrings on her lobes. "Do you own it?"

"I do. Almost ten years now. Here, let me help."

"Wow. Ten years." She moved her hair back so I could clip the earrings into proper place, one then the other.

I stood back.

"So do you have a business partner or is it just you?"

"Just me," I said, turning her around to look in the mirror. I quickly changed the subject. "What else are you wearing to your event?"

"I . . . don't think I've decided yet . . . It must be hard to run a business all on your own."

"I have Elizabeth and a few part-timers."

Her questions were inching to places where she wasn't invited.

"You're doing things a little backwards," I said. "You shouldn't start with the earrings. Start with the dress. Bring it in and I'll help you find the right jewelry."

"I didn't mean to offend you when I asked if you were running your own business. I'm sure you're quite capable of operating on the planet without a partner. I certainly have."

"Yes, but that could change," I said. "That guy from the patio? He was cute. Maybe that'll turn into something."

Should I tell her who he was? Can she sense my jealousy? I did mean it as a compliment, but I seemed to have alarmed her. Oh god, I *was* coming across as peculiar!

"Trust me, talking to cute guys is not a skill I was born with. I had to learn how to do it. And frankly, I'm still quite new at it. When you've been single for a long time, like I have, you forget how to approach men, you know? But it's really just muscle memory. I just needed a little . . . boost."

I felt her words slice right through me. *Yes. That's exactly it. That's what I need. A boost.*

She lowered her voice. "I had to get some help in the 'men' arena. Big-time. That's how I met Matilda."

I could hear Matilda and Elizabeth laughing and chatting at the back of the store.

"Is she a dating coach or something?" I asked.

"You could say that," Cassie said, spinning the earring rack, examining a pair of gold hoops that seemed more suited to her. "She has a lot of confidence, a lot of knowledge about this stuff."

"Well, sign me up for the next round of lessons," I said, laughing.

"I will!" she said, as though it were a real thing, these lessons, this kind of coaching.

Matilda and Elizabeth returned from the dressing room, triumphant.

"I never knew I looked so good in yellow," Matilda said, the gown draped in her arms. "You can find out all sorts of things about yourself in a place like this."

Something in me knew that Cassie and Matilda hadn't come to the store just to buy dresses or earrings, a fact confirmed when Cassie returned on her own two days later, just before closing time.

"I thought I'd take you up on the offer to help me accessorize," she said, pulling a little black dress out of a shopping bag.

"Oh great, yeah."

I was surprised at how happy I was to see her. She followed me to the dressing rooms, my nervousness making me uncharacteristically chatty.

"I have a pair of gold hoops and a cuff that'll look amazing with that dress. What size are your feet? You need to try everything on with shoes."

"Eight," she said, slipping into a stall.

I dashed to my office ahead of her, catching myself in the mirror: cat glasses, cream-colored twinset and A-line plaid skirt. I looked like an extra on *Happy Days*. I didn't even *need* glasses. Ugh. Why did I suddenly care what I had on? I flipped through my index cards and cross-referenced them to the second drawer of the third filing cabinet where I stored my gold hoops; the drawer below held my cuffs. I was saving the big hoops for a Cher-type outfit, but on Cassie, with a simple black dress, they'd be stunning. Cassie poked open the office door, trying not to look shocked at my hive of inventory.

"Wow. There's a whole other store back here."

"Trust me," I said. "I know it looks like a lot of stuff, but I know exactly where everything is."

I pulled her in front of the nearest mirror.

"The top is a little snug. I haven't worn it since Jazz Fest," she said, tugging at the halter.

She looked gorgeous in black and I said so. I was about to snap the cuff around her wrist when I noticed her charm bracelet; it was unlike anything I'd seen before.

"That's a *stunning* piece," I said, holding up her wrist to get a better look at it. Normally, charm bracelets did nothing to charm me. They were often so trinket-y, but this one was distinctive. It was made with my favorite kind of gold too, pale yellow, with that rough hammered finish. The chain was thick, almost masculine, and each charm had a Roman numeral engraved on one side, a word on the other.

"*Curiosity . . . Generosity . . . Courage*—where did you get this?" I asked.

Cassie gently pried her wrist free.

"It was . . . given to me."

"It's about as beautiful a thing as I've ever seen. Whoever gave this to you thinks very highly of you."

"I think you might be right about that," she said. "But does it go with this dress?"

"Mmm . . . Not really. It overwhelms it. Why don't you try this——?"

I traded a simple cuff for her bracelet. When she dropped it in my palm, it felt heavy, pleasing; it took everything in me not to slip it on my own wrist.

"No necklace?" she asked, sliding the cuff over her bare wrist.

"Not with a halter dress," I said with authority, my attention still drawn to the bracelet in my hand. "These hoops will add a bit of sparkle. But I would keep the sides of your hair up."

She took the earrings from my other hand and held them next to her lobes.

"See? Perfect," I said.

"You're right. That's perfect. Wrap them up."

She passed me the earrings and held out her hand. It was the strangest sensation, my reluctance to return her bracelet.

"I'll tell you how I got it," she said, noticing my hesitation. "In fact, to be honest . . . that's why I'm here. Can I sit for a second?"

She took a deep breath, looking about as nervous as I was alarmed. What was going on?

"What I'm about to talk about is pretty strange, so bear with me. It involves an adventure of sorts."

I felt a surge go through me.

"I'd love to do more traveling, but I don't fly," I said pre-emptively. "Plus, I'm the sole proprietor, and that makes it hard for me to leave—"

"I'm not talking about a trip, though some travel might be involved."

Her voice and demeanor became steadier and steadier.

"Maybe it would help," she added, "if I tell you about my own adventures."

And that's when she began to recount her life, how the death of her husband almost seven years earlier had upended her life completely. Not because she loved her husband, but because she realized she hadn't for a long time, which made her even sadder. For years she'd been numb from head to toe. I knew about that feeling and told her so.

"Yes. Matilda talks about a sort of 'aura of sadness,' that settles around people. She says she can see it. She saw a bit of it on you. I don't have that ability, but I do believe you might know something about feeling stuck."

I don't know how to explain why it suddenly felt so easy to pour out my heart to Cassie. Maybe it was her stillness, her compassionate eyes. But I found myself telling her about Luke's betrayal, his book, and how he and Charlotte broke my heart, making it difficult for me to trust not only men but women too. She listened patiently, and I knew without her even saying so that she understood.

"So, tell me what you're really here for," I said.

"I'm here to make you an offer. But to accept it, you're going to have to place your trust not just in men but in a whole bunch of women."

And that's when she said the name—S.E.C.R.E.T.— and described its incredible mandate: to orchestrate sexual fantasies that make women feel great about themselves again, or in some cases, for the first time ever.

"S.E.C.R.E.T.," she said, "introduced me to part of myself I had never known before. In your case, I think it's more about reigniting a part of you that's just been dormant—am I right?"

"Yeah, for about eight years," I said.

"Oh. That's a long time. I didn't have sex for *five* years and I thought that was bad!"

"What? No! No no no no. I've had *sex* since then, just not very good sex, and not with very good men. I meant that it's been about eight years since I felt any real passion, any *connection* with a man."

Cassie winced and nodded. Then she described exactly how this group of women went about reigniting passion.

"We orchestrate sex fantasies. Yours. Nine of them, which take place over the course of a year, a charm for every step," she said, holding up her bracelet. "The tenth is also a decision— to remain in S.E.C.R.E.T., as I did, or to go out on your own, maybe try a real relationship if you're ready. See this?"

She flipped through her charms until she came to one that said *Step Ten* on one side *Liberation* on the other.

"I completed my steps, which liberated me from so many things, mainly fear and self-doubt. And staying in S.E.C.R.E.T. was a free choice, and it remains so."

"Secret sex fantasies? In New Orleans?" I asked, barely stifling a giggle. "Forgive me, Cassie, but it's the most absurd thing I've ever heard in my life."

Part of me wanted to stand up, call the police and escort her out of the store. The other part was welded to my seat, my eyes, ears and heart wide open.

"I know it sounds ludicrous. But I'm telling you, it's the best thing that has ever happened to me. All that's required of you is to either accept or decline the offer."

"And you did this?"

She nodded.

"Last year?"

She nodded again, this time a smile turning up the corners of her mouth.

"You experienced *nine* different sex fantasies with *nine* different men?"

"I *did*," she said, looking almost as astonished with herself as I was with her.

"And you made the decision to stay in this . . . group, and to help other women?"

Her features fell slightly and her eyes darkened. "Actually, no. I made the decision to leave S.E.C.R.E.T. because I thought . . . well, I fell in love. With an old friend. But timing is everything, as they say, and ours was disastrous, really. Things fell apart. Being a member of S.E.C.R.E.T. is really the only thing getting me through."

"I'm sorry to hear that."

The silence that followed was heavy in the room, both of us contemplating the strange words just spoken.

"Holy shit" was all I could eventually mutter. "Why me?"

"Timing. We saw you and met you. And, well, I think we might be right—that you need this."

I looked around my over-stocked, over-organized office.

"I guess I do," I admitted. "But why do you think experiencing wild sex fantasies will fix everything?"

"It won't fix everything. But it does the trick of fixing one thing, which creates a sort of cascade effect in your life. At least, that's how it has worked for me. I shouldn't tell you much more than that. You'll hear more at the Committee meeting, if this intrigues. A year ago, I was barely able to make eye contact with anyone, let alone chat up some cute random guy. And now here I am sharing one of my most intimate secrets with a total stranger."

She glanced at her watch. "I have to get to work."

I felt suddenly panicked, like if she left I might never see her again. "Now what? What do I do?"

"Are you interested?"

"Yes! No! A little. Oh . . . I need to think about it."

"Take your time. If you decide to accept the offer, call me. I'll arrange everything. And then . . . it'll all begin."

What would begin, and how, and with whom, and where?

And how often? And what time of day? The control freak in me needed to map this out carefully. I had to have all the exits covered and the downsides discussed, everything measured and weighed and balanced out. As a kid I stood on the end of every dock and pool for much longer than the other kids, brow knitted in deep contemplation. Could I see the bottom? Could I touch it? If not, I didn't leap. And now, here was an offer from this confident, assured woman who claimed to once have been as lost and confused as I was now.

We went to the cash register, passing a flustered Elizabeth, who was manning the floor alone. I mouthed *I'm sorry*, pointing theatrically to Cassie as she walked in front of me.

"I'm glad you liked the bracelet and earrings, Cassie," I said, a little too loud, while punching in the purchase. What was I trying to camouflage?

"Think about everything I said," Cassie whispered, handing me her credit card along with her personal card, her name and number beneath the word *S.E.C.R.E.T.* At the door, she gave me a quick wave, then disappeared down Magazine Street towards the French Quarter. I pulled my sweater in a tight hug around me.

Did I want to continue working seven days a week, opening up then closing an empty store to go home to an empty apartment and an empty fridge? Did I want to live life with nothing to look forward to? I looked down at her card. For once, I wasn't going to make an easy decision difficult. First thing tomorrow, I'd call her. Right after I finished with the estate-sale boxes. But before the lunch crowd. Or maybe later, when the store was quieter. Or maybe when Elizabeth started her shift. Or before I opened the store. Yeah. That's when I'd do it. I'd call her then.

CASSIE

We didn't get a lot of customers in that quiet time between lunch and dinner, when the staff was whittled down to just me waiting for Tracina to spell me off. And we definitely didn't get a lot of handsome six-foot six-inch African-American district attorneys in three-thousand-dollar suits coming into the Café Rose at that hour. But Carruthers Johnstone was campaigning for re-election, his face on billboards all over town. I told myself he was probably there to drop off pamphlets. But when he asked if a "pretty little black gal, long legs, about ye high"—he held his hand at his chest—worked at the Café, my brain started humming.

I knew exactly who he was: the guy I'd seen Tracina straddling in that dark garage after the Revitalization Ball, the night I fell under Pierre Castille's charms. While nearly naked in the back of Pierre's limo, I spotted Tracina, her arms and legs around this man, kissing him against a big white Escalade. Ever since, I'd tried to put that scene out of my mind, filing it under "absolutely none of my business." But now this "business" was standing right in front of me, wiping his brow and looking around the Café uneasily.

"Tracina's not in. May I mention who is looking for her?" I played dumb, afraid of becoming somehow complicit in whatever drama he had brought through those doors.

"Yes . . . uh, tell her Carr came by. Give her this," he said, handing me a card.

Carr? She called him Carr?

Oh, I will, I wanted to say, but instead muttered, "Sure," slipping his card into my pouch. As tempting as it was to pry further, the less I involved myself with Tracina's problems, the easier my life would be.

But now "Carr's" card was sharing space with Mark Drury's phone number, which had been burning a hole in my apron for four days. I had written it out on a little piece of paper because Will didn't like us to carry around our cell phones on shift. But now it was becoming faded with all the folding and unfolding. I kicked myself for not insisting he take my number too. But I wanted to make the first move for the first time in my life. *I* had asked him for his number, hadn't I? One whole week had gone by since I'd met him on the patio at Ignatius's. That was also the day I first met Dauphine, and it had taken her a day to call me and accept the life-changing offer of joining S.E.C.R.E.T.

One day.

So what was I waiting for? It was just a damn phone call. An hour later, Will's truck pulled up in front of the Café to drop Tracina off for the afternoon shift, which I had asked her to start a little early so I could attend Dauphine's S.E.C.R.E.T. induction, scheduled that afternoon. Tracina waddled up the threshold. I could tell she was going to be one of those pregnant women who gained weight only in the front. I ducked into the kitchen. *Dammit. Call him. Now.* I picked up the wall phone in the kitchen and dialed the number.

After five rings, he answered. *Arrgh. Call him from home,* I told myself, hanging up after his groggy "Hello." I punched open the staff washroom door. Tracina was standing on a milk carton admiring her belly in the vanity mirror.

"This is new," Tracina said, quite literally navel-gazing. "This line thing has a name, I can't remember what it is. I'll ask Will. He knows everything about pregnancy."

"How are you feeling?"

That was the only thing I could ever think to ask her these days.

"The first three months were a bitch, but I'm heading into my second trimester and I'm feeling great now."

"Someone came by to see you today. A Carson Johnstone or something," I said, intentionally mangling his name while avoiding her eye contact. I handed her his card. "Big guy. Expensive suit."

Tracina's face tried very hard to stay placid. I whipped off my dirty T-shirt and pulled a clean one out of my locker. We faced each other, both in our bras.

"What did you tell him?"

"Nothing. I said you weren't in."

"What did he say? Did he say he was coming back?" She spoke slowly, but her voice was pitched high; she was either very happy or very sad. I couldn't tell which.

"He just said, 'Tell her *Carr* came by.'"

She blinked for several seconds, shook her head and then changed the subject back to me, her voice normal again.

"So, Cassie, how are you doing these days? We never get a chance to talk. It's like we're ships in the night or something." She was being friendly, eerily so.

"Fine. I'm fine. And you're fine. And Will seems fine too, which is great. We're all fine, I guess," I said, reapplying deodorant.

"I guess we are. And you're right, Will is *super* happy. That's for sure. But he's also very anxious about the baby. Worrying about my health. So much so he's, like . . ." She stepped closer to me and lowered her voice, cupping her hand around her mouth. "He's . . . afraid to have sex with me. I mean it's not like we *don't* have sex. We do. But not as much as I would like, and—"

"Okay!" I held up a hand to stop this information from coming any closer to my brain.

"He thinks it's going to hurt the baby—"

"Whoa. I don't need to know that either. I mean . . . he's my *boss*."

"But you're my friend, Cassie. Friends tell each other everything," she said, plucking her waitressing pouch off the top shelf of her locker.

Friends? I couldn't believe what I was hearing. We were many things—colleagues, co-workers, *rivals*—but the last thing I ever would have expected was for Tracina to consider me a friend.

"Don't friends keep each other's secrets?" she went on, securing her pouch below her belly. "Sometimes my friends tell me other people's secrets. But it's by accident, of course. Have you ever done that?"

Her tone chilled me. Who were her friends? Angela Rejean and Kit DeMarco, to name a couple. They had danced together for several years in a row in Les Filles de Frenchmen Revue. I knew Kit babysat Tracina's brother Trey now and again, and Angela offered to host Tracina's baby shower. These three women had history. Lots of it. And though Kit, Angela and I shared S.E.C.R.E.T., who's to say the bond Tracina shared with these woman was any less sacred?

Tracina cocked her head. "You look like you've seen a ghost, Cassie. What's on your mind?"

Wanna know what's on my mind? I wanted to scream. *The endless ways in which I'd like your boyfriend to fuck me.*

"Nothing."

I applied some lip-gloss in the mirror next to her.

"Hot date?" she asked.

"Actually . . . yes," I said, lying. But in a way not lying. I *would* call Mark. I *would* have a date with him. That wasn't a lie.

"Ooh, with who?"

"Just some guy I met."

"Anyone special?"

I thought for a second. "I don't think so. But, you know, I might just fuck him anyway."

And I left her alone in the washroom to pick her jaw up off the floor.

Why did I say that? Because I knew she'd tell Will. Hell, I *wanted* her to. And because sometimes you have to say things out loud to gather the gumption to go through with them.

❧

The Coach House door was open. I tiptoed past the foyer into the reception area and found Danica on the phone. She covered the receiver with her hand.

"You're early. Matilda's at the Mansion, but she'll be here in a minute. Go on in," she whispered.

"Dauphine's not here yet?"

"I'll watch for her. A new girl! So exciting!"

The boardroom door was ajar so I slipped in and saw for the first time the mythical Fantasy Board, to which only the Committee was privy. It was usually kept hidden behind a sliding wall. But there it was in all its colorful glory. Some of the men's names were struck out. Some I recognized. My heart sped up when I saw "Theo" on a purple card—my sexy French ski instructor—but there was a black slash through his name. There was also "Captain Archer," the helicopter pilot who'd led me to "Jake," the tugboat captain. Next to that was a card with "Captain Nathan" and a question mark; I didn't recognize that name. I inched the board back a little more and saw more strange names, then two that made my heart feel like a deep bruise with a finger pushing on it, including "Pierre Castille," covered by an X. My fantasy with the Bayou Billionaire had been extraordinary. The Ball, that sexy limousine ride home; he was incredibly hot and so assured. But his attentions turned toxic after the burlesque show, when he just assumed I'd pick him over Will for my final fantasy. I figured the X meant the Committee had dumped him from the fantasy roster, something I would have suggested had I been asked.

But the other familiar name was Jesse, my third Step fantasy, and his card had a number two scrolled on it. *Jesse!* My sexy-as-hell, tattooed pastry chef. Had it been almost a year since he overcame me in the kitchen at the Café Rose? Each of the men I'd had sex with was amazing in his own right, but I had made a special connection with Jesse, one strong enough to almost cause me to quit my fantasies early for a chance to get to know him better. Matilda convinced me to stay in S.E.C.R.E.T., to push through. And though I was grateful in the end when Will and I tumbled into bed, now I wasn't so sure I'd taken the right risk with the right man.

"Cassie!"

I almost leapt out of my skin at the sound of Matilda's voice.

"You scared me!"

She stood in the doorway, her arms crossed.

"Cassie, you know better than to come in here unsupervised. You aren't supposed to see the board unless you're a full Committee member."

"I can handle it. I mean, I knew some of these guys were coming back. What's the rule? Three turns through S.E.C.R.E.T.?" I asked, keeping my voice from breaking. Why was I suddenly so upset?

"Yes, that's right."

"And how many more fantasies does Jesse have left as a participant?"

"He's performed two. So . . . one more," Matilda said gently.

"Pierre's name is scratched out, I see."

"After the way he treated you at the burlesque revue? The Committee feels he is no longer S.E.C.R.E.T. material."

"I agree, which is such a shame. He's very . . . well, you know. Have you told him yet?"

"No."

"I'd love to listen in on that phone call, when the Bayou Billionaire's told his services won't be required."

"Powerful men aren't used to being rejected. Pierre Castille will probably be no exception."

"So . . . Jesse. Is he completely off limits while he's on the Fantasy Board?"

Why did I ask that? I knew the answer! Oh god, I sounded like a lovelorn teenager.

"Yes, he's off limits. Unless you're participating in a

threesome scenario or training him. We may tee him up with Dauphine if her fantasy folder indicates an interest in his type."

"Right. I see," I said, hardly camouflaging my disappointment.

"Cassie, if you want us to put you and Jesse together again, to see if there's still a spark, that can be done. But the rule is you then have to find a similar replacement recruit. Are you ready to replace him? To recruit a new man?"

She had me there and she knew it.

"I thought you only wanted to guide this year."

"I do. I'm happy to guide."

"So everything is as it should be." She looked at her watch. "Why don't you put some coffee on?"

I headed to the kitchenette off the foyer. I thought of the way Jesse had kissed me. That *kiss.* That hungry, searching kiss! The way he pressed me against the cool tiles. How he lifted me onto the prep table, bringing me to orgasm with his mouth, that *mouth,* just his mouth, because he never entered me . . . Oh god, there I was getting wet just thinking of the possibility of Jesse inside me, moving on top of me, his arm muscles flexing in the light . . . I had the sudden urge to waltz back into the boardroom and remove his name.

Danica stuck her head in the kitchenette.

"She's here. Dauphine. She's out at the gate. Ready?"

"Yup, sure, ready," I said, my hands deep in my front pockets. "Let's go!"

DAUPHINE

How many times had I walked past this mansion without any idea what went on in here? I lived only a few blocks away. The possibility of a lusher life had been right under my nose, and yet I couldn't see it and hadn't known it. It's funny how you don't know you're ready for change until it appears on your doorstep. I stood in front of that imposing, vine-covered gate on Third Street, contemplating entering. *You can always leave*, I told myself. *You do not have to stay. You do not have to do anything you don't want to do.*

My unspoken motto in life had always been: if I can't control it, I don't trust it. It had worked with my business—I trusted almost no one after buying Charlotte out (Elizabeth being the rare exception), and I took control of the store myself. But my controlling nature had also prevented me from moving, changing and growing. I had stopped taking risks. Jeez, I even cut my own hair because I didn't trust anyone else to do it. I'd sweep it to the front of my face and trim the ends in the mirror. Luke used to say it wasn't Charlotte that broke us up, it was the fact that I stood frozen in the tracks of my life.

When I saw Cassie coming out of the Coach House, she didn't recognize me at first. My hair was down and I wasn't wearing a dress. Instead I had picked out '60s-style side-zipper clam-diggers, a sleeveless floral blouse and espadrilles. I wanted to seem casual but not too casual; pulled together, but not completely buttoned-down. Cassie didn't look nearly as neurotic in her jeans and white T-shirt.

Okay, stop thinking, Dauphine!

"Am I late?"

"You're right on time. Ready?"

"Ready as the Arizona rain."

I followed her through the ivy-covered gate. The grounds behind the high fence were as I had imagined—impeccable, crew-cut green grass, vivid pink hydrangea bushes, white roses the size of a toddler's tutu dancing up the curved portico. Up close, the Mansion put a spell on you; you simply wanted to be inside of it. Cassie kept her hand wrapped around my upper arm, gently guiding me towards the red door of a square building to our left.

Matilda opened the door before we knocked.

"Dauphine, the woman with the beautiful name. Welcome to the Coach House. The Committee is very excited to meet you."

It all happened so fast that I didn't get a chance to take in the decor, though I thought I recognized two large abstracts lining the walls, the colors and brush technique distinct.

"Oh my goodness! Are those . . . Mendoza abstracts?" I asked, much to Matilda's delight.

"Why yes! They're the last two from our collection. We're the executors of Carolina Mendoza's estate. You know her work?"

"Design major. Modern Louisiana Art was one of my courses," I said, gazing up at the largest of the two paintings, which featured two fiery red squares that faded into yellow and orange at the edges. I quickly retrieved some facts about her from my filing cabinet brain: a young revolutionary from South America, a passionate feminist . . .

"She was a dear friend and one of S.E.C.R.E.T.'s founders," Matilda added. "The sale of her paintings every few years funds our endeavors. In fact, this year we're selling this one, *Red Rage*. We'll be sad to part with it."

"I bet. It's beautiful."

We passed a punky-looking young woman at reception with black hair and vivid red lips.

"Danica, this is Dauphine."

"Hi!" she said. "I'm a big fan of your store."

"Oh, yes. Thanks."

I vaguely recognized her, though members of the young hipster set sometimes blend into one another. And those types rarely bought intact vintage, always tweaking and altering expert tailoring to make it their own.

"Don't worry, your secrets are safe with S.E.C.R.E.T.," Danica said.

Matilda cleared her throat. "Danica, please set Dauphine up in my office to fill out the questionnaire." She looked at her watch.

"There's a test?" I asked, my heart pounding.

"No, no," Cassie said. "It's just a list of things you've done or would like to do. Sexually. It helps the Committee plan the fantasies. Takes about half an hour."

Danica reached beneath the desk, pulling from a small drawer a soft burgundy booklet about the size of a passport. She handed it to me. It felt like one of my sketching Moleskines from art class. The cover was embossed with an etching of three women, naked except for their long wavy hair. Beneath them was a Latin inscription: *Nihil judicii. Nihil limitis. Nihil verecundiae.*

"It means 'No Judgment. No Limits. No Shame,'" Cassie said.

I opened up the booklet. Inside was a preamble:

What you have in your hands is completely confidential. Your answers are for you and for the Committee only. No one else will see your responses. For S.E.C.R.E.T. to help you, we must know more about you. Be thorough, be honest, be fearless. Please begin:

"So . . . I fill this out?"

"Yes. We're just trying to understand your sexual history, your preferences, likes and dislikes," Matilda said, as I followed Danica to a cozy office, glancing over my shoulder as Cassie gave me two thumbs up.

"Tea? Water?" Danica asked, pointing to a black leather Eames chair and ottoman near the bookshelf.

"I'm okay," I said, glancing around the beautifully appointed room—at the white walls, oiled-walnut shelving, the mid-century modern touches. These were my kind of people, I thought. Then Matilda left me alone with my worries.

I would just have to be really clear with the Committee. I would tell them what I was willing to do and not willing to do. I would carefully list my rules: no flying, no lights on, nothing to do with beaches, no water. And if they couldn't honor those wishes, then fine. I would walk away. I wasn't here to change my life, just to enhance it, improve upon it. Somewhat. The sex part anyway.

But first they wanted basic information. I turned my attention to my little booklet again, scanning the questions, which veered from how many lovers I'd had, to one-night stands, threesomes, anal, oral—all with handy boxes, numbers and circles next to them. The first few questions were easy. I stopped counting my "number" after fifteen, so I rounded it up to twenty. Taking the five years with Luke into consideration, that made my lover count about two per year. I had always thought I'd been adventurous, but two men a year suddenly didn't sound like that many.

A few minutes later, Cassie poked her head into the room.

"How are you doing? Ready?"

"Ready as I'll ever be," I said, handing her my marked-up booklet.

I followed her across the main foyer, through two high white doors. We were now in a boardroom filled with women, and the chatter stopped instantly the moment we entered. Meeting new people wasn't my forte, and these were people to whom I would have to be vulnerable. *This is simply not a good idea.*

But before I could turn on my heels, Cassie pulled out a chair for me. As I sank into it, I slowly glanced around the all-white boardroom, a perfect backdrop for the ten women of various ages, colors and sizes who were all decked out in their vivid outfits, looking like the United Nations Commission on Perfect Accessories and Hair. I was dying to take in all their faces and at the same time half afraid to make direct eye contact.

"Ladies," Cassie said. "Thank you for meeting with us today. I'd like to introduce you to Dauphine. She is our next S.E.C.R.E.T. candidate, I hope. If she'll have us."

This sent a cheery applause through the room. There was a pause, and everyone was looking at me. That's when I realized I was supposed to speak. And say what? *Oh no, I haven't prepared properly for this! I've wrecked everything. Trust and control.*

"Hi. Thank you. I'm still . . . well, I have a lot of questions. And I'm not completely . . . It's just all so . . . new."

Despite my inarticulate introduction, the women all seemed reassuring, kind, and I began to relax into my chair. Cassie pointed and named each member of the Committee:

Bernice, Kit, Michelle, Brenda, Angela, Pauline, Maria, Marta, Amani and Matilda.

"Don't worry, the only name you really have to remember is mine," Cassie said. "I, of course, will be your Guide, while they, the Committee"—she indicated the whole room—"will guide *me.*"

"You'll both need the help," Angela said, winking at me. She was also ribbing Cassie.

Maybe because some of their faces were vaguely familiar— they ate, worked and shopped on Magazine Street, after all. Maybe because I recognized the painting of Carolina Mendoza on the far wall and decided to make her my private guardian angel. Or maybe because I knew they were women who, like me, had lost some of their confidence and were helping each other get it back. Regardless of why, it suddenly seemed normal to sign up for what they were offering: a sexual rebirth.

Danica placed a folder in front of me. It was burgundy, soft to the touch, embossed with the words *My S.E.C.R.E.T.*

"This is your fantasy folder. There is one page per fantasy. You can fill this out at home," Cassie said. "When you're done, Danica will courier it back to us."

On the right side were several sheets of cream-colored parchment. On the left, S.E.C.R.E.T.'s mandate was spelled out.

"Each fantasy must be:

Safe, in that the participant feels no danger.

Erotic, in that the fantasy is sexual in nature, not just imaginary.

Compelling, in that the participant truly wants to complete the fantasy.

Romantic, in that the participant feels wanted and desired.

Ecstatic, in that the participant experiences joy in the act.

Transformative, in that something in the participant changes in a fundamental way."

Inside the folder, in each flap, was a fantasy list. I scanned it, my face heating up: *secret sex in public . . . sex with an authority figure . . . a professor . . . a police officer . . . tied up* (Gulp! *Trust and control!*) *. . . served, spanked . . . serviced . . . waited on . . . sex with a famous person . . . water . . . nature . . . rescued . . . elevator . . . airplane* (Jesus, flying could be involved?) *. . . blindfold . . . food . . . taken by surprise . . . threesome . . . foursome . . . watched . . . being watched . . .*

It was enthralling, thrilling and terrifying in equal measure.

"Remember," Matilda said, "you choose your fantasies, set the limits and maintain total control. Anytime you want to, you can stop."

I looked around the room at the Committee. This time my eyes paused for a moment at each warm, expectant face. All these women made me feel like the biggest adventure of my life was about to begin. And yet, I saw myself fussing and worrying over every single scenario, slowly neutering my adventures, whittling them down to carefully choreographed interludes. I'd do this but not that. Or I'd be willing to try this but only if that were in place. I saw myself double- and triple-guessing myself over each decision. Then I remembered something my dad said, the day he finally pried me off the side of our backyard pool. Since I was a toddler, I'd been content enough to clutch the walls, to let my legs barely kick at the water. But he said: *If you don't wanna drown, sugar, you gotta learn how to go all the way under.*

So I had no choice but to do what I did next.

I tossed the fantasy folder to the middle of the table.

"Thank you all. But I'm not going to fill out this fantasy list. Not because I don't want to do this. Quite the opposite. I not only want to do this, I *need* to do this. But I have been making lists and labels and setting limits all my life, living within strict boundaries and according to certain rules. You've told me today that your job is to keep me safe. You've told me that I can stop the fantasies at any time. Those seem like reasonable limits. The rest, I leave in your hands, with my only instruction being this: Surprise me."

I had the attention of the whole table. Mouths were agape. Cassie was covering hers with a hand, her lovely bracelet dangling from her wrist, one I'd soon be wearing.

"So you accept?" she asked.

"Yes," I said, feeling defiant, triumphant. "I accept."

CASSIE

As much as I was thrilled by Dauphine's bravery and excited to guide her, I was also admittedly a little jealous. After all, I had caught a glimpse of her fantasy board, and some of the marvelous men she was about to experience. That's why I whipped out my phone right then and there on Third Street, before reaching Magazine. Enough of this silly reticence, these dumb fears. Dauphine had said, "Surprise me," in response to the Committee asking her what kind of sexual fantasies she hoped to enjoy. If I was going to be someone's Guide, I had better start getting brave myself.

I punched in Mark Drury's number with a new vigor.

"Hello?" he said in a voice that sounded like it had been stored in an oak barrel in a damp basement.

"I woke you up, didn't I." *Oh shit.*

"Yes, you did."

"But it's four in the afternoon."

"Is that *you*, Mom? I thought you passed away eleven years ago. This is such a nice surprise," he said, yawning.

"No, it's not your— It's the girl you met on the patio a few days ago. Cassie. Though, I am sorry about your mother."

"I'm just messing with you. I know who you are, and for the record, my mother's alive."

Okay, I'm dealing with a jokester. I can do this.

"Wait till I tell her what you just said."

"That's very presumptuous, assuming you'll meet my mom before you've even gone out on one date with me. Where are you?"

"In the Garden District, leaving . . . a friend's house," I said, glancing over my shoulder at the Mansion, now in the distance.

"So?" I said.

"So what?"

"So . . . wanna hook up?"

"Right now?" he asked, choking a little on his words.

"Yeah. Right now."

"Yeah!" he said, fully awake now.

He suggested Schiro's in a half hour. That meant no time to change, I thought, looking down at my T-shirt and jeans. And no time to change my mind. I was going to "hook up" with a guy I had just met.

A wave of nausea overcame me. Could I do this? That was what my year of S.E.C.R.E.T. was for, wasn't it? To act as a set of sexual training wheels? It was high time they came off. I knew what my needs were. Time to get them met.

Of course Mark Drury was late. Of course he knew the cute waitress, the hot girl eating alone, the androgynous sous chef who he stopped to high-five, and the curvy bartender from whom he ordered a pitcher of beer before taking a seat opposite me at the last empty table. Schiro's was popular with locals, the musicians and restaurant folks who ate at odd hours. It was almost 5 p.m., lunchtime for this crowd. The place was a study in plaid and piercings, and with a B & B upstairs it also had its share of international visitors. It was like a waiting room for heaven's misfits. I suddenly felt old.

"Hi," he said, grinning, pouring himself a glass of draft, then one for me.

I almost hadn't recognized him at first. He'd shaved, showing off his great face to full effect.

"Hi."

"I assume you like beer."

"Live for it."

He looked sleepy, his hair flattened and his green T-shirt—which set off his light blue eyes—was inside out. I had had butterflies in my stomach before he arrived, but curiously they began to calm down as soon as he sat. *He's just a guy. With needs. Like you.* He snatched a menu from the table stand and studied it, stealing a glance at me every few seconds.

"Let's get some burgers. They're great here."

"I haven't been here in ages," I said. "My ex and I used to come here for brunch when we first moved to New Orleans."

Why did I mention Scott?

"Your ex, huh?" He snapped the menu shut. "Would that be ex-husband or ex-boyfriend?"

"Husband. But he passed away a while ago."

"You're not messing with me now, right? Because I really *was* only kidding about my mom."

"No, I'm not kidding," I said.

He pried no further about that.

"How have you thusly fared in our Crescent City?"

"You mean, dating-wise?" I followed that question with a big gulp of beer.

"Yeah."

"Um. Hit and miss. You?" I asked, wiping my mouth.

"It's hard to meet someone who likes musicians' hours, you know?"

"And what about this? Is this a date?"

"You can call it whatever you want as long as you're naked by the end of it."

So bold! I tried not to register my shock. He was even bolder than my fantasy men, who all had helped me ease into things. But this was real life, as Matilda said. It was a lot riskier and messier and trickier than fantasy. In S.E.C.R.E.T., I couldn't be rejected, I couldn't screw up. In life those negative results were possibles, maybe even prob-ables. But I still had S.E.C.R.E.T.'s support, and Matilda's guidance while navigating this new terrain.

Now here was *someone*.

He was cute, funny and bratty. And what I had in mind was exactly what he had in mind. *You can do this, Cassie.*

I refilled my beer glass.

"How old are you?"

"Twenty-eight," he said.

I choked on my beer.

"You're almost ten years younger than me! That's disgusting."

"To *you* maybe."

The waitress came by. He ordered burgers for both of us.

"What if I was a vegetarian?"

"I didn't expect you to be perfect."

I used that moment to change the subject. I needed to catch my breath.

"So you're a musician . . ."

He shrugged, playing coy at first. Then he started chatting about his band, the Careless Ones. There were four of them in the group; they'd all grown up together in Metarie. And though they started as a Dixieland punk band, whatever that was, they were veering more into blues and country.

"But half of us want to go in one direction," he continued. "The other half in the opposite. And I'm the lead singer. Some days I feel like I'm in the middle of a custody battle for the soul of the band . . ."

He held his draft glass by the rim instead of its waist. His hair was damp and he smelled like apples. And his hands. Did I mention his hands? His fingers were lean, his forearms sinewy from holding guitars or microphones or signing autographs. Then he continued talking—about himself, his music, his band, his dreams, his aspirations, his influences, his inspirations. And I was spellbound. Not by his story, but by his total self-involvement. Rather than making me feel agitated, his youthful self-obsession suddenly, completely relaxed me. Maybe he was looking for my approval, but I wasn't looking for his. I just wanted two things from him. His mouth on my mouth. His hands on my body. I just wanted with him what I'd had with my fantasy men: sex, no strings attached.

Our burgers arrived and he popped a fry in his remarkable mouth. I took a bite of my burger. Then another one. I thought the silence was a cue for him to ask about me, but he started talking again.

"I mean I didn't, like, *study* music. For me it's all about the effect on the audience. That's the only way you measure music, by—"

"Stop talking."

"—the way it feels when it rushes over the—"

"Stop talking."

"—crowd."

This time he heard me.

It was my turn to talk.

"It's sweet how passionate you are about music, Mark. But if you want me to come upstairs with you, you've got to promise you're going to use that beautiful mouth of yours for something other than talking."

I watched his Adam's apple rise and fall. He dipped a fry in ketchup and took a bite. Then he signaled for the bill.

Up I went, landing on the laminate counter between a tiny fridge and a tinier stove, his lean torso wedged between my thighs. Off came my T-shirt. Then he grabbed my sneakers by the heels, pulling them off too, one then the other, tossing them over his shoulders. My jeans came off next, leaving me in a black lace bra and thong. It wasn't planned. These were lucky picks.

"Fuck you're hot," he whispered, liberating one of my nipples, which instantly hardened in his cool mouth.

"I told you, no talking." I leaned back into the metal upper cabinets. This was how I'd do it, how I'd get over Will, how I'd shove images of him and Tracina out of my head. I'd make new memories, with new men to think about when I needed relief or release. Starting with this one.

Over his shoulder I took in the dim, masculine room, a British flag for curtains, a small fat-backed TV perched on a hope chest across from a high double bed with drawers beneath. It was tidy, but it had a second-hand, temporary feel. No one would be here long, least of all a girl.

While he took my other nipple in his mouth, going slowly back and forth, slicking it down, I worked my fingers through his hair, and gathered up his T-shirt in my fists. Off it came, his smooth skin surprisingly free of tattoos. Both of his hands now clutched my thighs, spreading them a little wider. His palms felt hot against my gusset, which grew damp from the way his knuckle teased along my groove.

"*Ohh*, you're wet," he crooned, biting my bottom lip as a finger eased aside the elastic. Inflamed, he kissed me back into the cupboards, his finger now frantic, freeing more of my moisture.

My hands were now ripping the buttons of his jeans, pulling one, two, three of them open, digging down the front of his pants.

"Oh sweet Jesus," I muttered, folding my hand firmly around his erection, pulsing in my hand.

"For me?" I couldn't believe I'd said it, but it felt so good. *He* felt so good. I stroked him, making him harder still.

"Holy fuck," he moaned, lifting me off the counter, easily carrying me into the living area and dropping me backwards onto the bed with a bounce. His erection was apparent over his splayed jeans. My hands had measured correctly; he *was* definitely blessed, like the cliché of a rock star, and by the look on his pleased face he knew it. As he yanked his jeans all the way down, I lay there in my bra and underwear, feeling so sexy, so dirty, so right. I watched him stumble out of his boxer shorts.

"Oh my," he said, standing next to me on his bed, talking like a British TV detective. "What have we here? I think we have evidence of a very horny girl in my bed. Let's see what's under this bra and these panties, shall we?"

He slid a hand under my back to undo my bra, removing it and discarding it over his shoulder. It landed on a guitar in the corner, looking like a still life that might be called *Sex with a Musician*. Then I arched as his hand slid down the front of my panties, my hips bucking slightly to keep his fingers out of reach, to make him work to find me, enjoying the tease. Impatient, he grabbed the waistband and pulled them all the way down, leaving them roped around an ankle.

"That's better."

He moved to the foot of the bed and lifted one of my bare feet to his mouth. That mouth—his singing mouth, his humming and moaning mouth. His lips tickled my smaller toes, before completely enveloping my big toe, sending sweet agony snaking up my legs. Then he reached into a nearby end table and opened the top drawer, taking out a condom and rolling it on.

"Spread your legs, Cassie," he said.

"Say please," I teased, stretching my arms over my head and closing my knees. I froze the scene in my head. *Click.* A year ago, this would have been unthinkable. Something that only happened to other women. Yet here I was, a pleasure seeker, a pleasure giver, a pleasure taker.

He slipped his hands between my thighs, slowly opening them, and I lay there splayed and glistening, turned on by the determined look on his face. His size was exceptional, and despite my soaking wetness, his first thrust split me with the most perfect kind of pain imaginable. My thighs clutched around his lean hips. My hand grabbed his tense forearm. *Oh jeez.* I gasped as he thrust again, this time harder.

"Am I hurting you?" he asked, sweetly.

"Yes, but it's good, it's *so* good."

"It *is* good," he murmured, savoring the slow, deep thrusts, which began to quicken as he felt me clench around him, taking the whole of him in, finally.

"Oh yeah, you're so fucking *tight.*"

I watched him sink into me, faster and fiercer. *Yes. I can come like this!* I thought, lifting my knees higher, feeling him reach the very end of me.

Then he slowed to a stop. *No!* And pulled himself out, leaving me hungry, gasping. I almost screamed, *Don't stop!*— until I realized he had no intention of stopping anything. I felt his tongue swimming in my belly button, releasing another rush of wetness below. He opened me wider still, pressing my knees up and apart, holding me down, his face exploring me, kissing my thighs, the inner groves, nibbling greedily along my folds until he found my tiny, tight clitoris—fully engorged now—nosing it, lapping at it. He surrounded it fully with his mouth, sucking my lips and swirling his tongue around my tender, throbbing clit, making me utterly delirious.

"*Ohh* yeah," I sighed. *This is for you. Let him.* My hand clutched a fistful of his hair, while he cupped my butt, his thumb pressing into me, his tongue carving mad circles, pulling everything into focus.

"You like that?" he murmured between flickering tongue strokes. "Yeah?"

I couldn't help it. *I couldn't.* I gave way to an orgasm so intense I screamed into the ceiling as his fingers thrust and his tongue continued to circle and flutter through my cries. *Oh god oh god oh god, I'm coming, yes!* I had one hand on his headboard, the other clenching his hair, and I was bucking and gasping as it shot straight through my middle and out all four limbs. My eyes squeezed shut to hold on to the intensity of it all before it finally, cruelly subsided.

He inched his way up my weakened body, kissing my stomach, rubbing his wet lips across my nipples, then pushing himself back into me; he was so hard, so fucking *hard*. I had barely caught my breath when our bodies came crashing together, my hands clutching his hips, my knees bracketing him tight, the friction making me dizzy. My pleasure mounted again. *What the hell?* And then like lightning I came *again*, throwing my head back. *"Oh my god . . . Will! Yes! Oh, Will, oh . . ."* I cried out, just as he came, saying my name, groaning into my hair, grinding into my body . . .
Fuck.

I covered my mouth and shut my eyes, both at the intensity of the pleasure and at my stupid, *stupid* gaffe. When he gently pulled out and rolled off me, I hoped, *prayed* he hadn't quite heard what I had said. I mean, we were both so loud, and it was all so intense and so, *so* good . . . *Why did I have to fuck it up?*

"So . . . yeah. Will. That's your ex?" he asked the ceiling, while tugging off the condom.

Damn.

He looked at me and I nodded.

"Why aren't you with him?"

"It's complicated."

"It always is."

"I'm sorry. That was . . . an accident. And not worth discussing."

"If you say so." He sounded sincere.

Whew.

"But you know what *is* worth discussing?" I said, rolling onto my elbow to face him. I tried to offer a coy grin, something to signal a change not just in subject, but in mood. "Your captain's bed."

He bit.

"Just because it's got storage underneath doesn't mean it's a captain's bed. It's a small apartment. You have to conserve space."

My fingers moved up and down his firm stomach, following the soft line of dark hair that led to a neat thatch surrounding his penis, now spent and resting heavy on his thigh. This man was especially sexy when he wasn't talking.

"You are . . . amazing," I said.

With my finger I circled one of his nipples, then the other one.

"And you are funny," he said, still breathless. "And fun."

I put my finger over his beautifully formed, very talented lips.

"That's right," I said. "Funny. And fun. I think those are operative words here."

"I'm sure there are other *f* words we can incorporate," he said, wrapping his lips around my finger and sucking it.

I closed my eyes. Okay. We were good. *Liberation, indeed.*

DAUPHINE

Ever since my first fantasy on the Abita River almost a month ago, I felt as though an extra line of voltage had been installed in my body. How else to explain my energy that day? Not only did I send Elizabeth home, I sorted and priced the last of the estate-sale boxes, purged old stock and made the store so pristine, so sparkly, I had the urge to close up shop for good lest any of my hard work be disturbed by actual shoppers.

I even took a picture. And instead of feeling drained by the exertion, I felt victorious, energized. Then I spotted them in the front window—*the tables!* I forgot the folding sale tables on the sidewalk.

"Dammit, dammit, dammit," I said, quickly unlocking the door. It was after hours, so Magazine Street was almost empty. I stacked the scratched plastic bins, which contained everything from mismatched opera gloves, lopsided wigs, dyed-satin clutches with tiny stains, odd-sized fishnets, so-so rhinestones that I had left under a sign marked "Charity

Bins: $2 each—or $20 takes it all." I had been warned several times by the Magazine Street Retail Association that I wasn't allowed to put my inventory on the sidewalk unless it was Spring Fling, when the whole street shut down for an outdoor sale. Last year I was slapped with an eight-hundred-dollar fine when I ignored the rule on Easter weekend. But I was so proud of myself for making a dent, even a small one, in moving some of the dead inventory, I justified my infraction.

I saw a tall, imposing shadow cross the table in front of me.

"Miss Dauphine Mason?"

I slowly turned around, clutching a pink pageboy wig in one fist, two stray gloves under an armpit. I was eye-level with a taut blue shirt and a shiny brass badge.

"Well, shut my mouth," I said, my mother's accent flying out of me. Police officers do bring out the Belle in me, what with their close-cropped hair and broad shoulders.

And this one was particularly . . . arresting, with his grey-flecked eyes and a singular dimple in his cheek that disappeared when he chewed his gum. He stood cocking a hip, a man used to his own authority, with a set of handcuffs dangling from his belt.

"I need you to step inside the store, Miss Mason," he said, looking around, his jaw clenching.

"Who squealed on me this time?"

"Just step inside, please. Don't worry. There's no trouble."

He had the thighs of a runner—maybe from chasing bad guys?

"Jesus Murphy's cousin," I said, both hands on my hips now. "It's just a gosh darn table, Officer."

"Language, Miss Mason."

"If I am asked to pay another eight-hundred-dollar fine for putting tables on the sidewalk, I am not going to be very happy."

Without answering, he followed me into the store, where I could no longer contain my outrage. I flicked the lights back on.

"You know this is ridiculous," I said, tossing my store keys on the glass counter. "You should be catching criminals, not businesswomen eking out a living."

While I ranted, he moved slowly around the store, ducking his head into the men's side, peering over the high racks.

"Miss Mason, I have a patrol car parked out back."

"For what?"

"To save you the embarrassment of taking you into my custody on the street. But if you don't shut—"

"You want me to shut up? Well, I won't. I think it's unfair that—"

"Miss Mason, what I was going to say is if you don't shut the front door, lock it, then *accept the Step*, I won't be able to . . . arrest you."

With that, he moved towards me, dangling the handcuffs he had loosened from his belt. His smile took on a playful wickedness.

"Don't make me use these. Unless you *want* me to."

"I . . . I . . . You're from . . . *They* sent you?"

My anger subsided, replaced with embarrassment, then curiosity, then arousal.

"What'll it be, Miss Mason?"

"Are you a real cop?" I asked, my eyes narrowing. This was getting interesting.

"I don't have to answer that."

He was standing close enough to me that I could smell his peppermint gum.

I lifted my wrists in front of me. "Well, I guess it's time, then," I said. "I accept the Step."

If a cop could be balletic, that is the word I'd use to describe how he deftly turned me around, secured my arms behind my back and locked my wrists together in his snug cuffs. He put his mouth next to my ear.

"Where are the store keys?" he whispered.

A hot shiver snaked down my back. So this is what it felt like to be restrained. Frankly, it was not only one of my fears, it was also one of my darkest fantasies. I was beginning to see a pattern. First, conquering the water, now this.

"Aren't we staying here?"

"'Fraid not, ma'am. I'm taking you down to the station."

I looked at my plain cotton housedress, perfect for errands and cleaning but not for seduction. Not looking my best prior to having sex? Also a fear. Damn them.

"Am I . . . *dressed* for the station?"

"You'll be the best-dressed, or undressed, one there."

"What are you going to do to me?"

"Everything you want, nothing you don't."

Right. Good to be reminded. I felt calmer again. Then we got as far as the change room area and I suddenly stopped moving, my feet welded to the painted concrete. "Wait!"

"Courage, Dauphine," he said, his hand gently nudging my back.

"No. I need my purse."

He exhaled.

"Where is it?"

"Under the counter," I said, tilting my chin to indicate. "Thank you."

I was struck by the oddity of the picture—this tall, masculine image of justice returning with my coral leather hobo bag.

The air in the alley was cool, the night still. He locked the front and back doors of my store and then ducked me into the back seat of his dark vehicle, hand on my head, and tucked my purse in next to me.

"Thank you kindly. You're a gentleman."

"No. I'm a mean police officer."

"Right," I said. "I understand."

He has a role to play—let him, Dauphine. Trust and control.

When he settled into the driver's seat and took off, a tiny panic set in. I knew this man wasn't going to hurt me, or book me, or keep me someplace I didn't want to be, but I did not like being a passenger, let alone being caged in like this. Yet hadn't I also been afraid to let that beautiful man float me on my back in the Abita River? I was so scared when we turned off the Covington Highway that day, but so happy afterwards. That day still played out in my mind, like a bonus track. I tried to relax into my seat, but I found myself alternating between fear and excitement, which only increased my arousal. I started to understand the appeal of restraints.

It took only a few turns through the darkened streets of the Garden District for us to arrive at our destination: the Mansion. The gates opened and swallowed up the car. My heart quickened; so far I had only been to the Coach House. Then my heart sank as we slowly passed the side entrance, heading over a slight crest to what looked like a large garage next to the kidney-shaped pool, sparkling under the dark sky.

"No Mansion?"

"No more questions."

A garage door slowly opened and my policeman inched the car into a spot between two other vehicles, both fancy and expensive, though I couldn't have named them if the officer had put a gun to my head. He shut the engine off, exited the car and opened my back door.

"Step outside the vehicle, Miss Mason."

I propelled myself to my feet, wrists still cuffed. He sidestepped me to close the car door, and then pressed me up against his side. I could feel him hard against my hip.

"You're turning me into a bad cop, Miss Mason," he said, leaning in for a firm, insistent kiss.

I opened my mouth to his just as he pulled away.

"Are you ready for your interrogation?"

I nodded. *Okay. This will work.* He guided me by the arm through a door in the garage, we entered a small, warm office. There were two steel chairs facing each other on a thick carpet, a table to the side. The windows were covered with blackout curtains. The whole room was lit with one dim overhead bulb. He pulled out a chair for me and I sat. He took the chair opposite me, so our knees almost touched.

"Are you ready?" he asked.

I looked around the bare, still room. Not exactly the scene of high romance, but somehow it felt charged with sex.

"Ready when you are," I said, leaning back in my chair, my hands shackled behind me.

"You're being impudent."

"Authority brings that out in me." It was true. I decided if he wanted me to surrender, he'd have to make me.

"Stand up, please. I want to see if you're wearing a wire."

"A what?" I asked, laughing.

"Stand up and let me unbutton that dress."

He threw his cap onto the table beside us and rolled up his sleeves. I stood in front of him, chin jutting out. His big hands went to my top button. One after the other, he released them, leaving my dress gaping. Oh dear, my underwear did not match my bra. Why was that suddenly so tragic? It was hardly going to be a deal-breaker and yet I was disappointed. I would have dressed better, different. *Trust and control.*

He moved the dress off my shoulders so it bunched in back, over my cuffs.

"See? No wire, Officer." Was my voice quavering? Where was my bravado now?

"I'm not done my search," he said. He clearly liked what he saw, but I had never felt so vulnerable, being regarded like this so openly. "Come closer," he said.

He opened his legs so I could step between them, the outsides of my thighs touching the insides of his. He leaned back, resting his head in his hands, and looked up at my face.

"For such a bad, bad woman, you look very, very good right now," he said.

His eyes scanned my breasts, my skin, my hips. Not able to remove my bra, he reached up and lifted my breasts out and rested them pertly above the cups.

"Perfect," he said.

My heart sped up. Being cuffed, being unable to touch him, or push him away, scared me a little. But he had such an open, warm face, and those eyes . . .

"I'm going to remove your underwear, Miss Mason," he said. "I need to search all of you."

He placed his fingers tenderly in my waistband, his face stern, and slid the panties down. I stepped out of them. I could feel his breath on my skin, my stomach. Then he pivoted my whole body and held my hips firmly from behind.

"What are you doing?" I asked, fear coming over me now that I wasn't facing him. My eyes darted around the room.

"Checking all of you."

He moved aside my dress, still bunched around my wrists. He glided one of his hands over my ass, like he was admiring a sculpture up close, gently kissing the places his hands touched. I shut my eyes. Slowly, agonizingly, I felt his fingers slipping between my legs where I knew I was already wet.

"Just making sure you're not concealing anything," he said, coiling his finger up inside of me. *Ohhhh.* His voice was cracking with the kind of helplessness that only desire creates.

Was this really happening?

He pulled me down onto his lap. *Oh lord,* I could feel his erection against my thigh, my hands now near it, and I felt a growing ache. From behind, he split my legs apart, burying his face between my arms, my shoulder blades. He pulled off my ponytail holder, releasing my hair down my back. I watched as his hand moved across the front of my body, his fingers finding me again, so wet I almost apologized.

"You've been a bad girl, Dauphine."

"*Yes . . .*" I closed my eyes, leaning back into him, desire mounting as his fingers dipped and circled my wetness.

"I'm going to have to do some bad things to you. Would you like that?"

"Yes," I said. I could feel his erection grow, my hips lightly, instinctively grinding against it.

"Time for this interrogation to come to a close," he whispered, rising from the chair and taking me with him, moving towards the table.

He pressed me across it, my breasts against its cool surface. "If I undo your cuffs, do you promise to be good?" he asked.

I nodded as he released me, placing one hand, then the other, on the table in front of me. I rubbed my wrists as he dropped his belt. I peeked over my shoulder to watch him tearing off his uniform, peeling up his white T-shirt so I could finally catch sight of what I had been feeling: a firm, broad chest, the overhead light illuminating every ripple, an expanse of smooth skin, a line of dark hair from his belly button, the thick crown of his erection visible over the top of the table. *This is so hot.*

"Look at you spread out like this for me," he said, slicking a finger and dragging it down my spine to my ass, now high in the air. *Oh my god.* I closed my eyes as he navigated the fold between my buttocks, circling shamelessly around my dark nerve-intense pucker.

"Jesus," I murmured, clutching the sides of the table as with every dip and tickle he sent a shock wave of pleasure through my whole body. I had never been touched there before, not like this, so openly.

"What are you *doing* to me?"

"Naughty things to a naughty girl," he said, grabbing my cheeks firmly, widening the area he was pleasuring. He bent to take me in, all tongue now, slow and languid. The wicked sensations pounded through my whole body. I was pulsating, engorged, on the cusp of coming without him even going near my usual places. *Oh god.*

"Do you like that?"

Half delirious, I could only answer with a sound. Then I heard a drawer open in the table beneath me, the crackling of a condom packet.

"Turn around, Dauphine. I want to look at your beautiful face while I fuck you senseless."

And I did, in a trance now, eagerly flipping around to face his perfect torso. I had never seen a man built like him before, ripples on top of muscles, hairless, made just for this.

I propped myself up on my elbows, boldly watching as he unspooled the condom. He yanked my hips down to the edge of the table, teasing my cleft with his slickened head, inching it inside of me, then out again, never taking his eyes off me. I It stopped every few seconds so I could yield to his thickness, helped by his wetted fingers across my clitoris. When he was fully inside, I collapsed back on the table, his hands now caressing my breasts, freed from the bra. My nipples responded, tightening under his touch. When he saw how turned on I was, he moved with greater urgency. I reached back and grabbed the other edge of the table for better leverage and then we became a blur of frantic thrusts. *Oh yeah. So good.*

Then came the first wave, as his thrusts found my sweet spot deep behind my pelvis, and I lost it, my arms flung behind my head, bringing my wall down, letting go of that residual fear. Our eyes met just at the apex when my orgasm struck hot and fierce, then his did too as he pumped me hard and fast, murmuring, "This is all for you, Dauphine. This is for you."

He jerked and shuddered at the end, but remained in me and above me, coated with a gorgeous sheen of sweat, as I clenched and spasmed around him. Slowly my breathing steadied.

He smiled. *Laughed.*

"Wow," he said.

"Did you get . . . all the information . . . you needed, Officer?"

"Yes, and then some. Now I have something for you."

He eased out, then bent down to take something from one of the pockets of his uniform pants, which were lying on the floor by his feet. When he rose, he was dangling a gleaming charm between a thumb and forefinger.

"What does it say?" I asked, still splayed across the table.

"*Courage.* And rightfully so, Miss Mason."

He shot the charm into the air with his thumb like a coin, letting it fall on my damp stomach. Then he slapped a hand over it.

"Heads or tails?"

"What do I get if I call it?" I asked.

"Anything you want, Miss Mason."

"Tails."

He slowly lifted his hand from my stomach and peeked beneath it.

"Well, what do you know," he said.

His eyes scanned my body, and he lowered himself to kiss the charm on my belly. Farther down he went and I closed my eyes. His mouth worked me into another fever, bringing me back to that incredible precipice, that ecstasy, then letting me fall over it again.

Afterwards, I lay on the table, my fingers entwined in his thick golden hair, his breath on my stomach, my other hand dangling over the side of the table, clutching *Courage* in my palm.

CASSIE

I asked Matilda for a last-minute meeting a few days after Dauphine's cop fantasy. Being her Guide meant spending less time with my own, but my one-night stand with Mark had left me feeling a little off.

As she made her way to where I was sitting in Audubon Park, she looked the picture of Southern gentility. She had on a straw hat, dark glasses and an off-the-shoulder coral-colored sundress that showed off her red hair and the smattering of freckles across her smooth décolleté. She was nearing sixty but looked as fresh and sexy as someone half her age. And by the way she walked, you could tell she knew entrances were her particular talent. It was her idea to meet near the pickup soccer pitch by the Saint Charles entrance. She moved towards the bench, and even the players during a breakaway had to stop to take her in.

As we sat together, I caught her up on Dauphine, explaining how she was learning to give over control.

"That's a tough one, control," Matilda said, eyeing the

soccer game. "Too much and you never allow yourself to know others. Too little and you never truly know yourself. How about you, Cassie, how are you faring out there in the wilds?"

"Fine. Good. I . . . I did it. I had *sex*," I blurted out.

"Oh? How lovely. With whom?"

"Some guy I just met," I said, sounding oddly triumphant. "The one from Ignatius's that day. He's not really my type. But sexually, he was fun."

"So you're not going to see him again?"

"I don't know. He's almost ten years younger than me. Young. Self-centered. Sexy, though. Maybe I *will* see him again. The beauty of it is, I don't care whether I do or not. But the sex was incredible."

"So you *don't* want to hear from him again?" Matilda asked.

"Not really . . . I don't know. Does that make me a slut?"

Matilda turned her whole body towards me, her attention fully off the soccer game. She looked as though I'd just slapped her.

"The word *slut*, unless employed by iron-clad feminists or ironically by irony *experts*, has no business coming out of a woman's mouth, do you hear me? Not when she is describing her own sexual behavior and *especially* if she's describing another woman's. It's the kind of word that can scar, Cassie."

I was stunned. I'd never heard her use such a sharp tone.

"That word has been used as a weapon against women all around the world, since the beginning of time, to keep us feeling unworthy and separate. It can have especially tragic consequences for young women. Some shut down; some lose their confidence; some lose their desire to explore their sexuality; and still others end their lives over sexual shame."

I'd never really given the subject much thought, but I have, in my life, felt that shame, that sense that there was something wrong about wanting and enjoying sex. But since joining S.E.C.R.E.T. that shame had been fading. In fact, it seemed ludicrous to hold on to any of those old ideas. Then something else occurred to me.

"If shame is so toxic, why isn't S.E.C.R.E.T. more public? That would be a way to fight the stigma, the double standard. Why should 'slut' be an insult to women and not necessarily to men?"

"Let me ask you something. If we went public, would you admit to being an enthusiastic member of a group of women that arranges sexual fantasies for other women? Would you like to share with the world *all* the marvelous men you've met and *all* the marvelous things you've done with them, in S.E.C.R.E.T.?"

She lifted her sunglasses to look right into my eyes. She had me. There was no way I could face that potential scrutiny.

"We can't change the world, Cassie, but we can liberate one woman at a time. Reduce her shame. That's all we can do. Now, tell me all about this young man you slept with."

"Well, let's see. I *like* him. I like being with him. But when I'm not with him, I don't think about him. Then I feel guilty because I should have more feelings for him, shouldn't I?"

"Should. Shouldn't. Who cares," she said with a wave of her hand. "I think it's perfectly healthy, perfectly *necessary*, that a thirty-six-year-old woman like you has terrific sex with a younger man from whom she wants little else. Let me ask you something: were you honest with him about what you wanted?"

"Yes."

"Was the sex consensual?"

"Of course."

"Did you use protection?"

"We did."

"Well then, good for you! What fun it must be to be back in your body, to simply experience a man. So, no more talk of sluts, all right? No judgment. No limits. No shame. That applies to how you think about yourself too."

It felt like a good time to bring someone else up, someone who I *did* want to see again, for whom I still had lingering feelings.

"How's Jesse?" I asked, as casually as possible. "Is he next on Dauphine's fantasy list?"

"I believe he is," she said, looking out over the field. "He was your number three. We think he should be Dauphine's as well."

Ouch. I tried not to look at her, but she was eyeing a cute, sweaty player with his hands on his knees who was catching his breath. He looked about thirty, Latin, maybe South American or Italian. Not too tall, stocky, fit, with a head of messy black hair and teeth so white they flashed brilliant from ten yards away.

"See that one?" she asked.

"He's kind of hard to miss," I said. "Do you know him?"

"We're in the process of recruiting him. Angela was supposed to be my wing girl today. That task has now fallen to you."

"Now?"

"*Get the ball!*" Matilda screamed. "Honey, I know what you're thinking regarding Jesse. You can't have Will, and you don't want this young fella, so you're looking for a little something in the middle. That's okay. But I'm not sure pulling Jesse off the roster is a great idea. Besides, I have a special trip I'd like you to go on. You know we have to auction off *Red Rage.*"

"The painting in the Coach House?"

"That's right. We've decided to auction it off in Buenos Aires, in Carolina's home country. We think we can get the best price there, since there are only two paintings left. We need you to accompany the painting and represent our . . . consortium. You don't have to take any photos or answer any questions. You'll just put on a cute dress and sign a transfer of sale certificate."

Wow, Buenos Aires. The last trip I had taken was to Canada, where I had my ski instructor fantasy. I was due for a vacation . . . but with Tracina pregnant and Dell so old, it just wasn't possible.

"I wish I could, but leaving Will right now . . . it would devastate the Café."

"You really care about him, don't you."

Before I could answer, a runaway ball rolled close to our bench, followed by the guy Matilda had had her eye on. She smiled at him.

"Hey. Are you our coach now? Or just the ref?" he asked Matilda, breathless from running.

"You guys could use both," Matilda teased, tilting her head up to get a better look at his face over the brim of her hat. "What's your name?"

"Dominic. Yours?"

"Matilda Greene. This here's my friend Cassie."

"You guys soccer fans?"

"No," Matilda said.

Dominic laughed while one of his opponents razzed him to put the ball back in play.

"Don't go anywhere, Matilda Greene," he yelled, running backwards and folding into the play.

Every few seconds he'd glance over to make sure she was still there.

I was awestruck.

"How did you *do* that?"

"Do what?"

"Get the hottest guy in the park to come over and talk to you. Women half your age couldn't pull that off."

She shrugged, her eyes still on him.

"I singled him out. Separated him from his pack. Everyone recruits differently. But this is my method."

Dominic broke away with the ball again, heading fast to the other side of the pitch. "*Go! Go! Go!*"

"Are we recruiting right now?"

"Yes, as a matter of fact. We're down one since we dropped Pierre. That's why I'm reluctant to give you Jesse. Did you spot a wedding ring on our Dominic?"

"I wasn't looking."

"That's the first thing you have to look for."

I made a mental note as the soccer players headed to mid-field. At one point, Dominic pulled his shirt up to wipe his face, revealing his muscled stomach.

"Whoa," I said.

"Yes, he's really quite beautiful, isn't he. But they don't all have to be models to be recruits. They do have to know they're sexy. They have to be able to hold a conversation, seem interesting, even if they aren't. Attractiveness is sub-jective, but we like to stick to the 'classic' sexy, confident, masculine trio of attributes. And of course, they need to be in top health. This one is all that. And, what do you know, no wedding ring."

She glanced at her watch.

"Cassie, I need you to close this deal for me. *I* have to find someone to go to Argentina."

"Close what deal?"

"Get Dominic's number. Maybe he can replace Jesse," she said, winking.

My panic started at my feet and traveled all the way to the back of my skull like an ice cream headache.

"But he wants to meet *you*. He barely looked at me. What if he won't give me his number?"

Matilda stood and peered across the pitch, like a lioness lazily eyeing a gazelle.

"All you need to do is ask. In the meantime, be kind to yourself. This one-night stand's got you in a bit of a tumult. Don't let it derail all the progress you've made. You're coming into your own. I see it."

Matilda sauntered to the Saint Charles exit, missing Dominic's assisted goal. He carved a victory lap from the net to center field, where he messed up a redheaded opponent's hair, made one more circle to slap hands with sitting opponents, then finally landed at my bench.

"Hey," he said breathlessly. "Where'd your friend go?"

"She had to leave," I said, quickly adding, "but she did ask me to get your number."

"What? Very cool." He beamed.

All you have to do is ask. I was punching his number into my cell phone when his ginger friend came running up behind him.

"Meeting and greeting your fans, Dom? Does this one have a name?"

Was he looking at me? Yep. He was.

"Cassie," I said, shielding my eyes and squinting into his face, which, upon closer inspection, was cute. Added to that, he had a thick Scottish accent and freckled, muscular forearms.

"I'm Ewan. Listen, lose this bugger's number and take down mine."

"How 'bout this," I said, trying to keep the butterflies in my stomach from affecting my voice. "I'll give Dominic's number to my friend, and maybe I'll keep yours for myself."

"Can't imagine a better plan," he said.

Their numbers safely locked in my phone, I stood to leave.

"Well, fellas, it's been lovely."

Walking towards Magazine Street, I marveled at the fact that I had just made contact with two incredibly sexy men whose own fantasies S.E.C.R.E.T. might unlock. And if they were amenable and discreet, they'd be trained by one of the Committee members. Then they'd be lined up with a lucky candidate, perhaps Dauphine. I glanced around the park, now packed and buzzing with fit joggers, cute dads and hot cyclists. Had these men always been here and I'd never noticed them before? Or were they noticing something in me for the first time?

Matilda's words rang in my mind: *You're coming into your own. I see it.*

DAUPHINE

E lizabeth was the first to notice a stale petroleum smell wafting around outside the store. You couldn't blame Katrina or any of the other famous hurricanes. The infrastructure in New Orleans was long compromised before those epic storms laid bare its awful issues. But a possible gas leak would mean wholesale evacuation, and that meant shutting down eleven stores and restaurants in one of the most pedestrian-heavy parts of town. The Funky Monkey was looking at a month-long shutdown to replace old gas lines buried under the sidewalks out front.

"You do realize, Cassie, when they say a month in New Orleans, it could mean six. I have not been unemployed since I was a teenager."

My whining was taking place over margaritas at Tracy's. I must have been anxious; I was out-drinking Cassie two to one. We'd become friends. She had even filled me in on her drama with her boss, Will, and how she almost ended up with him. Maybe that's why I so boldly inquired about

Mark Drury. We were talking about men, sex and dating, so it didn't seem like I was prying about my weird crush.

"Yeah, we met. His name's Mark. A musician. Who. Talks. About. Music. Non. Stop," she said, rolling her eyes. "We've been out once but . . ."

"But?"

"He's just . . . he's not for me," she said. "I don't know why, or *what* I have to do to get Will out of my head and my heart for good. But Mark's not going to help me."

I hated to admit my relief. Not that I thought I had a chance with Mark. And I certainly wasn't interested in pursuing anyone while a stack of fantasies awaited me. But still. Then a look crossed her face, like a new and singular idea had just taken her brain hostage to the detriment of all other thoughts.

"Wait one sec. Let me make a phone call. I'll be right back."

When she returned a minute later, she was still talking on her cell.

"Yup . . . yeah . . . she's right here. Hold on." She covered the receiver, her face open and hopeful. "Matilda wants to talk to you."

Baffled, I took her phone from her.

"Hi, Matilda. What's going on?"

"Dauphine, honey, I understand you might have some time on your hands. I have a rather exciting mission for you to consider, and at the same time, you'd be doing S.E.C.R.E.T. a big favor."

Then she laid out what to a normal person would be a dream vacation: a free trip to Buenos Aires, where I'd stay in a five-star hotel and attend the auction of a rare painting, with plenty of time to see the sights and do some shopping. It sounded heady, glamorous and exciting. Except for the part about the plane.

"We'd pay your expenses and give you ample spending money, Dauphine. The auction is already arranged—you just have to show up and sign some papers on behalf of S.E.C.R.E.T."

I thanked her and told her it all sounded amazing, incredible even, adding I was flattered and humbled to even be considered. In fact, Buenos Aires was a city I'd always hoped to see. But there was one small problem.

"The thing is, Matilda, I don't fly. Ever."

Cassie was listening to our conversation, and when she heard that, her eager smile turned to a frown.

"Oh, honey," Matilda said, laughing. "Is that all that's holding you back? Once a fear is exposed it's no longer a fear. It's an opportunity for a decision—to stay stuck or to go forward."

I protested further, trying to explain.

"I hate being a passenger. I need to be at the wheel of things. I just . . . I can't give up that control."

"But you've let folks drive you around in a car, haven't you?"

I told her at least with a car, I knew I could force it to the side of the road and get out. "A plane ride is not only a full-on commitment, it's an act of faith, both in the plane's ability to remain aloft and in my ability to trust a pilot to keep it there. And as silly as it sounds, I don't have a lot of faith in either of those things, Matilda." I added, "I don't even have a passport."

"Pfft. Details. We can get you one in twenty-four hours. Trust me when I tell you, Dauphine, that you can and will transform this fear into faith. Trust us. Trust this process."

While Matilda continued to underscore the principles of flight, highlighting its best features and those also of Buenos Aires, Cassie carefully turned her paper coaster into an airplane, which she proceeded to fly over the top of my head. With sound effects.

What can I say? They wore me down, reminding me that I had told the Committee to surprise me.

After I accepted the trip and hung up, Cassie gave me a standing ovation in the middle of Tracy's. Later, when I told Elizabeth I was getting on a plane, she was so proud of me she dragged a piece of vintage luggage, the kind without wheels, to my apartment to help me pack. In my preemptive terror I told her where all the important papers were, with strict instructions that if the plane went down, the store and all its assets would go to her, not to my sister, Bree.

"She can have a fur," I said. "But not one of the minks."

"Okay," Elizabeth said. "But I'm sure it won't come to divvying up your estate."

"You never know. Life is weird. It throws things at you," I said, tossing a pair of kitten heels into the suitcase. Indeed,

I'd traveled from my initiation into S.E.C.R.E.T. to this, packing for a transcontinental flight. My eventual "yes" to Matilda came from the same place I found my yeses for my fantasy men so far, on a shelf below my doubt, in front of all my fears. Hopefully, there were a few more yeses left before boarding time a few weeks later.

Having never flown before, I so far hadn't found much about travel to recommend it. The airport was both chaotic and bovine, generating this awful "hurry up and wait" syndrome that triggered stress sweats and the jitters.

"I leading to Buenos Aires?" a deep, accented voice asked, poking through my trance and startling me.

I turned to face a crisp white dress shirt, stretched over the fit chest of an exceptionally tall, exceptionally attractive black man. He was behind me in line, loading his plastic bin with a heavy platinum watch, a black eel-skin wallet and a carefully folded suit bag. Though dressed like a casual businessman, he had an easy smile that made him look more like a movie star.

"How do you know where I'm going?" I asked. I dropped my S.E.C.R.E.T. bracelet in my bin with a clang. I had thought of leaving it behind, but now that I had a couple of charms dangling off it, I enjoyed wearing it.

"I guessed." He had a British accent. "Actually, it's on your ticket. And it's the first flight out this morning."

If the gods were truly on my side, they'd give me this man to lean on during turbulence.

"Is that where you're going too?" I asked, and yes, eyelashes were batted.

Before he could answer, a brusque security officer motioned me through the full-body X-ray. I stepped into the chamber, threw my hands in the air and spun, and then was reunited with my belongings. By the time I turned around to continue my conversation, the man was being ushered ahead of everyone in line, flanked by two men in uniform. He must have been someone important. He was definitely well dressed. Being in the fashion business, I noticed good buttons and well-chosen cufflinks and how a shirt that's been properly tailored hangs spectacularly down a man's V-shaped back as he walks away from you—turning back once, as this one did, to glance at you over his shoulder.

From the moment I sat down in my aisle seat in First Class, the cool blond flight attendant seemed specifically assigned to me.

"I'm Eileen. We were told this was your first time," she said. "You let me know how I can make this less stressful for you."

She brought me a hot towel, a small footrest and a stack of celebrity magazines, each time placing a reassuring hand on my forearm. During the taxi, she addressed her safety demonstration directly to me. And when the plane sucked me back into the seat on takeoff, a most shocking and intoxicating feeling, Eileen winked at me from her saddle seat. I almost

burst into tears at her kindness, let alone at the thoughtful-
ness of Matilda to let them know of my first-timer status.
Still, it wasn't until we leveled off that I loosened the grip
on my armrests, my fingers numb from clasping so tightly.

The seat-belt light went off, but I had no interest in
unbuckling. In fact, my plan was to pass on every beverage,
lest I had to pee while flying thirty thousand feet over Peru.
I decided if I sat very, very still, I could get through this
ordeal, a few hundred miles a minute, never leaving my seat,
never looking out the window, even though the seat beside
me was empty.

An hour and a half into the flight, we were all still alive,
and I began to move my legs a little, tilting my seat back to
settle in for the night flight. People began to close their
windows, and Eileen dimmed the cabin lights before passing out extra blankets. When she kneeled in front of me, I
thought for a moment that she was literally going to tuck
me in. Instead, she deposited a folded blanket on my lap
and leaned in to whisper, "Miss Mason, the captain would
be happy to honor your request to visit the cockpit while
the plane's on autopilot."

I burst out laughing. Never had anyone so seriously mistaken me for someone else.

"Oh, I didn't ask for any such thing. I would never—"

Before I could finish my sentence, Eileen gently removed
an envelope from the folds of my blanket and left it on
my lap. "I'm sure we're not mistaken," she said, eyeing me
steadily. "I'll return in a few minutes to escort you."

The envelope was unmarked, but I recognized the paper's creamy color. My heart started to race. Was I facing Step Three at thirty-five-thousand feet in the air? My hand was shaky as I ripped open the envelope. Sure enough, *Step Three* scrolled on one side of the heavy card stock and just one simple word was on the other: *Trust.* But who was doing the trusting—me, or every one of the passengers on this plane who wouldn't care to know how I was about to distract the pilot? I slipped the Step card into my purse and shook out a half-dozen Tic Tacs, which I barely had time to finish before the flight attendant returned.

"Are you ready, Miss Mason?"

I swallowed the remaining candy shards. "Um. Yes. I think so," I said, trying to disguise the terror in my voice.

"An old friend of mine once said that a fear uncovered is no longer a fear. It's an opportunity for a decision. Once you see how a plane operates, once you get an intimate look at all the buttons and levers, you can decide to end your fear of flying. Captain Nathan will be all too happy to help you."

She was quoting Matilda! Eileen was one of us. She gave me her hand, and practically had to pull me to my feet because my legs were rigid with terror.

"There. See? That wasn't so bad."

We made it down the short aisle. Standing in front of the cockpit door, she gave three quick knocks. A second later, a sandy-haired young man with thick glasses and a space between his front teeth poked his head out. *Oh dear.* I hated to admit that my shallow Southern heart sank, though I politely pulled my grin a little wider, reminding myself what the *C* in S.E.C.R.E.T. stood for. If my fantasy man wasn't . . . *compelling*, I didn't have to go through with the fantasy.

"Is this our lovely visitor?" he asked with a lisp. *Oh dear.*

"Yes," the flight attendant said. "Miss Dauphine Mason, this is our multitalented First Officer Friar. Miss Mason is keen to see what goes on in here. It might help her with her fear of flying."

"Ah, yes. Dispel the mystery and the fear disperses. That's Captain Nathan's specialty. He can show you around while I stretch my legs. Three's a crowd in here! Good luck!"

After mangling all those *s*'s, First Officer Friar made a beeline to the back of the plane. Out the window in front was a dark sky; below, nothing but black water. The high whine of the engines masked the screams in my own head as my legs now turned to cement. Eileen nudged me through the narrow doorway.

"I'll be back in a little while," she said, looking at her watch. "Enjoy your flying lesson."

She shut the door behind her.

The pilot sat silhouetted in the window. The only thing I could see above the seat was the back of his head. He wasn't wearing a jacket, only his white shirt, the muscles on his arms apparent beneath his sleeves as he flicked a number of switches from left to right on a panel in front of him. Thankfully, the white noise drowned out my pounding heart.

"Be with you in a moment, Dauphine. I just want to make sure autopilot's running smoothly. A robot takes over for most of the flight from now on. A very smart one."

There it was. That accent again. The man from Security! The man with the sexy British accent! The air left my chest and the pressure squeezed my lungs. Feeling tantalized and terrified at that same time had a bad effect on my stomach. I slapped both hands on the curved walls of the cockpit to steady myself as the plane rose and straightened. The pilot faced a wall of lights and levers that seemed to blink and shift on their own. Then he finally turned his chair around, aviators off, brown eyes on me. I gasped.

"Don't worry, we're on automatic, but we're not going to be alone in here for long, so I apologize ahead of time for the furtive nature of our interlude," he said, loosening the top button of his uniform. "But I need to know, before we continue with our tutorial on the safety of flight: Do you accept the Step, Miss Mason?"

I couldn't believe this was happening.

"Here? Now?"

"Yes. Here and now. Trust me when I say I can help you with your fear of flying. And a few other things too, I suspect," he said, leaning back into the plush leather of his pilot seat, taking me in from bottom to top.

"I've never been in an airplane before," I muttered, stalling.

"I understand that," he said, steepling his fingers. "But you are doing a fine job of your first time."

Standing four feet from a complicated instrument panel that the pilot was *no longer facing*, I watched dark clouds whip by the nose of the plane through the high, narrow windows.

"Are we . . . safe in here?"

"Very safe," he said. "Safer than driving. Safer than almost any other activity you can do at hundreds of miles an hour, high in the air."

"What if there's turbulence?" I asked, just as we hit a little bump. I yelped. My arms flew up to grasp the ceiling.

He took it as a cue to gesture me over to him.

Here we go! I slowly, carefully, closed the gap between us, and over his shoulder got a better view of the world before me. It was dusk, but light poked through the clouds, illuminating little towns and villages nestled in the foot of a mountain range. They looked like a strand of jewels dropped from a great height. It was beautiful, but still I felt gutpunched and queasy. Levers and buttons continued to move in a ghostly way all around us.

"Turbulence is just air pockets. The plane will ride through it. And I'm right here if anything goes awry."

I stood above him now, his head level with my breasts.

"Do you accept the Step?"

Handsome face, kind eyes, great smell, manly hands, but the clincher truly was his beautifully tailored shirt. Terribly shallow, I know.

"Yes, I accept."

"Then may I help you off with your knickers?"

I almost laughed out loud at the old-fashioned British word for panties. I was wearing a pencil skirt and pumps, and a button-up pink angora sweater. The low ponytail completed my '50s-housewife-on-an-errand look. It couldn't be helped; planning my outfits always calmed me, and today I needed to be calm.

"Tell me more about how safe I am," I begged, as his warm hands gently undid the back of my skirt, letting it drop to the floor.

"Well, Dauphine," he said, inching my panties, or "knickers," down, "takeoff is the hardest part. So much can go wrong. But we're well past that now."

Standing before him, I closed my eyes. I could feel his fingers unbuttoning my sweater, easing it off my shoulders. *Ohh.*

"Now the middle part of flight," he said, leaning forward to nuzzle my soft line of pubic hair, kissing it. "That's the easiest . . . sweetest part of the ride. But still, you never want to get complacent. Sometimes it's deceptively easy. You still need to be careful, to watch for subtle signals."

I stood over him, my legs trembling. He reached back to undo my pink satin bra, slid it forward and dropped it. Standing there naked, for a second I *forgot the plane was flying on its own!* It was black through the window. I wasn't sure if we were flying over mountains or water, but I closed my eyes. If I couldn't see it, it didn't matter. I placed my hands on the ceiling again, pressing my body forward into him. He was so at ease, so in command as he gently urged my legs farther apart, reaching up to pinch and circle my nipples, like I was an instrument panel he knew exactly how to operate.

"How does the autopilot know what it's doing?" I asked,

so deeply aroused by his thumbs now expertly parting my cleft, I thought my knees would give.

"It listens to me. I tell it what to do and it follows my instructions," he said, leaning forward to kiss my clitoris, now centered between his thumbs.

"Mmm, you taste so good, my darling," he murmured, his fingers now joining his mouth, slowly gliding in and out, agonizing me. I felt every knuckle against my most tender parts, prodding my clitoris forward, as his mouth fully encircled me. I grabbed his head as it moved beneath me. Then I felt that rush, fast and hot, and the mounting energy as his urgent tongue fluttered and flicked, his fingers darting in and out. All I could do was shut my eyes and arch back, dying and shuddering as I exploded with a new kind of pleasure, moaning into the ceiling, his tongue lapping relentlessly at me, my hand over my mouth to muffle my cries.

"Oh my god! Oh yes . . . yes!" I whelped, trying to steady my legs as he urged his pants down, rolled on a condom and eased me down. Still in a daze, I felt every vein, every ridge, as I wilted onto his lap, my thighs straddling him in his captain's chair, my feet barely touching the ground. A firm arm wrapped around my back, he moved up and into me, his brown eyes pleased as he took in my body, and I faced *the fucking front of the plane and the window and, holy shit, would you look at that view! No, don't look. Close your eyes, Dauphine. Don't look!*

"How much higher can this plane go?" I asked as he sped up his thrusts. *Oh!* The feeling of fullness!

"Much higher," he whispered, as he began to grind hard beneath me, his hips gyrating, his arms weighing my hips down. "You just have to know how to drive it properly. You just have to have a feel for the plane, and its limits."

With that, he turned fierce, and our bodies began pulsing harder on the chair. I grabbed the back to gain leverage.

"Oh god."

"Can you feel how hard I am, Dauphine, how hard you make me?" he groaned, pumping up into me, holding me down to increase the friction of his pelvis against my clit.

"*Yes! Oh yes. There,*" I murmured, but he knew. He didn't need my instructions.

I felt the heat building behind my belly button *again*, and *again* I came, falling forward as he turned the room into a blur, gripping my hips to take his own pleasure with a fierce resignation that came just after mine. He shuddered to a blissful stop, panting, my torso draping over him.

"That was incredible," he said, breathless too, running his fingers across my back as it rose and fell. I opened my eyes to the windows again, clusters of lights below signaling sleepy towns full of people with no idea what was happening in the darkening clouds above their heads. And I was okay and the plane was okay and we were so *alive*.

"Better get you dressed, my darling. I'm afraid we went a little over schedule."

He carefully lifted me off him and bent to hand me my sweater. As he stood to pull up his uniform pants and tuck and button his own shirt, I stepped into my panties and pulled my skirt up, finger-combing my hair back into its ponytail. We exchanged grins, each of us kind of proud of the other.

By the time Eileen knocked a few minutes later, the only thing that might have given us away, had Captain Nathan not snatched it from the floor and placed it under the plastic cap of an empty Styrofoam cup, was the condom. Then he reached around me for the handle to the cockpit door and pulled it open. I gave Eileen my widest, most guileless smile, my arms behind my back, my bracelet scratching the plastic wall.

"How is your visit going? A lot less stressed about flying, I hope?"

"Very much so," I said. "Captain Nathan has taken the fear right out of me."

"He does that well," she said, with no hint of lasciviousness. "Let's get you back to your seat, Dauphine. It's rather warm in here. Here's your Gatorade, Captain. We don't want you dehydrated."

She took me by the arm.

"Thank you, Captain," I said. "Flying will never be the same for me."

"I'm glad I could be of some help. Oh! Before you go, Dauphine," he said, reaching into his shirt pocket, "we like to give visitors a little something. For trusting us. You've earned this."

He handed me a small blue box.

"Dauphine gets her wings!" exclaimed Eileen with a little clap.

"Thank you," I said, as Captain Nathan stood and gave me a deep bow.

By then, First Officer Friar had returned. "It was good of you to keep the captain company," he said, squeezing past us. "It's lonely up here sometimes."

Eileen led me back to my seat. Was I imagining First Class eyes on me, noting my slight dishevelment, the flush in my cheeks?

Once seated and buckled up, I discreetly lifted the lid to the small blue box. Inside was a brooch shaped like wings, the airline's logo in its center. Under the cotton puff, another gold-hued ornament, my Step Three charm, *Trust* written on the back. I pinned the wings to my sweater. The elderly woman seated across from me gave me a thumbs-up. What she made of the charm I then secured to my bracelet, I'll never know. But after it was firmly in place, I pushed my seat back, slid my earphones on, closed my eyes and floated in a dream for the rest of the blessedly uneventful flight.

CASSIE

I t was only a matter of time before Mark Drury made his way to the Café Rose for Sunday brunch, a newspaper tucked under his arm, a sheepish grin on his face. He didn't have my number and I hadn't called him since our one-night stand weeks ago.

"Hello, Cassie," he said. "Fancy meeting you here."

"Very fancy," I said, "and very early. One o'clock in the afternoon. Did you have to set your alarm?"

"Funny."

I brought over a menu, flipped his coffee cup and filled it to the brim.

"I'll be right back to take your order."

"I'm in no hurry. Unlike you," he said, snapping open his paper. He was referring to the morning after, when I had left his place rather quickly. The last time I saw him he was tangled in mismatched sheets, softly snoring.

I rolled my eyes at him and headed to the kitchen.

When I returned, he ordered scrambled eggs, Boudin

sausage and toast, which he ate in a matter of minutes. When I removed his empty plates, he ordered a large house salad.

"For digestion. Like the Italians," he said.

After his salad he asked about the soup special.

"It was curried cauliflower, but we're all out," I said, just as Dell walked by with a platter of eggs Benedict.

"I'll thaw some of that minestrone. Won't take a minute," she offered.

"Sounds perfect," he replied.

"You're mighty hungry today, Mr. Drury."

"I've got a gig tonight. Always makes me hungry. Why don't you come see us? We're at the Spotted Cat."

He pulled a flyer out of his pocket and handed it to me just as Will, covered in white dust from head to toe, rounded the corner and headed upstairs. I wasn't sure he caught the tail end of our exchange, so I raised my voice.

"I will do my best to be there tonight, Mark. Thank you for the invitation!"

"Great!" Mark replied, confused by my sudden enthusiasm. "I should probably go now."

"No soup?"

"Just the bill. I gotta clean up my place in case I have guests after my gig."

"That's unlikely," I said, a little more quietly this time.

"We'll see about that."

When he looked at me, all the arrogance of his youth seemed to melt away and for a second he was just a young man who wanted to spend some time with me. And yet . . . and yet . . . all I craved was a nice long run followed by a cuddle with my cat, my couch and the remote.

I cashed out Mark's bill, for which he left me a too-hefty tip. Then I headed upstairs to tell Will I was leaving for the night. I hadn't been in the new space in a week and the transformation was astonishing. From a dim, dingy store-room with fading wallpaper and dusty floors, Will had created an airy modern dining room, with new casement windows facing the street, exposed brick on two of the walls, the floors stripped and oiled to perfection. He was painting the men's washroom at the top of the stairs next to the new skylights. I poked my head in to helpfully turn on the light, causing both of us to squint in the brightness.

"Whoa, I didn't notice the light was fading. What time is it?"

"Time for me to go home. Just letting you know Dell's on her own until Tracina gets here."

"Busy day?"

It bothered me that his voice could still freeze me in my tracks. It had been almost five full months since . . .

"Not bad."

It was also hard not to notice how his upper body was becoming more defined by all the manual labor, especially his forearms. He had bits of paint and plaster in his hair that I desperately wanted to pluck out.

"Plans tonight?" he continued, as I backed out of the washroom to check out the rest of the renos.

"As a matter of fact, yes, I have plans."

"With that skinny boy who was just here?"

"Maybe." I said. "I cannot tell you how beautiful it looks up here. I am beyond impressed."

"Are you guys dating?"

"Um . . . he's just a friend, Will," I said, refusing to go there, but quietly pleased he wanted to.

The main dining area took my breath away, the smoked-glass wall sconces, the refurbished metal light pendants that hung over the bar area. I could picture how beautiful it would look furnished and bustling, full of shiny, sexy diners falling in love over candlelight. That's when I saw something weird poking out from behind the new walnut bar—a brand-new twin mattress wedged between the wall and the fridge, a coverless duvet thrown on top.

Will came stumbling into the room, rubbing his hands on his jeans. I turned from the mattress to him.

"Oh," he said, looking from me to the mattress. "I've been sleeping here a few nights. Tracina, with the pregnancy . . . I mean, if I'm not keeping her up, she's keeping me up. And we both need our rest. When the baby comes, everything will be easier."

"That's kind of the opposite of what I hear about babies," I said. I desperately wanted to change the subject, so I did.

"It's so beautiful, Will, I mean it," I said. "Your work . . . you should be very proud. This'll be one of the nicest restaurants on Frenchmen."

"I want to have a really interesting wine list, you know? Bring some in from atypical places, like Uruguay and Texas. They have great vineyards in Hill Country."

"I didn't know that."

"You will. Soon enough."

"What are you talking about?"

"Well, you'll have to brush up on your wine knowledge, because you're going to manage this place for me. I want you to run it," Will said. "Your hours will change. You'd be here afternoons into the dinner rush. You'll have to wear nicer clothes. I mean, not black satin gowns, but not black T-shirts either. I'll pay you more. I'll pay you well."

The whole time he spoke, I stood there watching his mouth move. Being near him, working with him, seeing him every day—I wanted that. Watching him with Tracina and the baby, feeling the ongoing pain of being on the outside looking in on his family life, I didn't want that.

"I can't think of anyone else but you for the job," he added, taking a step closer to me.

"Does Tracina know?"

"I haven't run it past her yet, no. Cassie, we're not . . . we're not *partners*. Not like it would have been with . . . you."

We both felt the weight of his words fill the unfinished room. I reached forward, caressing his forearm with my fingers, electrifying us both. I meant it as a thank-you gesture, to punctuate this great opportunity he had just offered me, one that I would still need time to think about. But then my hand started to move, almost of its own accord, traveling up his arm, under the sleeve of his T-shirt where a new muscle had formed, the one that twitched when he punched in numbers at the cash register or rolled a layer of paint on a wall. My hand moved slowly over his chest, lingering above his heart, which sped up beneath my touch, sending a vibration through my arm. He grabbed me by the elbow and tugged me against him, placing a hand under my chin to tilt my face up so I was staring into his eyes.

"Do you understand how much I want you?" His voice was strained, hoarse.

I opened my mouth to say something, anything, but the words were stuck in my throat. And then I felt it, his mouth on the base of my neck, kissing me there. When our lips met, it was like they had missed each other for ages.

"Cassie . . ." He said my name between kisses, biting, nibbling my lips, one arm around my back, holding me against him, his other hand diving under my T-shirt, cupping my breasts lovingly, greedily. I felt him stiffen as I buried my head in his shoulder and shut my eyes. I wanted to freeze this moment with the only man I really wanted, holding me, wanting me . . .

"I won't stop, unless you tell me to stop," he whispered, his hand sliding down the back of my jeans, squeezing.

I didn't want him to stop, and if I hadn't spotted my flushed, guilty face in the mirror over the bar, I wouldn't have made him stop.

"We can't," I said, prying myself out of his embrace and

taking a step back. He recoiled too, not from me, but from his own actions.

"We were friends for years, Will," I said. "*Good* friends."

"I don't want another friend. I want you."

"Believe me. In a few months, you're gonna need friends," I said, tucking my T-shirt back into my jeans and straightening my apron.

"I'm sorry, Cassie. It's actually pretty shitty of me to offer you a promotion and then turn around and fall all over you like that."

"I won't lodge a complaint . . . if you promise not to do it again."

"I'm not making any more promises I can't keep. But can I ask you something?"

"Shoot."

"Will you think about my job offer?"

"I will."

"Will you be here tomorrow?"

"First thing."

"And the next day?"

"And the day after that."

"I guess that's gotta be good enough. For now."

I smiled. How could I not? I turned and headed out of the room and down the hall to the stairs.

"Cassie, just so you know . . ."

I turned to face him.

"It's you . . . it's always been you."

I braced myself on the balustrade.

"Did you hear me?"

"I did. I gotta go, Will."

Downstairs I yelled a "see you later" to Dell in the kitchen, who gave me a weird look. Then I snatched my purse from my locker and left, hot tears stinging my eyes. It wasn't until I hit Chartres that I realized the front of my black T-shirt was covered in white plaster and bits of paint.

DAUPHINE

The days of only seeing photos of beautiful places were over. That was the first thought that came to me when I woke as Captain Nathan, in his soothing accent, announced the plane's descent. I was expecting to see pasture out the window, but when I peered out, the sun was rising over a carpet of city, Buenos Aires stretching as far as I could see. Its scope took my breath away. I had read about the dazzling sprawl, but I was actually seeing it, and from high up. I'd never seen any city from this vantage point before, and it felt otherworldly, like having a superpower. Soon, I would be more than a mere observer. I'd be immersed in the city itself, the Paris of South America.

I privately thanked S.E.C.R.E.T. and, while disembarking, quite publically thanked my pilot by kissing him on the cheek as I passed.

"That's for helping me," I said.

"The pleasure was all mine," said Captain Nathan, tipping his pilot cap.

Two drivers stood behind a placard with my name on it: one would take me to the hotel; the other would bring Carolina's painting to a secure facility until the auction. Waiting for me in the back seat of a limo was a bowl of chilled fruit, pastries and hot coffee, which I savored along the way. I was ravenous, for food, for people, for life, my eyes scanning every detail out the window, as wide as saucers.

All in one block, I saw neoclassical French facades, Italianate cupolas, art nouveau gates and modernist glass block rectangles wedged between six-story walkups, laundry strewn over every balcony. I couldn't keep up with the feast of curves and cornices. People seemed oblivious to traffic lights, a hazard in a place where a quick turn off an eight-lane avenue could send you down a narrow one-way street with no sidewalks. *So this is what it's like,* I thought, *to be a stranger on an adventure in a new place.* My senses were alive, my whole body tingling with possibility.

My driver, Ernesto, was an eager tour guide, pointing out all the relevant signposts, like when the highway from the airport turned into Avenida 9 de julio, one of the widest streets in the world.

"It is . . . *comemorativo,*" he said with a crisp accent, "this one celebrating Argentina's *independencia.* Most streets in Buenos Aires are named in celebration of something or someone."

Approaching the hotel, we cruised through the heart of a dense and hectic neighborhood called Recoleta, a posh part of town, Ernesto said, where people still lined up to pay homage to Eva Perón in its famed cemetery.

Stopping in front of the Alvear Palace Hotel felt like we were pulling up to a castle. I chastised myself for feeling like a princess, something from which I thought my work-aholic tendencies had inoculated me. But there I was step-ping out of the long, sleek car with Ernesto's help, feeling utterly prized. A line of international flags whipped loudly in the wind, highlighting the fact that the hotel took up nearly an entire city block.

"This will be your home for the next little while," he said, removing his cap and bowing slightly.

I caught a better look at his face. His creamy dark skin and slightly Asian eyes were an alluring mix; for someone so young, he had an air of gravitas about him.

"It's beautiful, thank you."

My bags disappeared through the gold doors and I quickly followed them. That regal feeling was heightened when I took the elevator to my eighth-floor suite, where I kicked off my shoes. My sitting room faced a street already choked with morning rush-hour traffic, but the triple-paned windows meant it was as silent as a tomb. Good lord, this was a real suite, the kind where you ate in a room separate from where you slept. I flung open the heavy, gold floor-to-ceiling curtains, my bare feet caressing the deep pile of the Oriental rug. The porter left clutching his tip, and I stood for a moment in the middle of the rooms, squeezing my fists. Then I let out a high-pitched cry of joy, ran to the bed and flung myself onto it.

It was still a few days until the auction, the responsibility of which suddenly flooded my body. I was on a kind of mission, like a woman of mystery and intrigue, I decided. If I were afraid of anything, I would just pretend to be *that* woman, the fearless kind, the kind who took delicious pleasure thirty thousand feet up and received a suite of rooms for her daring.

After a hot shower, I peeled back the downy layers of bedding and slid between the heavy covers. Just a quick nap, I thought. I hadn't slept well on the plane. I closed my eyes and woke three hours later to a gentle knock on the door. I opened it to a bellhop, who rolled in a trolley. Perched between a carafe of coffee and a tray of crustless sandwiches was a thick, square envelope, *Dauphine* spelled out in that familiar S.E.C.R.E.T. scroll. It was odd, if not a little discombobulating, seeing something familiar in a place so far from home. I plucked the card off the tray and sliced it open with a butter knife. *Step Four* was traced out on one side of the heavy card stock, the word *Generosity* on the other, and beneath it the line "We are with you every Step, Dauphine."

It was happening! Another one.

Suspended on a hook above the trolley was a thick garment bag that felt hefty as I carried it to the bed. I unzipped it, exposing a fanciful red dress, sequins on the bodice, cascading to a riot of feathers around the hips and legs. It looked like a giant crimson swan. I held it up against my body in front of a full-length mirror. An invitation to a midnight tango show came drifting out of its wings.

Dancing? *No. Not dancing.* I avoided it almost as much as I avoided flying. As much as I loved music, I could never do more than nod to the beat in the dark corners of the clubs. Sometimes I danced alone in my apartment. I danced for Luke once, until I undermined the seduction by hamming it up, too self-conscious to pull off a real striptease. But the idea of dancing in front of strangers curdled my stomach. I wasn't lean or graceful, unlike my sister.

"If Bree only had Dauphine's discipline, or Dauphine Bree's thighs, we'd have had a ballerina in this family," my mother often said. I think she thought it was a compliment, but it gutted me.

I set aside my terror for a moment to marvel at the dress, the bodice's expert construction, hand-stitched and lined strategically to soften the boning that held it stiff. Its asymmetrical hem suggested tango, for sure, and while red looked good on me, I can't say that this dress was my style. No. Not at all. A sweat broke across my brow. I could not, would not, dance in front of people. Not with *my* body, in *that* dress. And S.E.C.R.E.T., as Cassie and Matilda kept reminding me, was about doing everything you want, nothing you don't.

~~⁀つ~~

It was hours before the tango show. I hit the streets wearing my trench coat and comfortable shoes. Buenos Aires was cool, loud and busy, the mix of old and new clashing on every corner. And *porteños* seemed to love their outdoors spaces as much as New Orleanians. Even on a crisp day, the Plaza San Martín was full of strollers and cyclists, and dogs of various sizes were pulling on dozens of leashes held by incredibly strong walkers. I felt a warmth overcome me. Were it not for S.E.C.R.E.T., I'd never be sitting in the middle of a plaza across from the Casa Rosada watching old men—wearing well-made tweed coats—playing chess, while nearby couples caressed each other in the sun.

I walked the neighborhoods from Recoleta to Palermo, from San Telmo to Boca, scouring second-hand shops, finding out who their suppliers were and how they priced goods. First thing I noticed in a city of tall, thin brunettes with aquiline noses (some inherited, most purchased) is that my curvy "Americanness" stood out. Nothing I tried on in the vintage stores fit, which left some of the shop girls more mortified than I was.

"Lo siento, señora," said the tiny, nervous proprietor of a beautifully curated vintage store near the Recoleta cemetery. At another store I couldn't do up a pencil skirt.

"My darling," said a kind, elderly store clerk in his perfect English. He'd sensed my funk while cashing out a set of tea towels and a linen tablecloth. "Do not let your body make you sad. It is a good body."

Thanking him, I left, carefully navigating the narrow sidewalks with the other pedestrians, trying unsuccessfully to act like a local as I tripped over the potholes while ogling the gargoyles and cupolas on some of the more stunning buildings.

In La Boca, eating sweet *alfajores* and sipping *mate,* a kind of tea, I watched an elderly couple dancing a slow public tango.

He was a few inches shorter than her and twice as small, and she was wearing too much makeup for daytime. But these oddities made them more attractive, more compelling. Their dance was achingly intimate, the way they performed for a crowd of strangers gathering in the square at dusk. I was moved nearly to tears by the music, and the expressions of pain and love on their faces. If she could be so vulnerable in front of so many people, in broad daylight, what the hell was I afraid of? Maybe that was true generosity. Giving of your-self, just as you are, for the sake of a dance.

That night I actually needed Ernesto's proffered hand to help me out of the back seat of the limo and to unravel the mass of red feathers surrounding my tango dress. I was not at all surprised that the dress fit perfectly, but I was shocked at how flattering it was. The bodice encased me snugly, my breasts spilling over the top. Below the dropped waist, the dress tufted into a mass of feathers that floated down to my calves. I felt like a goddess emerging from a scarlet ocean.

"*Gracias.*"

"*Por nada,*" he said, bowing again. "You look . . . *lindísima* in that dress, Señorita Dauphine."

I gave Ernesto a nervous smile and glanced down the narrow alley towards the tango club's neon entrance. Very few people were on this secluded street at midnight.

"I meet you right here . . . after?"

He motioned me forward with his white-gloved hands. *I'll be okay, I'll be okay.* As I inched closer to the mournful, lilting music wafting out of the dark club, a kind-faced doorman, also gloved, opened a gap in the velvet curtains hanging in the entrance.

"We've been waiting for you, Dauphine."

Oh dear. I ducked inside, feeling faint. A dozen couples turned to look my way, as though they had been expecting me. I was led around the tiny tables to a banquette against the far wall. As I took my seat, a sprightly waitress wearing a white tutu and black-and-white-striped stockings dropped a pink drink in front of me.

"We're about to begin, Dauphine," she said, in what sounded like a French accent. "Can I get you anything?"

Before I could open my mouth, a small, dimly lit band to the right of the stage struck up a ballad. The musicians were wearing blindfolds, their heads dipping and swaying as they played their instruments. Why were their eyes covered? The audience turned their attention to the band and the lone spotlight now illuminating the stage. I sank back into my velvet banquette, hoping just to watch. I could feel my heart pounding against my bodice, certain everyone could hear it too. Then I heard a low, gravelly a cappella voice.

A stunning woman in a dress exactly like mine, but black, slowly moved from the wings of the stage to center herself under the spotlight. Her hands surrounded the microphone, her lips a glistening ruby red. The song was in Spanish, but I could tell its lyrics were sad. Her eyes squeezed shut as she sang something about a girl and her heart and some broken dreams, I think. One of the couples rose from the front row, fell into each other's arms and dipped low in those familiar turns of the tango—each holding the other up, a leg jutting out, kicking here and there, no light between them. Another woman, in the tight blue dress slit to her waist, pulled her tuxedoed date onto the floor. Their dance released a cascade of four more couples, until the singer was surrounded by a dozen bodies moving in circles to the music. Then the singer turned to look my way, directing her passion to . . . *to me?*

The song was about passing time, about a woman who had regrets for a life not lived. Or maybe for living a life half awake. The singer was mesmerizing, I squirmed in my seat, uncertain how to react to her gaze. She seemed to be very publically seducing me. Or maybe this was just the nature of the tango. Feeling by turns charmed and embarrassed by her attention, I was relieved when a tanned hand beckoned me to stand.

"*¿Va a aceptar este paso?*"

The hand belonged to a tall man with short, black curly hair and beautiful black eyes. He smiled, displaying a row of white perfect teeth set against the olive of his perfectly smooth skin. I felt my knees would dissolve to pudding if I stood.

"I'm afraid I don't know how to dance," I said, as loudly and politely as I could without being louder than the singer.

"*No importa*," he said, still smiling, adding, "just give yourself to me and the rest will follow. We will take care of you."

We? He pulled me to my feet, overwhelming me with the expanse of his chest, a black shirt tight across his perfect torso, tucked into black pants that fit his dancer's legs perfectly. *Give yourself to him, Dauphine. This is about* Generosity.

"I accept," I said, my gut lurching.

Grasping my hand, he led me onto the dance floor.

He threw his arm around my back and drew me in until I was fully pressed against him, my heels between his shoes. He grabbed my other hand and held it aloft. Suddenly, I felt someone against my back. I turned, shocked to see the beautiful singer, her eyes closed, her hand joining ours aloft, her fingers entwining with mine. Her other hand crept up and around to my middle, just below my breasts, pulling me back into her, and her rose perfume mixed with my dance partner's soft musk.

"Let her help you. Feel how her body moves behind you," my partner whispered. "Move as she does."

She bent her left knee, bending mine too, her left hand caressing down my leg. Facing my partner, I felt the woman behind me pull up my skirt to reveal the top of my black garters. Before I knew what was happening, she was sliding a warm hand along my thigh, dipping me backwards against her body. The band picked up the tempo. I could feel her breasts against my back and the male dancer's chest brushing lightly against the front of me. We moved in heady unison around the floor. I felt carried along, a part of their dance. *I was doing it!* Soon, the other couples began to recede from the stage into the dark, and it was just the three of us.

Then, lesson over and timed to a flourish of the guitar, the singer twirled away from me and fell into the arms of a beautiful blond woman who appeared out of the shadows. Her hair was pulled tightly back, and she wore a mask and black tuxedo pants. She was taller than the singer, her white halter highlighting her lean, tanned arms. My male partner pulled me fully to his body, his hand tracing down my back, over my buttocks, as he pressed his pelvis into me. That had made him hard, and I could feel him pulsing against my side. As he lifted me off the floor, my legs scissored in the air, and after a quarter turn, he deposited me in front of the two female dancers. The blonde moved like a panther, her hand on the singer's lower back, their arms a limber vine.

"Watch them," my partner whispered. "What the singer is doing, you will do, and what she is feeling I will make you feel."

I mimicked the singer's hips, pivoting, *one, two, three, knee up,* as my partner caught me, pulling me against him and down, my hands on his chest. Then I watched as the women pressed together, *step, step, stop and pivot,* the blonde's hand moving down the front of the singer's body as she bent backwards, her eyes shut. It was so hot. *They* were hot, both of these women, clutching each other. This was turning me on as much as my own partner's hands. Then the blonde slowly unzipped the singer's dress, letting it die at her feet. She was in stay-up stockings and garters, no underwear, her pale pink nipples peaking over the top of her black demi-cup bra, dark hair cascading around her shoulders. I took in her beautiful body and the soft line of pubic hair highlighted against the tawny flesh of the blonde's hand as it traveled over her, fingers quivering. I felt my partner behind me, inching me closer to the singer. Then I heard it, the sound of my zipper as my dress slipped off and pooled around my ankles. The singer and I stood facing each other, both nearly naked, a foot apart, in garters and bras. I'd never been with a woman before, but her desire for me was obvious . . . and intoxicating. I wanted her, and him, all of it.

While our partners moved behind us, the singer pulled me in for an urgent kiss, and I let her! I was kissing a beautiful woman, her soft mouth humming, her tongue darting into mine. Her lips traveled eagerly down my neck, while her blond partner's fingers teased her, her long red nails now a blur of circles over her clitoris. Watching the blonde pleasure the singer, feeling the singer's ragged breath on my skin as her orgasm coursed through her, my own body heated and pulsed, arousing my partner behind me. Even after she came, she didn't stop swirling my nipples in her cool mouth, while my partner's warm, firm hands slid over my stomach, my pelvis, encircling me, his fingers finding my own wetness, using the same driving rhythm as the singer's tongue on me. I was gorgeously pressed between them, thrashing with pleasure; in a matter of seconds I felt it too, and my whole body quaked. I took what they were so generously giving me. With one hand in the singer's thick hair, I watched the tip of her pink tongue flicking my nipples as my partner's fingers fiercely massaged the knot of my clit in perfect circles, driving me crazy, releasing me, making me come, my orgasm crashing over my body in wave after wave.

"Oh . . . *yes*."

"*Hermosa*," the singer murmured.

My partner clutched me tight, his hand cupping me as I shook, then subsided. I felt faint as he kissed my shoulder and gently released me to the floor in a spent pile next to my beautiful dress.

As the band struck up a new tempo, the blonde tugged the singer into a stiff tango silhouette and they danced away from me, into the dark wings of the stage. My partner exited behind them, blowing me a singular kiss, stopping to touch the stage once with his hand, as if in gratitude.

Then he too was gone.

Good lord, what just happened?

I blinked, breathless, hearing the blindfolded band still playing as though to a full house. I felt coated in bliss, warm beneath the spotlight, my red swan dress sleeping next to the singer's ebony feather mass. Then I saw it, small and round and glinting on the floor of the stage where my partner had placed his hand: my Step Four charm.

Hermosa.

CASSIE

Mark Drury looked like I'd just rolled up a newspaper and hit him on the nose.

"You don't want to see me anymore?"

After he called twice in three days, I agreed to meet up
with him at Washington Square Park after my shift. Despite
a sign banning dogs and bikes, the park was a perfect place
to bring both on a hot summer's day.

"It's not that I don't want to see you . . ." I said.

"I thought we had a good time."

"We did."

"Then what's up with you?"

I squinted into the middle distance, keeping my eye on a
cocker spaniel puppy nipping at the leg of its owner, thinking that if Mark were a dog, that's the breed he'd be. Will
would be the stalwart chocolate lab over by the sandbox,
Tracina the yappy alpha beagle holding court nearby. I'd be
the flat-coated retriever under the stand of palms, the one
chasing its own tail.

"Mark," I said. "I think . . . you're great."

"Is it this Will guy?"

My shoulders sank. It *was* Will. Every time I made strides away from him, one look, one touch, one kiss and I was infected again.

"That's part of it." But the other, the part I didn't want to tell him, was that outside of bed I thought of him as my bratty brother.

Mark placed a tender arm around me.

"Love is hard, Cassie. I know. I'm a musician."

I almost snorted, but he was so damn endearing. I just accepted the gesture and leaned into him a little.

It had been three days since my interlude with Will in the new restaurant, since he'd pulled me into that kiss. In those three days we had sheepishly avoided each other at work, both of us over-apologizing for every awkward hallway passing, over-thanking each other for every favor of a poured coffee or a hammer handed over. Alone with me briefly in his office during a shift change, Will whispered that he wanted to get two things straight—and that it would be the last time he'd bring up what happened.

"One: I have no regrets for anything I did or said. And two: I still want you to take the job upstairs."

"Fine," I said, "I will. I'll take the job, but the other thing? That can't happen again. It's not fair to me, it's not fair to Tracina, or the baby."

In hushed tones, both of us listening for sounds of footsteps coming down the hall, he promised no more drama, no more stolen kisses, no more sneaking around. We even shook on it, the shock of his skin electric as always. And today, looking at Mark's attractive profile as he sat on the park bench next to me, I realized that since I didn't have the ability to keep away from someone I really wanted or to be compelled by someone I didn't want, I needed a man in the middle. I needed a wedge between me and Will, and me and Mark.

But the only other person who tweaked both my mind and body was Jesse, and he was cued up for a final go-around with Dauphine. Unless I could recruit a substitute. And that's when it struck me like a marvelous bolt of lightning.

" . . . anyway, look, I'm just gathering adventures too, Cassie, and maybe you're one of them. But if you're not into this, that's cool. No skin off my nose."

My thoughts drifted. They were both young and brash and lanky. They both had sexy smirks. They both looked good in a white tank top, a rarity for any man other than a '50s Marlon Brando. But while Jesse had a warmth, a kindness to him, maybe because he was a single dad, Mark was bratty. Jesse had tattoos, though I was still surprised Mark didn't. I tried to calculate exactly when Dauphine might have her Jesse fantasy. She got back from Buenos Aires in a few days, so it would take place within a month. A wave of nervous energy ran through me. S.E.C.R.E.T. recruits were put through a battery of tests that took weeks. I had to act fast—

Mark snapped his fingers in front of my face.

"Where are you, Cassie?"

"Sorry. I'm here. The dogs . . . they're so cute. I got distracted." I turned to fully face him on the bench. "You know, I liked what you said about gathering adventures. You're young. That's precisely what you should be doing. You shouldn't be tied down to one woman right now, right?"

"I guess," he said. "But I'm a musician. We like having girlfriends. They ground us while we create."

"Right."

The dogs were circling each other, sniffing. I turned to look him in the eye, my mouth set in a determined line.

"So if you're serious about 'gathering adventures,' I think I have one for you. It's a big one. An incredible one. The kind of adventure you're not going find anywhere else."

"Or *with* anyone else?" he asked, leaning in to kiss me.

I held him off. "This is an adventure you'll have . . . with other women. More interesting women than me. Adventurous women. If you are open to it."

And just like that, a slow smile spread across Mark's face. *Men do have it easier*, I thought. He didn't need a preamble or assurances before taking in my proposition, the same shocking one Matilda had dropped on me, the one I had offered Dauphine a few months ago. He didn't need to be warmed up, comforted or cajoled. He didn't need to be gingerly approached. He didn't have deep psychic obstacles to overcome or social conditioning to fight against. My offer didn't cause him to question everything he had been taught about his role in the world or his sexuality. When I dangled the possibility of more sex, *interesting* sex, lots of sex, exactly the way he liked it and the way women liked it, he simply clasped his hands behind his head and said, "You have my attention, Cassie Robichaud. My *full* attention."

⌇

Matilda wasn't as easy to convince.

"He has to go through a vigorous screening process, Cassie. That means medical, psychological, physical—"

"He'll pass," I said, tearing the label clean off my beer bottle.

"That's a sign of sexual frustration," she said matter-of-factly, pointing out my fidgeting.

"So is this request, believe me!"

Our usual meet-up spot, Tracy's, was quiet for a Friday afternoon. Come to think of it, my shift at the Café had been pretty dead too. Tracina was glad for it, so pregnant now that people didn't really feel comfortable having her wait on them because she looked like she could drop the baby right at their table. It was only a matter of weeks before she'd be off her feet entirely.

Will had posted for a replacement, but then his brother Jackson from Slidell asked if he'd take on his oldest daughter, Claire, a quirky, dreadlocked seventeen-year-old who wanted to finish high school at the New Orleans Center for Creative Arts, which had a campus not far from the Café. Between piercings and poetry readings, she promised she could work two nights a week and weekends, more shifts during the summer. Will was reluctant at first to have his unruly teenage niece also living with him, until Tracina pointed out the convenient babysitter possibilities once their child was born. So Claire started immediately, and immediately fit in at the restaurant by pissing off Dell and getting underfoot.

Matilda wasn't finished listing all the caveats of recruiting Mark.

"*If* Mark passes all the tests, he'll still have to be trained, Cassie. And the other women have to weigh in. It has to be unanimous."

"He'll appeal. And Dauphine has a thing for musicians."

"And then there's the matter of you and Jesse. He could turn you down, you know. I mean, he has one last go through S.E.C.R.E.T. and he may want to savor that opportunity. Are you ready for potential rejection?"

"Sure. Yeah. Of course." I shrugged, taking a sip of my beer.

I flinched because I was lying. S.E.C.R.E.T. had given me many gifts, but the ability to withstand rejection wasn't one of them. After all, there was no possibility of being rejected in S.E.C.R.E.T., only of turning others down. Of course Jesse could turn me down, and why wouldn't he? What was he going to be offered, anyway? A plain old date with me, a woman he had hot sex with once in a fantasy scenario, more than a year ago, one who balked when the possibility of more presented itself. Or the thrill of a new fantasy and new flesh pressed against his skin. Given the choice, wouldn't most men want the novelty? Wouldn't *I*? Well, no. I had had that novelty with Mark, and more than that with Will. Mark I didn't want. Will I couldn't have. And so, in my mind, that left Jesse.

"I'll meet with Jesse tomorrow," Matilda said. "If he says yes, you'll hear from him. If he says no, you won't. Either way, we'll pull him off Dauphine's roster this time, just to prevent any tension between you and Dauphine. That relationship is sacred. And whatever happens, she does not need to know about this conversation." Matilda paused to let this sink in. "Oh," she added after a few seconds, "by the way, Dominic passed. He'll be a new recruit."

"The soccer player?"

"He's actually a contractor. He's taken the tests and he's almost done with his training. If Mark doesn't work out, we can put Dominic next."

"What about Ewan, that sexy redhead friend of his?"

"He didn't pass the initial round. Funny that. We rarely get a unanimous vote on a ginger, which as a redhead I find rather bigoted. Marta just wasn't that into him."

"But he was so cute."

"Well, if you're on the Committee next year you can resubmit him, if he's still interested."

After splitting the bill and saying goodbye to Matilda, I decided to walk home. It was a balmy night, but spooky— no moon in the sky. I could hear sirens in the distance, discordant jazz pouring out of every other door, which got louder and stranger when Magazine became Decatur in the

French Quarter. I shivered. Fall was coming; I could feel it in my bones. In fact, the whole city felt suddenly as dark and unsettled as did I.

⁓

The next morning, I was barely out of the shower when the phone rang.

"Hello?"

"Hey, lady," the male voice said in a sweetly familiar Southern drawl.

It truly didn't occur to me it would be Jesse. Not so soon. Not at 10 a.m. Surely Matilda would have only *just* called him, would have only *just* offered him his options. Surely he'd need some time to think.

But it was him. My nerves ricocheted through my body, making the receiver go instantly sweaty in my hand. *Now what?*

"Who's this?" I asked. When I'm afraid, I push things away with both hands. I don't let go of them; I hold them at arm's length to gain the upper hand, hoping they'll come to me. I did that with Will; I was now doing that with Jesse.

"You know exactly who this is, Cassie Robichaud."

The S.E.C.R.E.T. Steps quickly ran through my mind; yes! I had access to all these attributes, I'd felt them, I'd experienced them. *I could do this.*

Surrender.

"I'm kidding. I know it's you."

"Yeah. So . . . Matilda says you wanted to see me?"

Courage.

"I do."

"Where are you?"

Trust.

"I'm at home."

Generosity.

"I was wondering . . . are you free for dinner next Saturday? I could cook."

"I have to wait a week? Where do you live?"

Fearlessness.

"In the Marigny, not far from where I work."

Confidence.

"I mean, if you're not available next Saturday, the Saturday after is fine," I added.

"I usually have my son on Saturdays," he said. "But I think I can figure something out."

Curiosity.

"Right. You have a son. How old is he now?"

"He's six, actually. I have him every Wednesday, and every other Friday and Saturday until six. Then I drop him at his ma's. His birthday was four days ago."

Bravery.

"Aw. Sweet. Well, why don't you come over after you drop him off next Saturday? I'll make us something to eat. Bring a bottle of wine or whatever you want to drink."

"I will do that, Miss Robichaud."

Exuberance.

"Great! I'm looking forward to it. I'm in the green house on the corner of Chartres and Mandeville. Second floor. See you then."

I must have leapt two feet in the air when I hung up. I had a date with a virtual stranger, a guy whose last name I did not know, a tattoo-covered single father whom I'd met during an amazing, anonymous sexual encounter because of our mutual membership in an underground group that orchestrated fantasies for sex-starved women. And I couldn't have been more excited.

"I did it," I said to Dixie, flat on her back, playing with the charms on my bracelet.

DAUPHINE

I should have known something was off when a different driver, not Ernesto, arrived twenty minutes later than the appointed time. I sat in the lobby of the Palace Alvear Hotel, in my new side-buttoned, black brocade dress with three-quarter sleeves, the better to show off my bracelet. I had found the dress buried in a rack in a shop in San Telmo, a gorgeous, form-fitting cocktail confection that stopped just below the knee, a conservative length set off by the way it hugged my curves. Watching the way my new driver took me in while striding confidently towards me in the lobby of the hotel told me the dress was worth every penny. His own uniform, on the other hand, was a little too snug, the hat too large, the sleeves too short. He just didn't have the physique of a man who sat behind the wheel of a limousine all day, which, in fact, was a high compliment.

"*Lo siento, Señora Dauphine,*" he said, apologizing for his lateness, his veined wrists peeking out from his cuffs when he extended an ungloved hand.

I felt a sizzle up my arm when I shook it. Where Ernesto had a boyish charm, this new driver was pure masculinity. But a second alarm bell went off after he settled me in the back seat.

"*¿A donde vamos?*" he asked. *Where are we going?*

If he had been sent by S.E.C.R.E.T., wouldn't he know the address? Matilda had said the auction was top secret and only a few well-heeled invitees knew its location. That information had been delivered via phone call, not by invitation, in order to avoid attention from the press.

I met his smiling green eyes in the rearview mirror. He was the kind of man who knew he had a certain effect on women.

"*Vamos al Teatro Colón, por supesto,*" I said, directing him to the historical theatre downtown. I couldn't help being charmed by his looks. *So shallow, Dauphine,* I scolded, resting back into my seat.

The next alarm when off on the slow drive to the theater, when, every block or so, he consulted a GPS, adjusting and readjusting his rearview mirror. And yet when we pulled up to the Teatro Colón, a block-long building that looked like a creamy marble wedding cake, my concerns about this man were immediately replaced by trepidations about the auction. A tuxedoed valet stood curbside to greet me. He ignored my driver as he opened the door and helped me out of the car.

"Wow," I said, sounding like the gosh-gollyest American who ever was.

"Miss Mason, it is a privilege to meet you. And I am sorry if you had . . . trouble finding the Teatro Colón." He eyed my driver. *"¿Quién es usted?"*

"Dante," my driver answered, as he grasped me by the upper arm.

My greeter exhaled dramatically and turned on his heel. Dante and I followed him through the throng of tourists snapping photos in front of the theater. We hurried past the marble statues in the gold foyer where other limo drivers gathered to wait, then passed the stained-glass ceiling and the signs that read, *EVENTO PRIVADO.* We pushed through the carved gilded doors into a darkened theater.

Teatro Colón was a mesmerizing spectacle of intricate balconies surrounding long sweeping arcs of plush red velvet seats. A dozen front rows were filled with restless bidders who'd been waiting for us. Thankfully, we weren't the last to arrive. Just before taking my seat, a tall blonde in a tailored blue business suit scrambled down the stairs, taking the last seat at the remote agents' table in front of a bank of telephones. Matilda had told me there'd be some buyers calling in from around the world, the phones manned by their local bankers.

Be cool, Dauphine. You're just here to sign some papers. I nervously patted my chignon, relieved I'd chosen kitten heels with the snug dress. My designated seat on the aisle of the last row was the best vantage point from which to watch the bidding before me. I leaned back to take in the sepia-stained frescos that circled a chandelier as big as the sun.

I eyed the buyers, mostly women. Money from the sale of the painting would fund S.E.C.R.E.T.'s rather unorthodox pursuits, as Matilda had explained. She didn't want it coming from people or groups that might pry too far into S.E.C.R.E.T.'s true mandate, or whose values didn't dovetail with our own.

Dante stood vigil to my right, like a handsome guard dog.

"It's . . . *lindísima*," I said, regarding the venue.

"Yes. It's spectacular," he whispered, leaning towards me. "It's been completely restored over the last few years. That dress is spectacular too, by the way."

So he spoke English! And with an American accent— no—a *Southern* accent! That was the final alarm bell.

"Who *are* you? Where are you from?"

A sweet smile crossed his lips just as a hammer hit a gavel and a curtain rose on *Red Rage*, gorgeously lit and perched on a matte black stand, its modernist style in stark contrast to the lush concert hall. Oohs and ahhs filled the room, and vigorous applause seemed to be Dante's cue to take a seat high in the empty part of the theater behind me.

The auctioneer took the stage and greeted the guests. After a brief preamble about the painting's history, he called on the room to acknowledge a representative sent to authenticate the transfer of ownership.

"Please welcome Señorita Mason, who accompanied *Red Rage* all the way from New Orleans on behalf of its anonymous owner."

I felt the blood drain out of my face. Without standing, I floated a hand in the air and quickly dropped it back down, sinking with it.

"We wish you great luck today, Señorita Mason. The auction will be in English. Headphones have been provided for translation. Let us begin."

Whack. Bidding opened at 2.3 million dollars American. Matilda hoped to double that. The auctioneer began navigating a forest of arms from both sides of the aisle. He was responding so quickly, he looked like he was doing a breaststroke. Anonymous telephone bids were also flooding in, and the blonde who had arrived later than me sat at the end of a bank of phones, her leg bouncing nervously.

"Do I hear two point four million? Two point four? Now two point six it is. That's two point six from the back. Three million over here. I hear three million up front . . ."

My head whipped back and forth to keep up with the fast climb.

"We have four million, four point two, we have four point two. Four point eight and now *five*, ladies and gentleman . . ."

At that price, a few of the bidders' representatives hung up their phones. By six million, half the room had stilled as I sat upright, literally on the edge of my seat. At seven million, most everyone else in the theater dropped out. But two remained: a stout woman in thick glasses competing against a particularly enthusiastic phone bidder, represented by the blonde, whose arm remained in the air, her finger registering "yes" to every uptick in the price.

"Now at eight point five . . . eight point five, and we have nine. That is nine million over here on the phone! Nine million *two* . . ."

Holy hell! It's going to ten million. That'll finance a lot of fantasies. I craned my neck to look for my driver, who was no longer shadowing me. Maybe he had joined the other drivers in the lobby.

"Ten million dollars, we are at *ten.* Ten point *four*, that is ten million, *four hundred* thousand . . ."

Left, right, right, left, the two remaining bidders each spurred the other on, the blonde on the phone never losing her cool, the woman in glasses becoming increasingly agitated. My heart played along, spiking with every raised hand. This was way more exciting than sports!

"Ladies and gentlemen, we are at eleven million and one hundred thousand dollars. Do I hear eleven two? We have . . . eleven two," said the auctioneer, pointing his hammer at the bespectacled woman whose arm was becoming heavier and heavier. The blonde's remained steadily aloft.

"Eleven three? Yes, we have eleven three on the phone. Will we get eleven four?"

The pause weighed on the room. All heads now turned to face the woman in the thick black glasses. Maybe because she wasn't some disembodied voice on the phone, I suddenly wanted her to win. But alas, the blonde's arm spiked calmly at the last price.

"We have eleven point four from anonymous bidder number eight up front . . . eleven point four . . . do we have eleven five?"

The woman in the glasses lifted a tentative hand.

"We have eleven *five*—"

"*Fifteen million!*" boomed a familiar voice from the back of the room.

It took me a second to realize who it was, because he was no longer wearing his uniform. My driver, Dante, stood there, in a dark suit that looked freshly pressed, a white shirt neatly tucked into the slacks, and his cap, sunglasses and ill-fitting jacket gone. He looked alarmingly sexy, a hand slung in a pocket.

"Are you a registered bidder?"

He pointed to the late arrival, the nervous blonde at the phone table.

"That is my company's representative, Isabella, from the Central Bank of Argentina. She can vouch for my funds. You can hang up now, Isabella. I am so sorry I'm late."

Dante—or whatever his real name was—raised the temperature of the theater from simmer to boil. The auctioneer, now flustered, turned to find the bespectacled woman's head resting in a hand, defeated.

"So then . . . it is fifteen *million* . . . going once . . . going twice . . . and *sold* to the gentleman in the dark suit. Carolina Mendoza's *Red Rage* goes for *fifteen million*. A record, ladies and gentlemen. A smashing record!"

Applause broke out in the theater, but my hands held firm to my armrests as I watched Dante stride over to the losing bidder to shake her hand. The crowd continued to clap as Dante posed for pictures in front of the painting.

The auctioneer, after a quiet word with Isabella, motioned me down the stairs to the telephone table, now cleared of everything except an elaborate certificate carefully centered on a leather blotter.

"Isabella tells me the fifteen million dollars has already been cleared. Unless you have any objections to an unregistered bidder purchasing the painting, you may sign the transfer of ownership," said the auctioneer, handing me a fancy pen with a feather tail, and adding, "It is an enormous amount of money. Impressive."

He also seemed unnerved by this handsome man who had infiltrated these somber, private proceedings in such a strangely dramatic way. But what do you say when someone drops fifteen million dollars, tripling what was projected? You say thank you, and you sign on the dotted line, which is what I did, with an appropriate flourish. I couldn't wait to tell Matilda about the windfall.

I handed the auctioneer the papers.

Dante, or whoever he was, came over to the table and completed the transfer with his own undecipherable signature. Then he met my still-confused gaze.

"Nice to formally meet you, Miss Mason. I can assure you that Ms. Mendoza's painting will be going to a very good home. I am a big fan of *all* her endeavors. So you can imagine how sad I was to be left off the list of bidders, and how grateful I am that you did not hold that against me."

"Who *are* you?" I asked, cautiously weaving my hand through the crook of an arm he offered. "And what was all that limo subterfuge? The not speaking English? Showing up unregistered? Was that really necessary? Surely you could have—"

"Dauphine, my dear, I will explain everything in good time. But we must leave now, before curiosity overtakes the room, swallowing us both. People will begin to ask questions. About me, about you and about the . . . group you represent."

"What do you know about that?"

"I know enough to ask you . . . if you'll accept the Step."

Of course! So he is one of them. He's one of us!

As a crowd gathered to photograph *Red Rage* before it was packed and shipped, he ushered me up the steps to the theater's exit. Now it was all making sense, though my heart continued pounding.

The foyer was empty, save for a half-dozen bored drivers checking their watches. Dante pulled me sharply in the opposite direction, through high glass doors covered in lace curtains. Suddenly, we were alone in a beautiful narrow hall painted ivory, lined with columns and wainscoting in the same golden hue as my bracelet. He let go of my arm, his whole body now facing me.

"So?"

"So . . ." I said, inching backwards until I collapsed onto an overstuffed settee beneath a bust of some famous composer. "Did you really just spend fifteen million dollars on a painting?"

"I did."

"Why?"

"To impress you. Did it work?"

I shifted over so he could sit beside me.

"Possibly."

Clearly, this was a man for whom everything came easy. But I wasn't quite sure I wanted to be one of those things. He leaned in, his face inches from mine. His nostrils flared like an animal's picking up the scent of fear . . . and liking it.

"I'll ask you once again: do you accept the Step?"

He lifted my hand and was about to examine my bracelet when I snatched my wrist from him, hiding it behind my back. He was sexy, and he knew about S.E.C.R.E.T., but there was a dark air about him that kept tripping me up.

"What's your real name?" I asked. "And how come you didn't know where the auction was if your banker was here, the blond one?"

"She was following us, having not received an invitation either. Now, I'll be happy to answer the rest of your questions, Dauphine. But there's really only one that matters. Do you accept the Step?"

His mouth now at my ear, he gathered a lobe between his lips, gently sucking it. A current flowed through me, my body turning to lava. Everywhere he touched me, the skin beneath melted. He was moving fast, so fast I'd soon be unable to stop him, even if I wanted to.

"I've been wanting to do this since I laid eyes on you at the hotel," he whispered, parting my knees, his hand making its languid way up my thighs.

I froze at the sound of chatter coming from the lobby.

"I locked the door. No one will find us in here," he said, my skirt now pulled almost all the way up to my hips.

I placed a hand on his shoulder and gently pushed him.

"Where are you from?"

He dove in again, his mouth finding my neck. He was having none of my questions. I was delirious with desire, my instincts beginning to dull because of his talented mouth.

"Dauphine, accept, and I'll tell you everything."

"I will accept," I murmured, eyes closed, "*if* you tell me . . . what Step I'm on."

His eyes searched for my bracelet again, but I'd cleverly tucked my arm behind me.

He straightened up, tugging the cuffs on his sleeves.

"It's not a hard question," I said. "Why don't you check the charm, the one you brought to give me afterwards? That will tell you the answer."

He paused for a moment, then said, "You know the rules, Dauphine. If you don't accept, I can't show you the charm."

I went over the S.E.C.R.E.T. acronym in my head. He was *Compelling*, that's for sure. And this would have been a *Romantic, Erotic* interlude. Perhaps it would have left me feeling *Ecstatic* and *Transformed*. But there was just one problem: I didn't feel *Safe*. That was what it all boiled down to. If Step Five was about overcoming my fears, his refusal to answer my questions kept me from feeling that.

"*You* know the rules too, Dante, or whatever your name

is. If I don't accept the Step, we stop here. It's over. I'm saying no. Who are you anyway? You sound like you're from the South—in fact, from Louisiana."

"Well, now," he huffed, standing. "For someone who refuses me, you sure demand a lot."

"It would seem so," I said, pulling my dress down over my knees. My chignon had fallen out in our brief tussle, so I undid the barrette holding it in place, releasing my hair.

"*Red Rage* indeed," he said, admiring my hair, reaching out to caress a tendril. I pulled away. "I would be happy to have my driver take you back to your hotel."

"That won't be necessary," I said. "I can make it back on my own."

"Then . . . I shall be on my way."

He stood and crossed the room, unlocked the door and quietly shut it behind him. Who in the hell was this man and what had he just tried to pull? I waited a few more seconds before heading back to the theater, where a handful of people still surrounded the painting. Was it too late to rip up the transfer of ownership? I had to try.

The auctioneer was locked in quiet conversation with the banker, Isabella.

"Excuse me," I said, interrupting them. "Before I leave, can you tell me if it's possible to stop the transfer? It's just . . . I feel I might have made a mistake in selling the painting to an unregistered bidder."

They looked at each other as though they had been discussing this exact thing.

"The problem is that you would now need his signature too," said the auctioneer. "He officially owns that painting."

"And he was a very keen buyer," Isabella added, in clipped but perfect English. "I did not realize he was unregistered; otherwise I would not have participated on behalf of Señor Castille."

"Señor who?"

"Castille," she said. "Pierre Castille. I assume he is well known in your city since his family owns half of it."

"A small part of this one too," chuckled the auctioneer.

Pierre Castille? Of *course* I knew the name. But I hadn't recognized his face out of context. There weren't many photos of him; he was private for someone so wealthy, but if you lived in New Orleans, that name was tantamount to royalty.

Why the hell would Pierre Castille, Pierre the Heir, the Bayou Billionaire, infiltrate a private auction, drop fifteen million dollars on a painting, then try to seduce me on a settee in a theater in Buenos Aires? What had I gotten myself into?

I felt the blood rise to my face. Cassie and Matilda were going to hear about this. Perhaps it was a sign. Perhaps stopping at Step Five was appropriate. I asked for directions to the cab stand and made my defeated way outside. I'd conquered enough fears, I thought, glancing down at my bracelet. Even half complete it looked quite pretty as it caught the glare off passing cars in the nighttime.

As I sat in the cab back to the hotel, my heart was still pounding, my skin feeling seared where Pierre Castille had touched me.

CASSIE

The last time I was invited to the Mansion I was naked beneath a full-length coat and led upstairs blindfolded, where a sensuous feast (and lover) awaited me. This time was a little different. It was Matilda waiting for me, looking somber on the porch in the middle of a hot Saturday. I already knew what preoccupied her. After I had gotten off the phone with an angry Dauphine the night before, I'd had a hard time sleeping, so I called Matilda and told her about the auction, and Pierre's stunt.

"I cannot believe Pierre," I said, greeting Matilda on the porch. "Dauphine's shaken."

"I don't blame her. In the almost forty years that we've been doing this, we've had trouble with only one man: Pierre. I should have trusted my instincts when he first joined, but we were all dazzled by his charms."

"Well, there's one consolation in all of this: his fifteen million will keep S.E.C.R.E.T. running for a long time," I said.

"*If* we keep it."

I had never questioned whether we'd keep the money. But the way Matilda was talking, giving it back suddenly seemed a possibility.

"Anyway," she continued, "whether we keep the money is a decision for the whole Committee, not just me. I'm heading to Dauphine's house now."

"Should I come? Can we postpone this . . . session?"

"No. This is a job for the head of the Committee and time is of the essence. I may be able to convince Dauphine to stay in S.E.C.R.E.T., but if not, I hope I can at least convince her to accept our apologies. Meanwhile, *you*, my dear, have an exciting task at hand that also needs to be completed. Are you sure you're ready?"

"Ready as I'll ever be."

"Nervous?"

"Yes."

"Has Jesse contacted you?"

"I'm seeing him tonight." I couldn't help but beam a little.

Matilda didn't echo my enthusiasm; instead, her tone shifted back to one of concern.

"After all that's happened, and how wrong I was about Pierre, I do hope I'm not wrong about Jesse too."

"I don't think you are," I said, wondering why she continued to plant these doubts about him.

I followed her into the Mansion, up the stairs, then down a long, cool corridor, where she stopped in front of a narrow door. She unlocked it. Inside the small room was a single grey club chair facing a wall of glass. Matilda pulled the chair out for me. The room on the other side of the glass was dimly lit but spectacular, with two floor-to-ceiling windows to my right, draped in thick burgundy curtains, cupids carved into the wooden valences. Ancient oil paintings of beautiful women in shoulder-baring gowns hung along the ivory-colored walls. The bed itself was a piece of art, each poster carved to look like a willow trunk, fronds decorating the oak fascia. In the center of the room sat a tufted chair, armless, with gilt legs, the seat and back embroidered with burgundy roses.

I felt more nervous than I had during one of my own fantasies.

"This is the Emperor's Room," Matilda said.

"So this is where the training happens?"

"Some of it, yes. You ready?"

I nodded, took a deep breath and gave her my most confident smile. I was about to watch Mark Drury's first training session with Angela Rejean. He'd passed all the tests, submitted to two prior sessions and aced his interviews. Now, before engaging in a fantasy with Dauphine, he had to pass final muster with Angela.

"It can be emotional to watch former lovers, Cassie. It takes fortitude."

"I'm fine," I said, as much for myself as for her. "He's for S.E.C.R.E.T., for Dauphine. Not for me."

"Good."

"Does he know I'm watching?"

"No. He knows *someone* from S.E.C.R.E.T. is watching, but we never say who. He was quite excited."

"Does Angela know she's being watched?"

She gave me a wry smile.

"Cassie, honey, this is her *thing*. All right then. Enjoy yourself. But study carefully too. We have to evaluate him— look for ways he can improve, to enliven a woman's fantasy experience. He has to find pleasure in pleasing. And he needs to learn how to make a woman feel completely desired, which is, without a doubt, the greatest aphrodisiac. I'll funnel any advice to him. Patience keeps coming up as an issue for him. Good luck," she said with a smile, adding, "you've come a long way, Cassie. Call me later. I'll let you know how it goes with Dauphine."

"Thank you. Truly. For everything," I said. "And I hope Dauphine stays. There's still just so *much*."

"I'll tell her just that."

She shut off the light and left, closing the door behind her. I was alone in my little dark room, unsure of what to do. I crossed and uncrossed my legs, waiting for the session to begin on the other side of the one-way glass.

A few moments later, Angela emerged from an ivory door flush with the wall in the Emperor's Room. Her normally straightened hair was arranged in a relaxed, sassy Afro, and she was wearing a white, wraparound dress, cut low, the material thin, almost translucent, her dark nipples alert. She wore six-inch pumps that set off her brown muscled calves to perfection. She ignored the glass, which would look like a mirror on her side of the room. She walked over to the marble mantel of the fireplace and leaned on it provocatively. There was a lot you could envy about Angela, but her calm, cool demeanor was at the top of my list just then.

From a door to the left, off the same hallway I had just navigated with Matilda, Mark slowly emerged, wearing a grin that only grew bigger when he took in his next "trainer." He looked so cute and clean in his chambray shirt tucked into baggy cords, his hair damp. I could almost smell his green apple shampoo.

"Holy mother of mercy," he muttered, at which point I realized I'd not only be seeing everything, but hearing everything through speakers.

"Okay, first thing: don't smile at me so much," Angela said to him. "You want our girl to feel you're happy to see her, but enthuse less, smolder more."

"Got it," he said, literally wiping the smile off his face with a sweep of his hand.

I laughed. I mean, it was funny—*he* was funny. But Angela was not amused.

"Take a seat."

Mark fell into the tufted chair like an obedient boy, which sent Angela's fist to her hip. *Oh, please don't blow this*, I thought. *If you blow this, no Jesse for me.*

"Yes, ma'am," he added.

"Don't 'ma'am' me," Angela scolded. "That is *not* going to turn any woman on."

"Sorry."

He examined the room, his eyes stopping on the mirror for a second. Angela followed his gaze. They were both looking directly at me. *No!* I sank in the chair, my hand to my throat, which was now closing in some kind of terror-induced anaphylactic shock. Angela snapped her fingers to bring his attention back to her. Whew. *They can't see you! They cannot see you, Cassie!* I reminded myself. Exhale.

She strutted up to him, stood close enough to almost touch his knees with hers.

"Remember, we only pair you with women who want what you want, who crave what you crave, who want to do what you want to do, or who want to try what you want to try."

He put one hand to the muscles in his neck to give himself a stretchy massage. Wow, he was nervous too.

"So, Mark . . . how shall we play today?"

How shall we play today? That was sexy. I tucked that phrase away. He looked down at her white pumps, regarding them thoughtfully. I followed his eyes as they made their slow way up her long legs.

"I'll play however you want to play."

That's my boy! I wanted to yell. *You can do this, Mark.* Angela moved her hand across the front of her dress.

"Why don't you take your clothes off, Mark?"

"I can get into that."

He stood, a full six inches shorter than her, to strip.

"You're a goddess," he said, kicking his shoes off, looking up into her face looming over him, her breasts level with his eyes. "I don't care if I'm not supposed to say that. It's what you are."

She cupped his chin, but instead of kissing him, she let go and turned to make her way to an ornately carved writing desk. She opened a drawer and took out a tangle of thick crimson ribbon. The only way to describe how she moved was feline. She was a woman who loved being in her body and she was used to being watched. He couldn't tear his eyes off her. Nor could I. She stood behind the desk now, watching as he ripped off his clothes, pants first.

"Mark, Mark, Mark. You're stripping like a frat boy. Put your clothes back on and start again, honey."

He did as he was told. Once dressed, he started again, this time removing his belt more slowly.

"Now you're a Chippendales dancer? Not sexy."

"*Fuck*," Mark said, clearly pissed at himself.

"Start with your shirt. Just use one hand to undo the buttons. Try that. Look at me the whole time."

He did, and it was much better. She held the ribbons in her hands.

"Now the pants," she said, as he casually undid his belt, leaving it in the loops, and dropped his pants and boxers to the ground.

He lightly kicked them aside. He was clearly ready, but she didn't draw attention to that fact. She pushed him back into the chair and dangled the red ribbons in front of his face.

"You should be naked too," he said, nervous laughter

escaping.

"I don't like that word," she said.

"Naked?"

"No. *Should*. It's not popular around here."

She moved behind him, firmly tying his wrists to the chair. Then she came around the front of him and nudged his thighs open. Keeping her eyes on him, she untied the side knot of her dress. She opened it up to him like an envelope. She had nothing on underneath.

"Let me put it another way," he said, taking in the whole of her body. "It would be great if you were naked *all* the time. For the good of mankind."

She flung her dress off her and stood in front of him, wearing nothing but her white pumps. I watched him taking her in. Then with one hand she squeezed a breast, while her other traveled all over her torso. I was spellbound, feeling her arousal as she gave herself a stir with her own middle finger.

"You're hard, aren't you? What are we going to do about that?"

"Holy *shit!*" he murmured, throwing his head back, his eyes riveted to her hands, her fingers. He wanted to touch her, to reach out to her, but he couldn't. Even *I* felt his frustration, his arousal arousing me. I had never felt that before; I hadn't seen much pornography and I was no voyeur. But this . . . this was intense. And hot. I sank a little lower in my club chair, slack with desire.

Both feet still in heels, she straddled his legs, leaned over and put her hands on his shoulders, her full breasts touching his chest as she bent to kiss him. She started slowly, languidly, arching her taut body, her ass high in the air. She moved her lips down his neck, stopping every once in a while to gaze into his eyes, to gauge his reaction. He was desperate.

"Do you think you can untie me?" he asked. "Fuck, I'd really like to touch you."

She thought about his words for a second. Then, kicking off her pumps, she lifted her leg and placed a bare foot carefully on his thigh. One leg propped up like that, she spread herself to him, keeping him an agonizing foot away from what he craved.

"You want to touch me?" she asked. He nodded, trying to keep his eyes on her eyes, but he couldn't help himself. They traveled down the length of her perfect body to watch what she was doing to herself with her hand.

"I like when a man does this to me," she said, the muscles in her arm flinching with every circle. "But I also like doing this for myself."

He made a sound, something between a grunt and a moan. "You think you could do a better job than I'm doing?"

"Yes . . ." he said, straining; this was killing him.

I felt myself heating up, surprised when my hand rose to my own chest, then dipped into my bra and found my right breast, squeezed slightly. This was so new to me.

I watched as Angela bent her knee more, drawing her cleft closer to his face. She put her hands in his hair, guiding his mouth forward towards her, almost lovingly. The top of his head moved as his mouth found her, and he lapped at her, his eyes gazing up every few seconds over the top of her thigh to check her reaction, his hands still tied behind his back. He was all mouth, only there to please and serve her.

Angela threw her head back. "That's good . . . That's very good, baby," she cooed, her hips lightly thrusting to match the rhythm of his tongue—and I remembered his mouth on me not so long ago, his hands . . .

"Holy shit, *yeah*," Angela whispered, grinding her hips into his face, his tongue. "Oh . . . mmm . . . you're going to make me come and then . . . I'm going to fuck you."

He nodded, weakened. This was like worship, the way his head bobbed rhythmically between her legs until she threw her head back in a spasm, gripping his hair and taking her orgasm from him, and he gave it to her eagerly. Spent, she dropped her foot to reach behind him and with a tug released his hands, letting the ribbons cascade to the floor. He immediately wrapped a fist around his erection, his own mounting desire impossible to ignore. Angela moved—a little wobbly—to the nightstand and took out a condom. Returning, she unfurled it on him with one swift movement. Then she straddled herself just above him.

"I'm going to fuck you, Mark," she said. "You good with that?"

He nodded vigorously, placing his hands on her thighs and guiding her down onto his throbbing head. She seemed to take him in partway, bobbing slightly, agonizing him, but not sliding all the way down.

"Your pussy is fucking perfect," he crooned, watching her slowly consume him.

"Shh . . . good boy," she purred, stroking his hair. She inched down, then, holding his shoulders, slammed onto him, taking his shaft all the way in, as he threw his head back, pressing his fingertips into her thighs. Then it began, her fierce gyrations, her exquisite hips pumping him for everything he had. She was all appetite and he was simply food for her, and he was *loving* it, probably astonished that his body could provide for a woman like this. She was *fucking* him, and I could feel myself grow hotter as his fingers dug into her taut flesh, his ropy neck muscles pulsing. At one point, he held her face and kissed her hard, like he needed a hit. After which she gazed down at him over the mounds of her own bouncing breasts, and came. Her cries were barely dying down when he stood, lifting her up in an easy straddle, pivoting, and tossed her onto the bed, making her laugh out loud.

"Nice job!" she said.

Strangely, I felt proud of him in that moment too, I really did. *Go for it, Mark, now make her yours!*

He stood over her now, slapping her knees apart, his to conquer. He entered her swiftly, sharply. *Oh god,* she cried out at the same time that I murmured it, my fingers finding myself, doing to myself what he was doing to her. And that's when I felt it too, watching them. I felt it travel all the way up my body. One hand tangled in her hair, he was relentless as she moaned beneath him, her legs wrapped around his lean waist, her arms flung over her head, letting him fuck her hard like that for a few moments—and soaking me in the process.

Then, in one impressive move, she flipped him over onto his back and she was now straddling him, in control again. He laughed at his pinned arms, using all his strength to lift her forward onto his still-eager mouth, his fingers separating her folds, his head moving in circles. She looked back over her shoulder at his unrelenting erection, flipped around and slid his condom off, the front of her pussy now before Mark's tongue. When she took him in her mouth, it was mere seconds before he arched beneath her, coming, moaning, "Angela . . . *oh Christ*," lifting his pelvis in service to her. I was awed by her skills, her enthusiasm, as she licked him clean. And when she came yet again, so did I, with an intensity I had never felt before, all my senses exploding, my moans mingling with hers. Collapsing back into my chair, feeling faint, I breathed heavily along with them.

After a pause, Angela crawled off Mark, flopping next to him in the bed. Both their bodies were swallowed up by a cloud of down duvet and pillows. The gentleness with which he held her, the soft way her hand moved up and down his stomach, *this* now seemed far too intimate to watch. Flushed and satisfied, I quietly exited the room, shutting the door gently behind me. I ducked into a small washroom next door to splash cold water on my face and hands.

My phone said three o'clock. Enough time to stop at the

grocery store, pick up some wine, and maybe even rest a little before Jesse was at my place. That boy had no idea how this training session was also about to benefit him.

⁓

I wasted almost an hour at the grocery store trying to figure out what to cook, half distracted by Dauphine's dilemma, but also by the incredible scene I had just witnessed. So when my cab pulled up in front of the Spinster Hotel, I had less than an hour to make bouillabaisse, set the table and take a shower. But having little time to think and pace and ruminate was a good thing. I picked out a pair of faded jeans, a blue silk blouse and silver bangles for my wrists. For some reason I didn't want Jesse to see my S.E.C.R.E.T. bracelet; it felt odd, too talismanic.

While I was towel-drying my hair with one hand and stirring the soup with my other, the doorbell rang. He was early. Really early. *Dammit, dammit, dammit.* I threw open my door and there he was: that grin, the stubble, those crinkly eyes, the Cajun accent. I was speechless and . . . makeup-less. Ugh! And my hair . . .

"Well, hello there," he said, ducking through the doorway.

"You're early."

"I'm right on time," he said, kissing the side of my damp head. He smelled so good, like cut grass and summer. "A habit of good single dads everywhere. Never make your kids wait for you; they grow up feeling unimportant."

"Good rule. But I need a few minutes."

"For what? You look good to me."

He handed me flowers and a bottle of wine.

"Sweet peas and cold rosé."

"Thank you. Lovely."

My place was small; the kitchen, dining and living area were all one long galley, the bedroom visible through French doors at the end of the room. Jesse's height also made my place seem like the low-slung attic apartment that it was. Both of us had grins on our faces like we'd just gotten away with something excellent.

"It's really good to see you."

He placed a hand on his chest and bit his bottom lip while eyeing me up and down, swaying slightly in his cowboy boots. My face shot hot.

"Really good to see you too. Help yourself to anything. I'm just going to . . . finish getting ready."

He kept his eyes on me as I pointed to the bathroom, walking backwards towards it.

"Be right back!" I said, and closed the bathroom door behind me.

I was completely breathless. *Holy shit. He's here. Calm down.* I was behaving like a teenager. I turned on the dryer and gave my hair a few minutes of heat before deciding, *Fuck it, this is what I look like, this is who I am.* I stared myself down in the mirror for one last pep talk, remembering Matilda's words: *He's just a guy. You're both just people.*

I found him in the middle of setting the table, a tea

towel slung over his shoulder, tattoos peeking out from under his T-shirt sleeves. He was carefully spacing out spoons next to mismatched bowls. A warm current spiraled through my body.

"Soup's almost ready. I hope you don't mind that I added a bit more bay leaf powder. But don't be afraid to buy whole leaves. You just pick 'em out after."

I forgot he was a chef—a pastry chef, but still he knew his way around any kitchen.

"Thanks. I can take over from here. You're *my* guest. And you've probably had a busy day already with your son. Did you guys do anything fun?"

Breathe.

"Nah, he has some little friends that live nearby. They came over. Played in the backyard while I fixed the lawn mower. Glamorous stuff like that."

"It actually sounds nice," I said, cutting up the French loaf and putting it on the table with some sea salt and butter. "I'd love to see some pictures of him."

"Sure. But first, sit for a bit."

He could tell I was nervous, flitting around the kitchen, plunking down salt and pepper shakers, wineglasses, pulling out my threadbare linen napkins, wedding gifts from a bygone era. I could barely remember who I was back then.

I lowered myself into the mismatched chair next to him, and my knees skimmed his.

"So. Why'd you bench me?"

"I didn't . . . bench you. I put in a request to see you again. Outside of S.E.C.R.E.T. And here you are. You could have turned it down."

"I'm teasing." He took a healthy bite out of a slice of bread. "I thought of you from time to time."

"I thought of *you* from time to time," I said, then chomped into some bread myself.

"I'm glad you made the request. Been feeling a little hungry for something . . . a little more substantial."

"Me too," I said. *Where was this going?* "But . . . I mean . . . I don't have any expectations. I realize how we met. It's just that I've been thinking, of all the people who I . . . Well, I felt a connection to you. So I . . . yeah."

He took the remaining chunk of bread out of my hand and threw it across the room. Then he put out his hands to me.

"I'm thinking I need to get you in your bed right now, Cassie, 'cause I get the sense you're gonna start thinking about this all too much. And then we're gonna get all gummed up in that mental machinery of yours." He gently tapped the side of my head.

"G-good thing you can't really overcook bouillabaisse," I stammered, rising unsteadily to my feet.

"Yeah, you can. But who fucking cares?" He bent down to throw me over his shoulder.

I screamed, thrilled and shocked. The Delmonte sisters downstairs probably had glasses to the ceiling to hear better. *Fuck them*, I thought as he carted me ten feet to my bed and threw me down, causing an eruption of pillows and at least one of the bed legs to thump hard on the floor that was also the sisters' living room ceiling. He pulled a condom out of his wallet, tossing it next to me.

Okay then.

"The neighbors," I whispered, as he slowly crawled up my body until I was flanked by two inked arms on either side of my head.

Jesse's face, which was so open in the kitchen, now took on a darker focus. Hovering over me, he fished around for my wrists, one then the other, pulling them up over my head, capturing them beneath his hands.

"So?"

"So?" *Jesse is here, on top of me! Holding me down by my wrists on the bed.*

"How do you want to play, Cassie Robichaud?"

I had a heady déjà vu.

"How do *you* want to play?" I was feeling out of my league all of a sudden. My heart thumped against my chest. I felt nausea rise. He lowered his groin until he had me fully pinned, his erection hard against my inner thigh. It was unmistakably clear what this was doing to him, *for* him.

"I'm happy to do anything with you, Jesse. But . . . I wasn't looking for some kind of fantasy scenario with you."

"I know it," he said, collapsing on his elbow, his eyes now searching and warm, his hands smoothing back my hair. "We don't have to do anything weird . . . I'm happy to just . . . neck."

It was the way he said it—*neck*—that caused me to erupt into a fit of giggles. And that made him laugh too.

"Y'all wanna just *neck* with me?" I said, mimicking his Cajun accent. "Okay, let's just neck."

He bent to kiss me, to shut me up, really, his palm cradling my head, his fingers entwined in my hair. Oh, *this* was the mouth I remembered, the hungry, searching mouth. The other hand slowly unbuttoned my blouse, landing warmly between my breasts, then made its agonizing way down, undoing the buttons of my jeans, sliding them off along with my panties.

"All gone," he said, slipping a hand underneath me to unclasp my bra, flinging it across the room.

He stood up next to the bed to remove his jeans, then his boxers, making it immediately apparent how much this was turning him on. He took my hand and guided me to him.

"Touch my cock, Cassie," he whispered. "Say it."

It was so hard, so smooth.

"Say what?" I said, running my hand up and down his *cock*.

"Say you want my cock inside of your beautiful pussy," he murmured, his eyes flashing under my inexpert touch.

I'd never seen him totally naked before, but here he stood over me, all muscles and sinew, tattoos and desire, and he knew he had me, this shameless, potent man.

"What do you want, baby?" he asked.

"I want you inside of me, now," I begged.

"You want me to fuck you, Cassie?"

"Yes, Jesse."

"Say it."

"Fuck me," I muttered.

"Say, *I want you to fuck me hard, Jesse.*"

I closed my eyes, my whole body feeling an incredible want, as he pressed my knees apart into the mattress.

"Mmm, look at you and your pretty little pussy," he drawled. "What's a guy gotta do to make that his?"

"You know," I said, wishing sexier words came to me more easily. That was something I could do with Jesse, learn to let go more, be freer . . .

"Say it, Cassie."

"Fuck me, Jesse. I want you to fuck me hard . . ." I said, almost delirious with want.

He bent over the foot of the bed, his mouth moving up my leg to the curve of my inner thigh, his tongue tickling the smooth groove where my tender skin met the line of soft down. *God* he was teasing me. He was driving me crazy.

"Jesse, fuck me," I demanded, as his hand caressed my thigh, his thumb slicking down my folds, merely fluttering over my clitoris. The ache becoming too much to bear, my hips began to rock to make him touch where I needed touching, to fuck where I needed fucking. But he merely let a lazy finger grace the opening, finding me so wet I gasped, and I arched fiercely now towards him, never hungrier.

I writhed beneath him as he gathered one of my breasts, my nipple tightening in his cool mouth. He did the same to my other one as I moaned in response, now desperate. And oh, *the ache*. My knees began to nudge the side of his torso, to maneuver him between my thighs.

"More?"

"*Yesss.*"

He sat up between my legs to roll on the condom, his taut forearms flinching, his eyes savoring me. I realized why I wanted this man, why I had ached for him, because it was an ache that *could* be soothed. With Will it was all hunger, one we could never satisfy. I needed Jesse *because* I wanted Will, and Jesse was the only man to quell that want. In fact, I was going to let him fuck it right out of me.

And he did, entering me sharply, fiercely, sinking into me inch by agonizing inch, his thrusts insistent and growing fiercer as my hips bucked against his. He took my wrists again and pinned them down next to my head.

"You like this?" he said, filling me up, his voice a low growl.

I nodded, feeling like he was actually fucking pleasure *into* the very end of me. The more he thrust, the more his stomach muscles clenched and contracted, turning his whole body into an oiled piston. My knees bent high to clutch his torso, now coated in a sheen of sweat. Then it happened: my whole core squeezed around him and he could feel it too, his face registering a shock, taking it as a cue to ride me higher still, pump me harder, my clit now pinned between his pelvis and mine, his keening hips kneading it perfectly, beautifully, rolling into a hot build. I wanted to scream as the whole of me surrendered. I was calling *"Oh god"* as I came, setting him off, his beautiful lips curling as he came hard into me too, saying, "*Oh, Cassie . . . yeah,*" neither of us caring about the neighbors or the noise as we finally collapsed, gasping into a heaving pile of limbs.

"I think my heart . . . stopped. Shh . . . I need to listen for it," he mumbled into my hair. "Am I . . . dead? Can you hear anything?"

"I think you're gonna be okay," I said, as he eased out and off me. I shifted to face him, coated in his sweat, and sleepily traced the outlines of the tattoos on his shoulders. I spotted a scar there. He grabbed my fingers.

"How'd you get that?"

"Dirt bike stunt. Fourteen years old," he said, between kissing my fingertips.

He sat up so I could see his full body paint and turned around to give me a better look at his back.

"Is that an oak tree?"

Almost like adolescents at show and tell, we slid from hot sex to sweet stories as he began to tell me what was behind the more prominent tattoos—the tree whose branches twisted into a skull cradling his shoulder, the other shoulder covered by a cluster of birds.

"Yeah. It's the oak from my grandma's property in Kenner. I grew up there after my parents died. This one hurt," he said, pointing out a beautifully rendered face of a handsome young man on the left side of his rib cage. "My older brother. He taught me how to read when I was ten. Late bloomer. He died in the first Gulf War." So much tragedy on his body— dead family, old memories. "And that's my 'tramp stamp,'" he said, bending to show me his lower back, where indeed the word *Tramp* was stamped on his sacrum.

"Ha!"

"Were you expecting a butterfly?" he asked.

"I think with you expectations might be a bad idea," I said. Was I fishing? Was this me seeking assurances that I could have expectations of this man? I wasn't sure. He stretched out next to me to cuddle.

"That's probably wise, Cassie," he said, sounding sincere and serious, throwing his thigh over me. "I was thinking the same thing about you."

Me? I almost did that female thing, that thing where I reassure him and tell him, *Oh no, no, no, I'm here; you can expect things from me. I'm all in.* But I knew better. Just because a man has his entire life story drawn out on his skin for all to see, that doesn't make him an open book. And just because I had sex with him, that didn't make me his. We were both still carrying shadows from our past into whatever our future held. But for the first time in my life, I was okay with that. I was beautifully, perfectly okay with it.

DAUPHINE

had never been a traveler, so I wasn't expecting to feel such a rush of pure joy upon returning from Buenos Aires and seeing my porch, my potted marigolds and heavy mums wilting in the late summer heat. Upstairs, I dropped the last of my luggage, sighing in gratitude at my dusty, sunlit apartment. My trip, which had begun as transformative and restorative, had turned dark and frightening after my interlude with Pierre Castille. Being home felt grounding, safe. And I now discovered it was true what they said about homesick Southerners: there's no sorrier lot.

After I hosed down my plants, I drew a bath and soaked off the stress of the return flight (the turbulence was a little meaner and no Captain Nathan to offer "comfort"), and the Customs officers were a little nosier, poking through my purchases with the help of a beagle I wasn't allowed to pet. The officers were looking for sausage and ivory, probably the *only* two things I didn't bring back with me from Argentina. I had bought two extra suitcases for the costume jewelry, linens, housedresses and four vintage tango dresses I bought to sell at the Funky Monkey. Such is the life of an "international buyer." But while the beagle was nosing through my belongings, I was heartened to realize that I *had* intended to sell all this stuff. I didn't want to insulate anymore, which was really the purpose of keeping that treasure trove to myself. All those imaginary futures where I'd have just the right thing to round it out, that future was happening now.

When the doorbell rang, I jumped, my nerves still a bit rattled. As expected, it was Matilda, her apology written all over her kind face.

"Dauphine, honey. Can I come in?"

Seeing her face, I realized that my anger about the security breach with Pierre had faded. Still, I didn't greet Matilda with a hug.

"Of course. Please come in. I'll make tea."

Typical Southerners, we exchanged pleasantries and travel highlights. I included discreet mention of my visit to the cockpit and my night on the tango stage, both of which left me blushing and grateful.

"I'm so glad you enjoyed those Steps. But I don't blame you, Dauphine, for wanting to quit us. I just came to tell you how relieved I was to hear how you thwarted the worst part of Pierre's plans."

"Cassie always stressed to me that I could opt out of any situation that didn't feel a hundred percent right . . . He didn't."

"You have sharp instincts. You know yourself. That's

enviable. For that, I want to give you something," she said, reaching into her purse, removing a small purple box and carefully placing it in front of me.

"Is it my Step Six charm? Really?"

"Open it," she said.

Truthfully, one of the things I'd thought about was that if I quit S.E.C.R.E.T., I'd miss out on all the rest of the charms. What can I say? I love my bling. Which was why it was hard to contain my glee after I opened the box. It contained not just my Step Six charm for *Confidence*, but all the others as well.

"Oh my goodness," I said, reaching into my purse for my bracelet, which I kept in a velvet roll.

"You earned *Confidence* when you trusted your instincts about Pierre. I'm so glad he didn't shake that from you. Seven's for *Curiosity*," Matilda reminded me, laying each charm out on the Formica. "That's for asking Pierre all the right questions. Eight's for *Bravery*, of course, and how you stood your ground with him. And Nine, that one's *Exuberance*—and I do hope you still feel a measure of that, Dauphine, after all you've experienced with us."

I secured them one by one to my bracelet, shaking it in front of my eyes. It was dazzling.

"This is so thoughtful, so generous," I said. "I'll treasure it, and my time in S.E.C.R.E.T. Always."

"I have one more offer," she said, leaning forward in her chair. "Of course you can say no, but I urge you to consider it. We'd like you to experience a final fantasy, one we're quite confident will be worth the leap of faith. We are all very upset about what happened to you in Buenos Aires. So we'd relish the opportunity to make amends. I can assure you we'd do this not only to restore your feelings of safety, but to solidify everything S.E.C.R.E.T. stands for. And I have it on good authority that this fantasy will exceed every one of the fantasies you've experienced before. In fact, we suspect this last one will blow your mind."

Maybe it was her face, beseeching and earnest. And maybe I suddenly saw the folly in punishing myself *and* S.E.C.R.E.T. because of the deed of one bad man. I looked at my bracelet, nine charms dancing around my wrist. What do you say to an offer like that? You throw your arms around the person proposing it and you say, "Yes, fine. One more."

I was surprisingly calm the day my final fantasy card arrived three weeks later. It was Elizabeth who had a hard time containing herself after I asked her to dress me for a "casual but sexy" date at Tipitina's.

"Seriously? A *date?* You're going out? With a real live man? To a concert? All this change is too much for my little heart to bear."

She was still absorbing my new mandate, the one I had carried home with me from Argentina along with all my beautiful finds.

When she asked me, as always, what was for sale and what was for keeps, I replied, "Sell everything, all of it. All the excess stock that I'm keeping for no good reason. Everything in the back. All the gold hoops and the silk pajamas and the leather gloves and the pillbox hats," I said, adding, "and whatever we can't sell, we'll give away. I need more room to grow."

Elizabeth looked overcome, teary, as she held a set of blue-tinted *pince-nez* between her fingers.

"Dauphine, do you know how long I've been waiting for you to say this?" she asked.

And today I was asking her to help me again, this time to see me through her eyes, so I could gain a new perspective on myself.

She was breathless. "Okay. There are a few looks I've had in mind for you for a long while. Will you let me give them a try?"

Elizabeth whirled around the store, plucking scarves and blouses, bracelets and T-shirts, dresses and jeans. This culminated in a stop in the office treasure trove, where she pulled bangles, cuffs, stilettos and a brand-new lavender camisole. Nothing Elizabeth chose for me was vintage; the pieces were all tight, edgy, the colors mostly blues and purples, which I rarely wore. But when she pulled out her hair straightener, I knew we were looking at a game-changer kind of evening. If I didn't wear my unruly red hair piled on my head or tied back, I didn't know what to do with it.

After an hour and a half of being dressed and undressed, while we ate takeout fries and smoothies, and waited on customers between modeling "looks," I settled on black leather pants, a camisole under a white sheer blouse and a charcoal blazer, topped with a hail of thin gold chains, a gold cuff and black suede ankle boots with wedges. I looked bold. And, I had to admit, sexy.

"But see how that hint of lavender camisole gives the whole look a soft feminine appeal too," Elizabeth said, thoughtfully examining me in the mirror like I was her creation.

"Why have I never let you do this before?"

"No clue. You look like a rock goddess," she said.

I looked like me, just a more current, modern version. I felt potent, punchy and free.

"How does this look instead of the cuff," I said, fetching my charm bracelet.

"Oh *yeah*. God that thing's gorgeous. You have such a good eye, Dauphine. Such a good eye."

"And *you* are getting a raise," I said, grabbing Elizabeth by the cheeks and kissing her square on her Clara Bow lips.

The limo fetched me at home, at ten sharp, the cool night air hitting my face, signaling that fall was just around the corner. The last time I was at Tipitina's, I had been with a very reluctant Luke during Jazz Fest, on one of our last outings as a couple. Music never was his "thing." So far the ladies had me pegged. If this fantasy was just me listening to great music with a great guy who was into it too, that would be good enough for me.

"We're here, Miss Mason," said the driver, noting the line snaking around the building and up the block.

My heart skipped at the sight of THE CARELESS ONES, lit up on the marquee. Yes! Their music could not be a more perfect soundtrack for whatever this fantasy was going to be. So far, so right! *Just breathe*, I told myself.

The kind driver, sensing my nervousness, ushered me through the throng of fans, acting like we owned the place, like I was a VIP. Nearing the front of the stage, where the opening act was performing, I spotted two familiar-looking women holding out a chair for me.

"Dauphine! You're here! You remember us? I'm Kit and this is Pauline," Kit yelled over music. "We're your dates until your *date* gets here. Have I mentioned just how much I *love* my job?"

"You look amazing!" Pauline enthused, sexy in her clear-skinned, short-haired way. She had on a black mini-dress downplayed with a denim jacket and banged-up black ankle boots. Kit was in cutoffs and a baggy white dress shirt, a dramatic grey streak highlighting her now-ebony hair.

"Thanks for being here," I said. "It means a lot to me." And it did. I wasn't used to going out like this on my own, or going out at all, for that matter. "So . . . is he here?" I asked, sneaking a glance around the crowded room.

"He's on his way," Pauline said, exchanging looks with Kit.

"You'll tell me when he gets here?" I asked, nervously patting down my straight hair. It felt like silk.

"You'll know when he gets here," Kit said. "Don't worry."

A glass of chilled Chablis appeared in front of me, my favorite, and after the opening band left the stage, the packed room went completely dark. Minutes later, when the Careless Ones fired up their instruments with a familiar riff, the hair stood up on my arms. It was *him*, Mark Drury, lit from behind at center stage. As Mark reached for the microphone and pulled it to his mouth, the floodlights hit his amazing face full force. For a few seconds the only sound in the cavernous room was his breath on the mesh of the mike. He had the body of a musician, all lank and sinew, bones seemingly hollowed out for music to move through them. Clothes hung on him perfectly, but they were incidental to his voice. Everything was. Why he didn't do it for Cassie, I'll never know, but a glance around the room at all the glassy-eyed women swaying in their seats confirmed he wouldn't lack for attention for long.

For a few seconds he said nothing; he just stood there with his eyes closed. Then *flash*—lights exploded as he broke into the band's best single, "Days from Here," adding a honky-tonk edge, bringing the house to its feet. For the next forty-five minutes of their set, I forgot the fantasy, stopped searching for the man I'd soon be with, and simply marveled at Mark's talent to pull emotions from his body and pour them over the crowd. That's what the best live music does: it makes a whole room of people feel the same thing. There I was, up front, on my feet, clapping and grinning with two other women from S.E.C.R.E.T., my body filling to capacity with joy. Whoever my fantasy man was, he'd be getting the best of me tonight.

"We're going to change up the temp a little bit. Get you cozy," Mark said, pulling up a stool, perching his acoustic guitar on his knee. "This last song's for my girl. She's right over there," he said, nodding to indicate a table near ours.

See? Of course he has a "girl."

Instead of feeling bitter about his "girl," I suddenly felt . . . magnanimous, like there was enough love, enough affection, enough of this joy to go around. Mark made his hand into a visor, peering into the dark crowd over my shoulder. I turned around to get a look at this lucky girl. I couldn't tell which one he meant, so I turned back.

"There she is," he said, *looking right at our table,* "the gorgeous redhead in the front. That's my baby. You good?"

The hot white spotlight then centered over me and pulled in on my terror-stricken face. *Me?* I felt Pauline's firm hand grab my forearm as though she were preventing me from fleeing, or floating to the ceiling.

"Her name's Dauphine," Mark announced to the crowd. "And I'm hoping y'all will help me get her to do something for me," he said, plinking his guitar strings and *smiling right at me.* "I'm hoping she'll . . . accept the Step."

He started strumming the intro to a song, and I saw stars! *Is this really happening? To me?* His band members looked slightly confused, but when they recognized the riff, they joined the intro.

"I know y'all don't know what the hell that means," he said to the crowd, smiling, "but *she* knows. Don't you, baby."

That smile. The crowd began to urge me on. I heard, *Accept the Step! Accept the Step!* Even Kit and Pauline were chanting now, both of them laughing and clapping.

"So what do you say? After this song, maybe we can go somewhere," he said, and now I laughed, my hands covering my mouth. Then I drew my hands away and yelled out, "Yes!" and when I did, the crowd erupted, and Mark launched into the most aching rendition of Margaret Lewis's "Reconsider Me." For the next three minutes, I forced my heart back down my throat and into its proper place behind my ribs. I felt flushed, and thrilled that he'd boldly shared our connection with the whole room—yet no one knew a thing about us except Kit and Pauline.

After the song, during a standing ovation, he placed his guitar on its stand and made his way directly towards me, the whole room in paroxysms as time stopped and he pulled me to my feet and into a lush kiss.

"Let's get the hell out of here," he whispered into my ear.

"Okay," I said, unsure my jelly legs would hold me upright. I waved a goodbye to Kit and Pauline as Mark tugged me through the still-clapping crowd and backstage into the bustling green room. We swept past his sweaty, chatty band members, one changing his shirt, another standing with a wife or girlfriend, another hovering nearby, blowing smoke out the back door. We pinballed through the room, exiting through a narrow, dark hallway where we made a right, then a left, until we hit upon a small office with a metal desk and a bleak bulb swinging overhead.

"Wow, you take me to the nicest places," I said, a little tipsy from the attention and from the wine.

He shut the door behind us, sending a yellowed calendar crashing to the floor. And then Mark Drury came at me slowly, hungrily. I moved back until I could feel the concrete wall behind me. Reaching me, he placed one arm, then the other on either side of me.

"So it *is* you," he said, peering into my face.

"What do you mean?"

"They gave me a name and a picture. I thought I recognized you. But I didn't believe it until I looked out into the crowd and saw you there. I've seen you at my shows," he said, his perfect lips inches from mine.

"You have?"

"Yeah. And I always go to find you after and you're always gone. Then I saw you on the patio of Ignatius's a few months ago, but I got pulled into a conversation with someone else."

"You mean with Cassie?" I said. "She's . . . she's a friend of mine."

"Mine too," he said. "Life's funny, how things sort themselves out, don't ya think?"

He was right. He was totally right. And I nodded. We could hear the next band cueing up on the other side of the wall, their opening beats pulsing through my body and his hands.

"I'm supposed to take you to the Mansion," he said, nuzzling my ear, smelling my hair. *Oh god.* "We have a car waiting for us out back. But I've been wanting you all night. Knowing you were in the crowd . . . knowing it was you. I don't think I can wait."

He smelled so good, a hint of apples, his breath warm, minty.

"May I?" He inched my jacket off my shoulders. "This too?"

I nodded as he began unbuttoning my blouse. As I stood there in my lavender camisole, he dragged a palm across my clavicle, circling a breast, the pad of his thumb waking up a nipple through the silk. He sweetly lifted the camisole up and over my head, then released my breasts from my bra.

"Fuck *me*," he said, taking them both in his hands, kissing them and leaving a wet path from one tense nipple to the other. He slipped a hand down the front of my leather pants, looking astonished to discover how wet I was.

Sweet Jesus.

I couldn't do anything but cover his mouth with a firm kiss that quickly turned ferocious. I melted into him, his whole body pressing me against the wall.

"I'm going to make you scream," he said, as I sighed at the feel of his mouth making its way down the front of my body. On his knees before me, he peeled off my pants, and started with tender, tentative licks, along my hip bones and over my belly button, coaxing my legs apart with his beautiful face, his talented tongue. Lifting one of my thighs, he buried his face in my cleft, nearly toppling me over before I found footing on a nearby chair. I was pinned against the cool cement wall of Tipitina's, by *Mark Drury!* I looked down as his tireless teasing found my clit and he swirled it inside his warm mouth like found treasure. My hips cocked forward as his tongue circled and flicked, his fingers darting in and out and taking me right to the edge of my senses, parting me more, and more, until his whole mouth owned the very center of me.

Then I felt it, the hot rush that pulled me under as I came—quickly, loudly, fully—heavy waves crashing over me, my fingers raking his hair. *"Oh god, oh god, oh god, Mark"* was all I could say, until I finally, completely, wilted over his body. He rose slowly and kissed his way back up to my face, cradled it with both his hands. But my legs were shot as I sank into the nearby busted office chair, my knees flung apart, my pants around one ankle like a black leather cuff.

"Holy shit," I breathed.

"All day I've fantasized about doing that," he said, wiping his sexy mouth victoriously.

"What else do you fantasize about?" I asked, already wanting more of him.

"This is *your* fantasy, Dauphine. It's supposed to be about you. Don't get me wrong. This works for me too."

I leaned forward and pulled him by a belt loop to stand in front of my face. I flashed my eyes up at him, my mouth slackened, looking for silent permission.

"And that works too," he said, as he stroked himself through his jeans.

My hands, shaking slightly, unbuttoned him, freeing his perfect erection, *my god,* taking his smooth tip in my mouth, never hungrier for anything. I looked up at him again as my tongue began circling his tip, and he died a little, his face collapsing at the site of my growing enthusiasm. Then I took him fully into my wet mouth, moaning at the same time, my firm hand pumping ever so rhythmically along his shaft, my other one under him, cupping him, feeling him rise with aching arousal. He closed his eyes as I took him deep into my mouth. I sucked in my cheeks, my lips a firm ring, my throat relaxed, my low moan moving through his groin. He whimpered. I was good at this, had always been good at this, but I had never wanted to be *the best* like I did now.

My mouth and hands were working their magic, but it was the eye contact that did him in, just as I slid a wet finger back and around, pressing in on him at the exact moment he came, hard and loud, deep into the back of my throat, one of his hands stroking my hair, the other one outstretched on the wall, as he said *god* and my name over and over again until spent. After a few tender strokes, I let go of him, flinging myself back in the chair, deeply pleased. My eye caught the calendar splayed on the floor; it was dated five years ago. *Just who was I back then?*

"Holy *shit.* That was . . . mind-*fucking*-blowing, Dauphine." His hands were on his knees, his jeans bunched around his ankles. "I've never . . . it was so . . . what the *fuck.*"

"Best ever?"

"Uh . . . *yeah.*"

"Well, that was my fantasy," I said. "Complete."

"Oh, but it's not over yet. Let's get the hell out of here. The Domino Suite awaits!"

"What's that?" I said, reaching down for my bra.

"I don't have a clue, but we're going to find out."

"So there's more?"

"So much more," he said, plucking up our clothes and pulling me up to my feet. "More than you know."

We dressed stealing soft glances at each other. And then we slipped out the back door of the club, where the same long black car that had dropped me off now took on an extra passenger. He held my hand in the back seat, and somehow this gesture was more intimate than what we'd just done to each other with our mouths at Tipitina's.

"That Margaret Lewis song . . . so good," I said.

"You know her?"

"*Know* her? I have all her records. Vinyl."

"Who would have thought this is how I'd meet my dream girl," he said, raising my hand to kiss the back of it.

His dream girl?

He noticed my bracelet for the first time. "You earned them all, right?"

I nodded.

"I think you get some do-overs tonight," he said, kissing my fingers.

Matilda was right: this fantasy was unrolling in a way that I could not have imagined myself. We kissed the rest of the way there, coming up for air only when the limo glided through those ivy-covered gates. The Mansion was dark, one window lit on the second floor.

"This place is so freaky, don't you think?" he said, exiting the limo in front of a small fountain with little angel statues.

"You've been here before?"

Mark looked at me.

"Right," I said.

"I'm going to assume you've been here before too."

"Once, and only back there," I said, pointing over the crest of a hill to the garage at the end of the driveway.

"What were you doing back there?"

The look on my face told him it was best not to ask.

"Right. This is so insane," he said, grinning widely. "I fucking *love* it."

The side door was open, and instead of taking me to the right, where I assumed the front foyer would lead us upstairs, he tugged me to the left, down a long, black-and white-tiled corridor with swinging oak doors at the end. We were quiet as mice, creeping hand in hand into the massive kitchen. A single light over a stove cast shadows on appliances the size of cattle. The pots and pans hanging from the ceiling were big enough to prepare meals for Vikings.

Mark pulled open an industrial-sized fridge stocked with enough food to feed an army. Snatching a large serving tray from an upper cabinet, and a box of crackers, he bent into the fridge to scoop up handfuls of chocolate truffles, grapes and cheese rounds.

"All they have is romance food," he said as he handed me the tray so he could continue to load it up. "They need to start buying cold cuts and bread."

"Ahem. Hello." The voice came from the kitchen door.

In my fright I screamed rather loudly, and Mark tossed the box of crackers in the air as a diminutive woman in a starched maid's uniform turned the lights on full force.

"I'm so sorry to have frightened you. I'm Claudette. We waited for you earlier, but the driver told us there was a slight delay. Are you finding everything you need?"

"Yes. Thank you," I said, trying to calm my heart.

"I'll show you to your suite," she said, taking the tray of food from my hands. "I'll carry this, my dear. We'll send up some drinks as well."

We were like a couple of school kids caught breaking into the cafeteria, but instead of getting punished, we were being offered keys to the whole school.

The Domino Suite was up the side stairs and down a wide hall in the west wing. It was, as its name implied, entirely decorated in black and white, its key feature a marble claw-foot tub at the end of an all-white platform bed dotted with round black pillows.

Claudette placed the tray on a glass-topped banquette that faced a floor-to-ceiling window framed with black velvet curtains. A second later, another woman, also dressed in uniform, dropped off a bucket of chilled champagne and several bottles of sparkling water.

"Just call down if you need anything," Claudette said as they left, closing the double doors behind them.

We waited a beat to make sure we were really alone. Then, with grins smeared across our faces, we leapt onto the platform bed, landing in a pile. I was happier than I'd been in a long, long time.

"This is so cool," he said. "You are so cool."

I noticed the iPod and speaker on the mantel of the fireplace.

"Any requests?" I asked, getting up and skipping across the room.

"Surprise me," Mark said, echoing my instructions to S.E.C.R.E.T.

It occurred to me then just how well the organization had done that. They'd surprised me over and over again. But this was by far the biggest surprise—my favorite musician singling me out in a crowded room, pleasuring me in the back of a club, then bringing me to this beautiful place, making me feel wanted, special, treasured, if only for a night. I wheeled through the iPod menu, stocked with some of the best Louisiana blues and jazz, and chose Professor Longhair, which made Mark convulse with joy on the bed.

"Yes! He's the king!"

"My favorite's 'Willie Mae,'" I said, joining him again, working my hand under his T-shirt. "Don't you wish you could have seen him play at Tipitina's?"

"Tipitina's. Yeah. From now on, I can only think of it as the place where we met," he said, pulling me on top of him.

We launched into a luscious make-out session, the kind I hadn't enjoyed since high school. Then he flipped me onto my back, his kisses rich and deep, his arm beneath me as I arched into his tight body.

"I've never met anyone like you," he whispered. "I could talk with you all night long."

"Me too," I said, meaning it. "But there are lots of other things I could do with you all night long too."

My fingers aimlessly circled a strand of his hair as we lay together, just like that, for a few songs, taking quiet bites of grapes and chocolate and cheese, nodding to the songs that he would play for me and I for him. Rapturous with the music and with each other.

CASSIE

had to admit it was a little weird to see Angela Rejean
frosting a cake in her kitchen while wearing an apron and
a sundress, her now-straightened hair pulled into a low
ponytail at her nape. Last time I saw her she was on the other
side of one-way glass, making a meal out of Mark Drury.

Dauphine would have had her fantasy with him last
night and I assumed because I hadn't heard from her that it
had gone well. At least, I hoped it had. I hated the idea of
her fleeing S.E.C.R.E.T. in anger and resentment. And I
liked to think I had picked well with Mark.

Angela told me to take a tour of the place, while she put
last-minute touches on Tracina's fancy baby-shower cake
and Kit tied bows on little gift bags for invitees. The narrow
living room in her mint-colored Creole cottage on North
Roman was decorated with pink and blue paper flowers
around the windows, since the sex of the baby was unknown.
But the goofy decorations didn't take away from the
grown-up style of her place. Red Oriental rugs were strewn

about the living room's original pine floors, where two surprisingly comfortable antique loveseats, reupholstered in bright purple paisley, faced each other. The walls were painted a dark coral, not pink, more like the color of the lipstick she always wore. Framed photographs of Nina Simone and Billie Holiday dotted the narrow hallway to her bedroom, where an imposing four-poster bed sat draped with billowing white netting, her even more imposing tuxedo cat, Boots, sitting moored in the middle like a fat boat. On her antique dresser was a collection of Haitian dolls, and above it, a framed black-and-white aerial photo of Port-au-Prince from the '60s, next to that a wall-mounted flat-screen TV. The whole place was feminine, not girly, cozy without feeling cramped.

"Hand me that tea towel, Cassie," Angela said when I returned. She was wiping the extra frosting off the platter with her finger. "Would you mind putting out the little plates? They only had blue ones, but that doesn't mean she's having a boy. I hope people don't think that she's having a boy. I mean, we don't know what it is. I should say something. Do you think? Or just leave it. I'll just leave it."

It was sweet seeing her flustered. She was usually so in control. She was a good friend to Tracina and clearly wanted to make her baby shower perfect. In that moment, I was truly happy that Tracina had a friend like this, since I certainly had been no friend to her. Between my unwillingness to cover for her absences and my stupid dalliances with Will, which still remained secret, thank goodness, my presence in Tracina's life had only added complications. While placing a big yellow bow on a box of newborn diapers, I vowed to be a better friend to her and the baby, regardless of my feelings for Will, a vow made a lot easier by the presence of Jesse Turnbull in my life. That was his last name, I'd learned—Turnbull—a small fact that went a long way towards making him seem more real to me.

Since our first date, which had ended in my bedroom, we'd seen each other twice more—once for a matinee, where in the back row he had astonished me by putting his tongue in my ear and his hand down my jeans, making me quietly, *oh so quietly*, come. Afterwards, he kissed my forehead on the sidewalk outside and left to pick up his son. The other time we took a trip to Metarie to look at a motorcycle he was thinking of buying. He'd pulled me down a nearby alley and ravaged me against the cinder-block wall of a garage. All of our encounters were hot, brief and sweet, and each time I felt that if I never saw him again, I wouldn't be surprised. He was like a friendly tomcat, one that's genuinely happy to see you, to be fed and caressed by you, but that can easily survive on its own.

While I tossed a salad, Kit carted several TV trays into the living room and set them up in the corners for the finger food and candy. It was just the three of us for a spell, so we naturally launched into S.E.C.R.E.T. chatter.

"It's a lot of money to just give away," Kit said to me. "But the Committee voted this morning. It was unanimous."

"Fifteen million down the drain," Angela said, with a whistle.

Kit smacked her arm. "You voted yes."

"How could I not, after Matilda's impassioned stance against 'accepting money from an inveterate misogynist.'"

"I don't know," I said. "Maybe it's time we did more for women than just improve their sex lives."

"Are you complaining?" asked Angela, holding the carrot she was peeling directly in my face.

I bit down on it and smiled. "Nope."

"Speaking of sex," Kit said. "Matilda said I could invite whoever I want for Dominic's threesome." She was going to be one of the soccer player's trainers. "What about you, Cassie? You game?"

She knew the answer before I even opened my mouth.

"Kidding. By the way, how's Jesse? Is it *love*?"

I knew *they* knew I had pulled Jesse out. But we hadn't discussed it yet.

"We're just testing the waters," I said, shrugging like it was no big thing. "I have no expectations."

Kit and Angela exchanged *yeah right* glances.

"Will you stay in S.E.C.R.E.T. while said waters are being tested?" Kit asked.

"We're not there yet," I said.

"I always regret not doing that 'drive fantasy' with Jesse after we recruited him," Angela said, popping an icing-covered finger in her mouth. "He's a speed freak, you know. Not speed the drug, speed as in going fast. Weren't we lining him up to take Dauphine in a convertible somewhere through the desert? Was it Sedona? Little weekend trip? She did so well with that pilot, we thought that would be fun, but, alas . . . Cassie wants him all to herself."

"Who trained Jesse?" I asked as casually as possible.

"Pauline freshened up his oral skills. I remember because I got to watch. *That* was *hot*," said Angela, shaking her hand like it just got singed. "And then I think . . . Didn't Matilda practice bondage on that boy?"

A hot wave flashed through me. *Ouch.* What was that? Jealousy? No, something different, deeper. Whatever that was, it stung, and I quickly camouflaged the effects the news had on me.

"Jesse's a favorite of Matilda's. She was even looking to change the rules to keep him longer than three turns. Until you pulled him. Sigh."

Matilda and Jesse. *Why didn't she ever mention that to me?* Maybe that's why she was always so hesitant to discuss pulling Jesse out of S.E.C.R.E.T., even way back, when he was my Step Three fantasy and I had thoughts of stopping and getting off the ride. She convinced me not to. She convinced me to stay. As for bondage, again, why was I so surprised? Of *course* she'd still train male recruits. Why wouldn't she? Why shouldn't she? She's still gorgeous, still sexy. God, when would that magnanimity kick in, the confidence, the kind that Angela and Kit had? I felt like such a fucking schoolgirl, with so much still to learn.

"Matilda's got some plans to train Dominic now. Apparently, he likes to rock climb. Likes getting all trussed up."

"Ooh, I like the sound of *that*," Angela said.

"Bernice put her name in for Dominic," said Kit. "He also likes black *and* curvy."

"That's not fair. I'm black!"

"You ain't curvy."

"But I wasn't even offered—"

"Hey, girls!"

Tracina snuck in through the side door, accompanied by her fifteen-year-old brother, Trey. He was a nice kid, but because of his autism it was difficult for him to play with his peers. Still, Tracina had begun to make more of an effort to involve him in adult social activities, and sometimes Will let him help upstairs to keep him busy, when coloring books stopped working.

"Who likes curvy black girls?" she asked. "'Cause that's all I am, just a big ol' curve!"

"New bartender at Maison I got my eye on," Angela said. "Did you two walk here?"

"Yup, Trey was my big helper. Baby, go play with Boots. Girls gotta talk."

Angela patted around on top of the fridge. "Here's the remote for the TV," she said, tossing it to Trey. "You remember how to use it, right?"

He nodded and headed to the bedroom, then Angela launched into big-sister mode.

"You're gonna have a baby in less than *three* weeks and you *walked* here? Will's gonna get a kick right in the middle of his skinny white ass."

"I told him I wanted to walk. And Trey needs more exercise too. Will knows to pick us up—and all the *presents*," she said, shaking her behind in joy.

I watched the three of them, Kit, Angela and Tracina, gauging their level of intimacy. Did Tracina know about S.E.C.R.E.T., or had they kept it from her? It was impossible to tell.

Tracina offered a wan "Hey, Cassie" over her shoulder, followed by "Will's niece Claire's working out, don't you think?"

"Yeah, Will lucked out with her," I said, arranging baby carrots on a veggie tray.

"No, *we* lucked out. Me and you," she added. "She's gonna babysit for me, and work your night shifts. Let the young'uns take over is what I say. Dell should just pull up a stool at the cash register and call it a day. And I'll be damned if I'm going to lift a finger in the new place. I don't want to wait tables ever again. All I want to do is make the schedule, sample the menu and taste the wine."

Had Will told Tracina that he'd offered me the manager job? Did it matter? She'd find out sooner or later, and hopefully when she'd be too blissed-out over her baby to care.

The rest of the guests began to arrive, including Dell, who wore her pale yellow church hat and matching gloves. Tracina carefully navigated the small room, passing out punch, frequently coming perilously close to toppling Angela's vases and framed photos with her belly. Angela abided by Tracina's only request—"no stupid shower games"—but she was forced to wear the bows from every gift on a paper plate hat. Maybe because the room erupted into laughter over the last of the gifts—a set of Luna beads from Kit for "post-pregnancy fitness"—no one heard the knock at the door. Even I, sitting right next to it, didn't hear it until it became so insistent I finally got up to answer.

Standing there was a stony-faced Will, and he was not alone. Next to him was Carruthers Johnstone himself, who'd just won re-election as the D.A. of Orleans Parish. Something told me he wasn't here to thank his constituents. I took a step back as though whatever ire now possessing the two men was catching.

Tracina's face was grim—grey even. She was sitting in her silly "chair of honor," wearing a now terribly ridiculous hat covered in festive bows, holding a set of ebony Luna beads in her hand.

"Tracina, everyone, I'm sorry to barge in on you all like this," Carruthers said, not sounding like a politician at all, but like a broken man. "I saw you walking down the street and I've been circling the block for half an hour . . ."

"Who's this guy?" Will muttered to Tracina, fully entering the hot crowded room.

Tracina looked from one man to the other, her mouth slack. It took her a moment to speak, and when she did, she went from zero to sixty on the emotion meter.

"Why are you here?" she wailed at Carruthers, trying to stand without assistance, nearly toppling forward. "I told you I do not need anything from you!"

"I'm here because I love you, Tracina," Carruthers boomed. "I told you it wasn't going to be so easy to get rid of me. And if that's my baby, it's going to be impossible."

Every woman in the room drew a sharp breath at the same time, emptying it of oxygen. Maybe that's why Will looked like he was about to faint, his hand feeling for the wall behind him. I wanted to rush to him, but there were too many people between us—real obstacles, not just metaphorical ones.

"What about your *wife*?" Tracina boomed, still standing, her tiny fists on her hips.

Carruthers' head fell forward. "I told her. It's over."

The rest of the room took this as their cue to examine the floor as well. When I looked back up, Tracina's eyes were full of wonder. And Will's face held an expression of unadulterated shock. The whole time, Dell sat stock-still, her fork poised in admiration of a slice of cake in front of her as though this awful business were not happening at all.

"Well, I'll be damned," Tracina muttered.

"Will someone please tell me what the fuck is going on?" Will demanded.

Carruthers turned to him. "I apologize for the public manner in which all of this is coming out. But I believe I am the father of this baby," he said. Then, to Tracina he added, "And I'm sorry to ruin your lovely party, but you won't see me and you won't take my calls, so you left me no choice."

"Is what he's saying true?" Will's voice was now devoid of all emotion.

Tracina's eyes softened as she gazed at Will, her expression saying it all, even if her words ("I don't know") didn't. As if to punctuate the drama, a sudden stream of water trickled down her legs, pooled at her feet on the pine floors. She peered down, trying to see over her belly.

"Oh my *god*, I'm peeing myself."

"No, honey," said Dell, finally bringing her fork to her mouth and chewing a bite of cake. "That's your water breaking."

"My *what?*"

Angela screamed first. Carruthers scrambled over to Tracina and eased her down into a chair. Will stood motionless watching all of this, while I ran to fetch towels. Water was still cascading down Tracina's legs when I returned, and Carruthers' D.A. personality was in high gear.

"We're not waiting for an ambulance to come to Treme," he said, pointing at Will's phone. "My Escalade's outside. I'll take you now, baby," and to me, to *me*, he yelled, "grab her other arm." And that's how I got sucked into the maternal entourage, Tracina barking orders over her shoulder for Kit and Angela to *watch Trey, keep Trey, tell Trey not to worry.*

As we piled into the back seat, I got a last look at an ashen-faced Will, his whole body shaking as he tried to get his truck door to open, then rushed around to the passenger side and slid across. *I should be with him,* I thought, *helping him through this.* That I ended up being the one to hold Tracina's hand instead of Will's was the oddest surprise of the day.

A contraction seized Tracina and she dug her fingers into my thigh.

"Am I gonna be okay?"

"Of course. Of course you are! Just breathe," I said, as calmly as possible, smoothing her hair off her sweaty face.

"Hold on, honey. I'm gonna get you there as fast as I can," Carruthers said as he pushed on the gas.

Tracina turned to me. "I'm an awful person," she whispered, tears falling down her cheeks. "I feel so awful."

"Don't worry about anything else right now except this baby, okay?" I felt her hand tighten in mine, saw her eyes squeeze shut.

I turned around and spotted Will's truck behind us, weaving perilously, trying to keep up. Poor Will. If this proved to be true, if he really wasn't the baby's father, it'd gut him. Despite all the drama and uncertainty that surrounded the pregnancy, the only thing Will had ever seemed sure of was his devotion to this baby.

Carruthers was driving fast, but every once in a while he checked on Tracina via the rearview mirror. "You're gonna be okay, baby. You're gonna be okay."

Tracina never answered, her clammy hand gripped in mine, nothing registering on her face now except waves of pain.

We made it to the Touro Birthing Center in record time; Carruthers had called ahead on a hands-free phone so a nurse was standing by with an empty wheelchair. Once

Tracina was in the chair, she reached up, looking around for me, and grabbed my hand.

"Cassie, stay with Will. He's gonna need a friend," she said.

What? Had I heard her right? She let go of my hand, and reached for Carruthers' as she was wheeled into the center.

I found my way to the delivery area waiting room. A few minutes later Will came huffing in, eyes wild, a line of sweat down the middle of his T-shirt.

"Where'd they go?"

"Down there," I said, "but I don't think—"

He didn't wait for me to finish. He busted through the doors and disappeared down the hall. I was so jangly already that the vibrating in my purse didn't register at first as a phone call. I answered over the sound of a loud and braying intercom announcement, plugging my ear to hear better.

"Hey, lady. Where y'at? Sounds like the racetrack. Don't bet your whole paycheck."

It was Jesse, his voice mellow and grounding.

I explained the baby shower, the early labor, the dramatic drive, the empty waiting room in maternity where I was now taking over a few seats. I stopped short of saying I was sitting vigil while a delicate paternity question was about to come to a head. A nurse pointed to my phone and then to a sign behind her: CELL PHONES NOT PERMITTED IN EMERGENCY. STEP OUTSIDE TO TALK. I lifted my index finger, the universal symbol for *Just one minute*.

"So, I guess dinner and a movie are out of the question," he said.

"I should stay here."

"You're a good friend," he said. "Hey, I've been thinking."

"Yeah? About what?"

"About you and . . ."

Oh dear. Why did my heart clench?

"And . . .?"

"And me. And the fact that I'm glad you got in touch. I didn't know it until now. But I think I might've been waiting for a girl like you."

I was stunned.

"Too cheesy?" he asked.

"A little. But . . . I like cheese. What about our 'no expectations' plan?"

"You didn't expect me to follow that plan, did you?"

I laughed. Now was not the time to get into it with him. I told him I'd call him later, and then I hung up and shut off my phone.

Just when you think you have things figured out, a stranger shows up at a stupid baby shower and threatens to change everything. And that's only what *I* was feeling. I could only imagine what was going through Will's and Tracina's minds. Carruthers, on the other hand, seemed to have made his mind up before he knocked.

I stared at the double doors. The only certainty now was that whoever came bursting out first would tell me something that might change . . . well, everything. But right now, all I knew was that Jesse Turnbull was in. He was all the way in. Isn't that what I wanted?

DAUPHINE

W e probably should have left immediately when Mark and I realized that not only was I leaving S.E.C.R.E.T., but I was taking him with me. There were house phones everywhere, in every room we visited. We could have called some-one, anyone. We could have summoned the car or Claudette . . . or phoned Matilda. Or we could have simply left the Mansion.

Instead, after our tumble in the Domino Suite, we were both hit with a weird, giddy second wind. When he offered to take me on a secret tour of the Mansion, including some of the rooms in which he'd been trained, I threw on a bathrobe, totally game.

"Lead the way, Romeo," I said.

I saw the lushly decorated Emperor's Room with its one-way mirror, and something called the Den, with what looked like S & M equipment strewn about.

"Are you into this stuff?" I asked nervously (*excitedly?*), fingering a table with leather restraints, not sure which answer I wanted to hear.

He shrugged. "I feel like with you I could be into anything," he said, scooping me up and carrying me out of the room backwards.

"I think you're right about that." I dipped down to kiss his mouth—*those lips!* I didn't want details about his escapades any more than he wanted details of mine; the only thing we cared about now was how our experiences would benefit each other.

My favorite room in the whole house was the Harem Room in the basement, with its brass stripper pole, massive floor cushions and indoor hot tub.

"What did you learn down here? How to be a sheik?" I teased, spinning around the pole once, twice, until he convinced me to open my robe and do a little bump and grind for him, while he lay back on the cushions stroking himself.

"No touching," I said, turning around and bending over to agonize him.

It was all so fun with Mark, so silly, so joy-filled!

It's true, we probably should have let someone know. Instead, we soaked for a half hour in that hot tub; then, wrapped back up in those handy bathrobes, we raided the bar fridge, grabbing water and fruit meant for cocktails (mostly orange and pineapple halves and maraschino cherries) and headed up a different flight of stairs, this one leading to the workers' quarters on the third floor. At the end of that hall, we came upon a cozy, pretty bedroom with exposed brick walls, its pine floors painted white, and wicker furniture placed strategically about. It reminded me of a guest room in a lovely seaside cottage. We climbed into the high bed, pulled the heavy eyelet duvet over our sex-battered bodies and talked. I told him a little about my past, my fears, and how Luke and his stupid book had put such a dent in my confidence.

Instead of offering to punch Luke in the face, he said he'd write a song to set the record straight.

"You don't have to do that," I said. "I am so seriously over it."

"Then that's what the song's gonna be about."

And then we slept deeply, surrounded by downy pillows, orange peels and at least four empty bottles of water.

In the morning, we had sex one more time, tenderly, slowly, my legs covered in tiny bruises from his hands. He lifted them this way and that, his hip bones thrusting, but tenderly, moving so beautifully, our bodies made for each other. Entwining his fingers with mine, he flipped me on top of him as my head dropped back, and I rode him as carefully as I could, as his fingers traveled over my breasts, down my stomach, his face marveling at the way the sun must have danced through my hair, turning it a blazing golden red. I came like that, so easily, his ability to stroke me perfectly—a miracle for only knowing my body one night.

After that, there was no hesitation, no long discussion, no doubt, no fear.

The first call I made was to Elizabeth. I told her I was too sick to come into work, a lie that thrilled her because she saw right through it: it meant my date had gone well.

"How well did it go?"

"I can't talk right now."

"Because *he's still there!* Okay! That is so *good!*"

The second call was to Cassie, which went straight to voice-mail, and the next, to Matilda.

⁓

She now sat on the other side of her desk in the Coach House, where she had told us to meet her when we dressed. Mark was in the seat next to mine, holding my hand tenderly between his.

I couldn't believe, still, that this was happening.

"You both look like guilty dogs," she said. "Why? And Mark? You're leaving us too, then."

I looked at his profile. My rock star, so bold on the stage, looked so sheepish in front of Matilda.

"I feel the same way as she does, ma'am. Lightning doesn't always strike like this. I just want to be with her," he said, seeming as surprised to say the words as Matilda *was not* to hear them.

"Why wouldn't you feel this way, my dear? You're not a complete idiot. Maybe I'm even a little envious. Because you're right, what's happened between you two doesn't happen often. But it's quite special when it does." She paused.

Not just special, I wanted to say—*momentous, life-changing, mind-blowing.* I had worried she'd try to talk me out of this, that she'd caution me not to confuse great sex for true love. But we were getting a ringing endorsement.

"This means finding your replacement, Mark, and looking for another S.E.C.R.E.T. candidate, Dauphine, but that's what we do. Now Mark, I'd like to have a quiet word with Dauphine. Why don't you wait for her in the courtyard? We won't be a minute. And thank you for your service, however brief. Clearly, you were . . . revelatory."

"The pleasure was all mine, ma'am."

He stretched to standing and looked at my face, his hand reaching for my chin.

"And Mark——" Matilda added, sweetly, as he got to the door. "Never call me ma'am again."

He nodded, embarrassed, as our eyes followed him out the door. When we were alone, I turned to her.

"I tried to reach Cassie, but her phone's off," I said.

"She's at the hospital. Her colleague went into labor last night. I'll tell her," she said, placing a hand over mine. "Listen, you should know the Committee voted yesterday to donate the money we received from Castille Industries, all of it, to various causes that help women. Pierre won't give us the painting back, but we decided that we cannot operate an organization dedicated to liberating women by taking money from a man dedicated to manipulating them."

"But what about all the women you could help with his money?"

"S.E.C.R.E.T. has had a marvelous run. Almost forty years. We have another few years in us, I think. We'll make them really count. And if needed, we have one more painting, though it's one I hope not to part with."

She shook off the sad turn of events, then gave me a genuine smile.

"You'd have made a terrific Guide, Dauphine. But we'll be in touch. I want to know how you're doing, how every little thing's going. I'm sure Cassie will want that too."

"You don't know what y'all have done for me, Matilda. You've given me back my spirit, my joy. I can't tell you how grateful I am that this organization exists."

I came around the desk to squeeze her tight. As much as I loved this place and all its magic, I couldn't wait to get back to my dusty hovel and my tidy store and my wonderful customers and the lovely Elizabeth.

And Mark.

My man was waiting for me outside in the sun, his hair a wreck, his smile delicious, his arms warm, his stomach growling madly.

"Baby, I need a big fat greasy omelette, I need home fries, I need bacon, I need toast," he said, kissing my neck. "And I need you."

This wasn't a fantasy. This was real. *Look what happens when you let go of control and make a little room,* I thought. *The whole wide world rushes to you.*

"You read my mind. Let's get out of here."

CASSIE

Tracina picked out the baby's name—Rose Nicaud—in honor of the Café, which itself was named after one of the first African-American female entrepreneurs in New Orleans.

"We'll nickname her Neko," she said, cooing into the baby's tiny forehead, no bigger than a silver dollar.

To say the baby was small would be to describe only a part of what made her so extraordinary to look upon. She was almost translucent; a network of teeny pink veins covered her whole face and body like a pale web, giving her a light purplish hue. When she wasn't being held, she was splayed in a portable incubator next to Tracina's bed, a diaper—the size of a coffee mug—completely swallowing the lower part of her body, her fists no bigger than rosebuds. Tracina had a private room, courtesy of her baby's wealthy father.

"The doctor says she's going to be fine," Tracina whispered to me, not because she wanted to keep the noise down, but because her voice was nearly gone from the screaming during the birth, at Carruthers and at Will, both of whom she allowed in the delivery room, just in case.

Now Carruthers, the seeming victor, in hospital greens and a cap, had clearly made a home for himself in the giant armchair, his suit, vest and tie strewn about the place. He slept with his hand resting protectively on the incubator's glass cover.

"I might have to stay here for a few more days, but there shouldn't be any complications," Tracina said.

Medical complications, at least.

Everything else I would learn came later, when Tracina and I inched towards a kind of friendship in the weeks and months that followed the dramatic birth, when I would discover I had a lot more in common with her than I thought.

She told me her insistence on waiting as long as possible before a cesarean was because she knew there'd be a test and she wanted to delay Will's heartache as long as possible. No one doubted she cared about Will a lot, but it became clear during the delivery and after that Carruthers was the man she loved. Still, she felt that Will would have made a better father—more reliable, more hands-on, less complicated with his love for the baby. Carruthers was a high-powered politician; he had a wife (now soon-to-be-ex) and two college-aged children. And yet, it was touching the way he stayed by Tracina's side all night, ducking out to take and receive phone calls, even trying his best to treat Will with some kindness, though Will struggled to return the gesture.

That's why she told all those lies. Like me, Tracina didn't want to be a wedge in someone else's relationship. Even though Carruthers had been ardent from the beginning, he just wasn't ready to leave. Tracina knew how easy it would be to fall into the role of mistress and she wasn't having it, never wanting to hide and lie, especially when Trey was getting so smart, and a good man like Will was so available. She broke it off completely. Then she discovered she was pregnant. Not having had a father around herself when she was growing up, she wanted to do everything in her power to make sure her baby had one who was. And she felt that as long as she kept her mouth shut, only someone ignorant of her and Will's family trees would question the paternity just because the baby's skin might not perfectly match Will's. He had two African-American grandmothers; Tracina had white relatives on both sides. The baby's skin color, like her parents' before her, was always going to be the result of a spin on a blessedly infinite wheel of hues.

Still, a blood test was administered, and the results were immediate. If Will, head hung low, could have dragged a dirty "blankie" behind him through the maternity ward, Tracina told me later, it wouldn't have made the scene any sadder.

She tried to get him to stay and talk. Even Carruthers offered to go for a walk around the block with him. But Will kept walking.

I almost missed him while checking messages at the pay phones, my cell phone long run out of batteries.

"Will! Wait!" I yelled, leaving the receiver dangling, unsure of what went down, though it was pretty easy to glean from his face what the test results must have showed.

I called his name three, four times through the parking lot before he finally stopped and turned, and by that time his key was stuck in the lock of his door, again.

"Do you want me to drive? Let me drive you home, Will," I said, bending over with my hands on my knees to catch my breath. It was officially fall, but the noonday sun was hot as mid-summer hell. We'd both been at the hospital for a full twenty-four hours, taking turns sleeping in the cab of his truck.

Will turned around slowly, leaving the keys dangling.

"Know what the worst part is?" he said, not meeting my eyes, still searching the air around me for answers. "I *never* wanted kids. I don't think I ever told you that. All my friends had them—my brother, cousins, all of them—but I was like, *Nope, there are just too many of 'em in the world.* And I work too hard, and I don't make enough money to do it the way it's supposed to be done. My dad owned that café. He was never around. And he was always broke. But I tell you what," he said, pointing to the whole hospital, "I wanted *that* baby. Ah . . . *fuck.*"

His emotions overcame him. Everything he'd been bottling up over the past several months, all of his doubts and fears about becoming a good enough father for a child whose mother he struggled to love, let alone like, all the while expanding his business on precarious loans and his own blood and sweat, all of it—it came out and he cried. But not for long. In fact, less than fifteen sharp seconds. I threw my arms around him, inhaling the smell of hospital in his hair. He didn't embrace me back. Instead, he kept his paint-spattered hands tightly covering his face. And when I let him go, reluctantly, he stepped far away from me and shook off the pain, so all you might have gleaned from our body language if you drove into the empty parking spot at that exact moment (which, in fact, Jesse Turnbull had) was that two acquaintances had just had a quick catch-up and were now saying their goodbyes.

That's why Jesse leaned out the window of his own truck (a newer, better one, of course, than Will's) and said, "Hey, babe. Thought I'd bring you a coffee on my way to work," handing me a medium takeout with soy.

He wouldn't have said "babe" if he knew who I'd been hugging and what Will had just been through—what we'd been through. He wasn't that kind of guy; he wasn't boastful, territorial, dickish. And Will was rarely impolite. But in that moment, his skin so thin, his heart so bruised, all Will could do was ignore Jesse, shoot me a pained look, rip the keys out of the lock of his stupid busted truck, whip around to the passenger side and enter the damn thing from there. It was awful and awkward watching him slowly inch from the spot next to us, only to fishtail out of the lot like those idiot show-off teenagers testing their wheels in a WalMart parking lot.

"That your boss?" Jesse asked, handing me the coffee.

I nodded.

"He okay?"

"You know what? No."

"Sorry to hear that. Can I drop you somewhere?"

"Nah, I'm way out of your way. And I feel like I need a good long walk. Then a good long nap. It's been that kind of night, and morning."

"Everything all right?"

"Baby's fine, mom's fine . . . the dad's fine. It's Will I'm worried about."

"I thought . . . So he's *not* the father?"

I winced by way of an answer.

"*Ho* boy. How about you? You okay?"

I said I was fine, just tired, but I hadn't really taken my own personal temperature just yet. Hospitals have a way of taking the focus off anyone not on a gurney or bed. But what else could I say to Jesse in that moment? I couldn't tell him I was happy to see him but that I was also harboring a darker, deeper joy at this sudden turn of events that had left Will free. I was happy to see his face, Jesse with his blue-tinted sunglasses, his hands with their rugged backs, and smooth, soft palms from being elbow deep in coco butter and marzipan all day, the same hands that had begun to make their brilliant acquaintance with every inch of my body. I wanted him even now, my body automatically drawn towards the door of his truck like a big magnet, my face inches from his. He put his hand on the back of my head and pulled me in for a long kiss that tasted like good coffee.

"Okay, babe. I'll call you later," he said, and drove off, leaving me with a new round of thoughts now buzzing to life.

I want Jesse. I want Will. Do I want Will? And who's to say Will even wants me after all this drama, or that he'll want any woman, for that matter? Besides, he probably thinks I'm now swimming in men. First, a lanky musician comes by the restaurant, and now some other punk drops coffee off for me. I had to laugh right then and there. Imagine if Will thought I was a "player," or worse, a "slut," a word that Matilda banned . . . but still. There was something in his eyes just now that had sent a chill my way.

So I did what I always did when I couldn't think about a thing straight. I started walking. I walked the ten blocks towards the Mansion and the only person who'd ever offered me clarity.

~⁓

It was a Sunday, but Matilda was there. And she was alone.

"Know anything about corporate charitable tax deductions?" she said instead of hello.

I followed her into her office, where half a dozen ledgers lay spread out on her desk.

"'Fraid not. Are you in the middle of something?"

"Oh, just cooking the books. Trying to figure out operating costs. How much longer we can stay afloat. How's the baby? Is she just dreamy?"

"Tiny and cute, yes."

"Has Dauphine called you yet?"

"My phone was off, the battery's dead. Oh my god! Her Mark fantasy! I completely forgot! How did it go? Did you talk to her?"

"Yeah, I did."

"Did it go well?"

"Maybe a little *too* well."

She filled me in on all the juicy details, and I had to admit I was envious. And though I had known Mark was her type, I had no idea they were both so ripe for something deeper, and so soon.

"It happened to Pauline two years ago with a recruit," Matilda said. "Same sort of thing. But Pauline stayed. Dauphine's out, I'm sad to say. Mark too. They both seem very happy . . . And now I have a feeling we're going to lose you too. Am I right?"

"You mean to Jesse? We're not there. Not yet. Or do you mean with Will? With Will, that would be a non-starter."

"Are you sure?"

I filled her in on the paternity drama and the strange conundrum I faced. Will or Jesse? I couldn't have both.

"Has Will asked you to be with him?"

"No."

"Has Jesse?"

"Kind of. I mean, he's, we're . . . it's *good*, you know? I really like Jesse and the sex is amazing. But I think . . . I think I *love* Will."

"Have you told Will this?"

"No."

She steepled her fingers in thought.

"Well, what are you waiting for? You can't keep catching him between women, Cassie."

"But what about Jesse?"

"Something tells me Jesse will survive. And he always has a home here."

My stomach dropped at the thought of him with anyone else. Matilda had a soft spot for him, that I knew. *What have I done? What do I do?*

"When you have it sorted, let us know. I was hoping you'd join the Committee next. At least with your vote we might finally get a redheaded man past the initial selection round. Meanwhile, these were just mailed to the press and other important guests," she said, sliding open a drawer. She handed me an invitation. "I hope you can make it. And be sure to bring a date. Either one of them."

S.E.C.R.E.T. cordially invites you to a public unveiling
of our Major New Charity Initiative, Benefiting
Underprivileged Women and Children in NOLA

at

Latrobe's on Royal
Black Tie

I was shocked to see *S.E.C.R.E.T.* written in that familiar curly font on a public invitation.

"Matilda! That's the group's *name*. I mean, you put

S.E.C.R.E.T. out there so boldly! I couldn't bring Will to this. He'd start asking questions. He'd be all *What's this stand for, Cassie?*"

"Oh, that. Don't worry. We're giving away the money we raise under S.E.C.R.E.T.'s *official* name, the one that's on the books: The Society for the Encouragement of Civic Responsibility and Equal Treatment. See? You can surely belong to *that* group, can't you?"

She turned around one of the ledgers to show me where official invoices and receipts indicated its full name, not the one I was used to.

"We pay our taxes. We have a mortgage. We're good citizens. And when people ask us what we do, we say we improve the lives of women in need. You're safe to bring someone like Will to a public event like this; we take our anonymity very seriously. And of course, there'd be none of these concerns if you chose to bring Jesse instead."

"That kind of sums up my predicament."

"Indeed. But what a wonderful predicament. I'd call it progress," she said. "Wouldn't you?"

Indeed.

CASSIE

After my meeting with Matilda, I was bone-weary, but I knew Dell was probably a walking corpse by now, having closed the Café the night before and opened it today. So instead of crawling into bed, I showered, changed and took the long way to work to check up on Will.

His truck wasn't at his place in Bywater or parked in front of or behind the Café, and he wasn't answering his phone, so I assumed he had taken a drive somewhere to clear his head—or to cry openly, for longer than he was able to with me.

The restaurant was empty. Claire burst out of the kitchen in an artfully placed hairnet that did little to contain her blond dreadlocks, her hands coated in oil and bits of kale. I liked her open, guileless face, and how a few weeks living at Will's had removed her sullenness, turning her into a full-blown chatty teen. She was growing on Dell too, who taught her food prep right away, something that had taken her months to show me.

"Where's that disinfectant hand soap? The pink stuff Dell uses."

"I'll show you," I said. "Are you by yourself?"

"Yeah. Dell was of no use to me after the lunch rush and went home."

For seventeen, she was mature beyond her years, which wasn't necessarily a good thing, I decided. Sure I was sexually stunted (well into my thirties), but Claire and her new friends from school were unsettlingly accelerated. They scared me a little when they came into the Café with their smoking and piercings, their seductive "selfies" and their casual "sexting."

A week ago I had asked Claire how she could be a vegan *and* smoke.

"For the same reason you can be nosy *and* nice," she teased.

I felt around on the shelf above the sink, found the bottle of pink disinfectant soap lying on its side and squirted some on her hands.

"Has Will been by?"

"Haven't seen him," she said, drying her hands on her legs and immediately checking her vibrating phone.

Will let her carry it around in her waitress pouch. His reasoning was that she didn't talk on it, only checked texts, so it wasn't as rude. I told him if she worked upstairs that wouldn't be allowed.

"Nor the piercings," I said to him.

"Fine, you'll be the boss. You'll make the rules," he had said.

Still, Claire was a hard worker, so I didn't complain. And she was a natural in the kitchen.

"I got a head-start on salad prep," she said. "Kale's done. I'll tackle the carrots next."

"Thanks. I can probably handle the floor on my own tonight," I said.

"Oh good. I want to go see the baby."

I almost blurted out everything that had happened at the hospital between her uncle and her almost-aunt, but this was officially now a family issue, something she'd have to navigate with Will.

While helping Claire prep and blanche the carrots, I thought about Dauphine and Mark, probably passed out somewhere, arms and legs entwined. I envied their seeming certainty, Dauphine's decisiveness to just grab this man and go with it. But sometimes people just know; it's in their nature. When that option was available to me, to test the waters with Jesse outside of S.E.C.R.E.T., I was only on my third Step. I was certain of a connection with him, but I hadn't yet made one with myself.

Had I now? How well did I know myself: my body, my mind and my heart? Maybe the better questions were, *where did these three things overlap and where did they remain separate?* S.E.C.R.E.T. dealt in pleasures of the body, an area of my life I'd always ignored. I had lived so far in my head I had also let my heart atrophy. Mark and I had definitely made a physical connection. Jesse and I had too. Plus, he was making quiet inroads into my heart. But Will had long ago conquered all three. I loved his body, his mind *and* his heart, never more so than today, when his absence not only preoccupied me but pained me physically, as I imagined him somewhere sad and alone.

So even before I was sure about Will's feelings for me, I took my cell phone out back into the alley while Claire manned the floor, the last favor I'd ask before sending her home.

Jesse picked up on the first ring.

"Hey, babe, you still at the hospital?"

"No, I'm at work. You?"

He told me he was about to go into a meeting with clients who wanted a five-tiered wedding cake.

"You must be exhausted," he said. "So I take it plans tonight are out too."

"Yeah . . . I have to stay here, Jesse."

The silence that followed had mass; I could feel it actually weighing down the phone. Maybe it was the way I had said his name, like it was punctuation, with a hint of gentle finality.

"Okay . . . I'm getting the feeling that tomorrow's not going to be good for you either."

Inhale.

"Jesse, I think . . . no, I *know* . . . I'm in love with someone else."

More silence, this time lighter, now that I'd injected it with a bit of truth.

"I see. Huh. Who's the lucky guy?" he asked, a hint of sourness in his tone.

I told him it was Will, my boss and my friend of many years. I didn't go into the details; Jesse didn't need to hear about our eight-year mostly platonic odyssey, the pining, the fears, the insecurities, the jealousies, the betrayals, all the drama that had conspired to keep us apart.

"Does he love you back?"

"I don't know, Jesse, but I need to find out. And I don't want to string you along or use you as some kind of net in case he does reject me. And he might. But I need to be all in on this one. After what he's been through, I want to be able to be honest if he asks me about you. And you deserve that too. You're a good man, Jesse. So so good."

"Wow. You sound so . . . I *hate* to say you sound really fucking sexy, because I'm getting my heart ripped out, but I really wish I were the other guy right now."

What more was there to say? Tender well-wishes followed on both our parts. They felt genuine and necessary.

"I don't like the phrase 'I hope we can still be friends,' Jesse. It sounds so lame. But I really do hope we can be . . . *something* to each other."

"Cassie, don't take this the wrong way, but I'm not great at being friends with women I want to sleep with."

The silence widened; there was little left to say.

"I understand."

We said gentle goodbyes and hung up. I kissed the screen on my phone. I'd been blessed by such good men in S.E.C.R.E.T., men who, beyond awakening me sexually, also helped me forget the not-so-good ones I'd experienced before. And then there was Will. I hoped I was letting go of something good in hopes of getting something great, but for all I knew Will was done with me.

Still, it was unusual for him to disappear like this. I looked at my watch, then up and down the quiet alley, worry setting in. The news of the baby was a devastating blow, but what if he really had been in love with Tracina? What if he was feeling this only now, now that he not only couldn't have her but was learning she had never really been his?

Out of the corner of my eye, I saw a curtain flutter out from one of the open upstairs windows of the Café. Will was still waiting for the custom screens. And that's when I knew. I burst in through the door, back through the kitchen and into the dining area, where two customers had grabbed a window table next to where Claire was bent over her phone, flanked by two new friends from school who were also looking at something on her screen.

"Claire!" They leapt like I'd interrupted delicate surgery. "Can you stick around for a little while longer? And please get those people some menus. I'll pay you double overtime. I have to check something upstairs. I won't be long."

I didn't even wait for her to answer. I would have been a crappy, bossy mother, I decided, as I quietly took the stairs. The knob for the new oak door was on back order, so I had to gently nudge it open with my shoulder. The door would eventually separate the old Café from the new space, once the stairs leading directly outside were complete, but right now Will kept it shut to keep the construction dust from wafting into Café Rose.

The space was dim for the middle of the afternoon. Then I noticed all the curtains were drawn. Newspaper trails still lined the floor to catch spatter from the ceiling paint. But the tables had finally been delivered, a cluster of twelve of them, with marble tops and wooden legs. I let a hand caress a cool, smooth surface. And then I saw them, Will's bare feet on the floor peeking out from behind the cocktail bar, a mickey of whiskey, one quarter empty, on top. Will wasn't much of a drinker, and he never drank during the day, so this was probably his idea of "making quite a dent in the bottle."

"Is that you, Officer?" he asked, his voice groggy.

"Why? Are the police after you?" I went along with him, slowly rounding the bar until I stood at his feet.

He was in his jeans, no shirt, using the duvet as a pillow, the mattress bent like a loose taco to fit the narrow space, his face wrinkled from sleeping, probably unsoundly.

"They will be after me when they find my truck out on North Peters," he said, clasping his hands behind his head, stretching awake.

I couldn't read his tone. I couldn't tell if he was still sad or mad or well past both and into an emotional zone even he'd never visited before.

Oh, Will. I wanted to crawl down there, wrap my arms and legs around his pain. Instead, I said, "What's your truck doing out there?"

"Took that bend at Saint Ferdinand," he said, using a hand to trace the truck's path. "And there was this huge possum in the middle of the road and *bam*—"

He clapped and mashed his hands together.

"Poor possum."

"Possum's fine. My truck is wedged in the ditch, stuck between fence posts near the lumberyard. Had to smash the back window to get out. At least, I hope the truck's still there. Actually, it might be worth more if I claim it was stolen."

He laughed softly, but I couldn't. *Should I ask? Where have you been and what are you thinking and can you be mine now? Can we be each other's?*

"But you're okay, right?"

"Okay? I'm fucking *great*. I'm a damn country-western song, Cassie. Guy loses everything he thought he had in one day. Losing my truck kinda rounds out the chorus, don't you think?"

There it was, the sarcasm hiding the sorrow, that man I knew so well. The one I loved so much. *Here is your opening, Cassie. Say it.*

"You haven't lost everything, Will."

"That's true. Day's not over yet. Or is it? I can't tell with the curtains shut. What do you think of them? They're pretty nice, aren't they?"

"They're beautiful. See? You have the curtains . . . and . . .?"

His eyes moved from admiring the curtains to studying me.

"What else do I have?"

He sat up on an elbow, his gaze heavy.

Say it, Cassie.

"You have . . . those marble tables. They're g-gorgeous," I stammered.

"That's true. They *are* gorgeous," he said.

I was nervously fidgeting with the edge of the bar.

"And . . . what else do I have?"

For chrissake, say it.

Say it now.

"You have everything, Will, right here in this room—"

"Do I have you?"

Enough, Cassie. It's here, all of it, right in front of you.

"Yes, Will."

"Are you sure, Cassie? Because I really want to have you, and earlier, when that guy drove up to the hospital parking lot, and it didn't look like I could have you either, that's when I thought—"

"Will. You have me."

I don't know if I dove to meet him or if he reached up to pull me down to the mattress, but soon I was kneeling in front of him, letting him pull off my T-shirt, my stupid bra, my dumb belt, kicking off my awful jeans, both of us hating every single thing that still stood between us, even if it was just our clothes.

Now astride him, our fingers entwined, I felt lucky and so, so grateful.

"You should see your face right now," he whispered. "So beautiful."

I was going to say, *You make me feel beautiful,* but it wasn't true. I felt beautiful before he said it, a miracle in and of itself.

"Thank you, Will." My fingers graced his sternum. He was all I ever wanted.

He reached up, curling a firm hand around the back of my neck, pulling me down on top of him until my breasts were pressed against his warm chest. His eyes were calm, his hair a tangle of anguish and sleep. I smoothed it back.

"Kiss me, Cassie. Kiss me like you meant what you just said. That I have you. That you're mine."

His mouth was slightly open and I sank down on it with mine. We weren't urgent, nor ferocious. Not yet. There was no hurry. I kissed him roundly, fully, once, then suckled his bottom lip, savoring him, kissing him again as his tongue darted hesitantly between my teeth, tasting me too.

"Will," I said between kisses, "I missed you so much."

He sat us both up, my legs still wrapped around him, his erection insistent between us.

"I missed you also . . . as you can see," he laughed, flicking my hair away from my eyes.

My hand instinctually reached for him, and I rolled my fingers over his smooth, round head, feeling him stiffen more. His eyes took in the parts of my body he now reached to savor—my neck, my shoulder, my breasts. His tongue circled hot around my nipples, his lips gently tugging them into tense peaks slick with his kisses. Satisfied, he nudged my torso away from him so I rested on my palms behind me. Suddenly, I didn't even like being this far away from him, but it was to allow his hand to slip beneath me, to tease out my wetness with a few feverish strokes of his fingers.

"I've wanted you for so long, Cassie," he whispered, sending two fingers higher still, curving up to hit a spot so sensitive, so perfect, I felt my eyes go wide. "I want to look in your face while you come. While I make you come," he said, licking his fingers quickly and covering my clit, now aching, under the soft pad of his thumb.

"I've been wanting to do this to you for so long, Cassie."

His lips curled as he increased the speed but not the pressure, hitting my perfect spot with an insistent, delicious tempo. "Come for me, Cassie. Come for *me*." Oh and I did, right then, right there, throwing my head back, pressing my knees out, my whole body arching towards him. I came, releasing all the ache, all the pain, all the longing into that dusty, perfect room upstairs, the one that grew more and more beautiful each and every time we found ourselves alone and naked in it. His fingers continued thrusting, as I moaned for him, until I had to beg him to stop, desperate to catch my breath, desperate to come down, to come back to him, my Will.

My whole center heaving, I reached to stroke his sleepy, stubbly face, vowing silently to take care of this good man better, to never let him go again. His mouth found my thumb and he sucked and swirled it, bucking slightly as I reached my other hand between my legs to take him in my hand.

"I've missed this too," I said, wrapping my hand around him as he rested back on his hands.

He watched my fingers flutter up and down, loosely, but quickly, my grip tightening with his obvious appreciation, my fingers moving faster, until that became too much for him, and he rolled his eyes heavenward. I quickened my pace still, leaning forward, my mouth next to his ear, my nipples grazing his upper arm.

"It's you, Will, it's always been you. It'll always be you," I whispered, as he moaned, saying my name.

He patted around for his wallet, stuffed in his jeans nearby, stopping my hand so he could slide a condom on. Then he gathered my legs around him again, arms encircling my waist tightly. "You feel so fucking good," he said, as he eased me down onto him, all the way to the end of me, filling me up more completely than anyone ever had or ever would. We stayed still for a moment, joined like that, my hands on his cheeks, my wet lips sliding sweetly across his, breathing in his breath, my hips grinding him slowly, feeling him all the way in me, one strong arm braced behind him, the other around me, holding my hips down. He moved beneath me, lovingly at first, reverently watching my face. Then his thrusts increased in intensity, and my hands braced on his shoulders as I felt him plunging up and into me, as I drove down onto him.

"*Oh god, Will.*"

"Cassie . . . oh, I love you, I love you like *this*," he said, his face twisted in sweet agony as I rode him, my whole being focused on squeezing him, my hips rocking hard enough to finally pull the ecstasy right out of him. He came. *I made him come,* and then he fell backwards, panting for a few seconds.

I savored my beautiful victory until his body missed mine, and he pulled me down against him, gathering me close again. We spooned, my ass tucked in his sticky lap, his hard thigh thrown over mine, quivering from what he had just done to me, from what I had done to him, from what we had done to each other.

"Promise me something," he said.

"Anything."

"Promise me we'll never let anything or anyone come between us again."

"I do," I said, closing my eyes. "I promise."

CASSIE

Despite the fact that Will and I had known each other for the better part of a decade and had seen each other naked (at least three more times since that glorious afternoon, once at his place, once at mine and again on that mattress before he hauled it to the trash when the new chairs arrived), the night he came to fetch me for the S.E.C.R.E.T. event at Latrobe's was, technically, our first date ever.

The weeks leading up to that fateful night were the happiest in my life. There was no more hiding, no sneaking around. With Tracina away from the restaurant and off building a new life, we were free to start ours, turning the restaurant into our discreet proving ground, a kiss here, an open embrace there, a hot look around every corner. And I didn't care that Dell rolled her eyes or Claire was a little confused, too young to be a confidante but old enough to know some "heavy adult shit just went down," as I caught her saying to her friends over smokes in the back.

After he said yes to my invitation, I took Will to the Funky Monkey to buy his first tux and to see Dauphine, so radiant with newfound love herself that it was like looking in a mirror. We kept our overwhelming joy at seeing each other to a normal level in front of Will, saying only that our acquaintance was the result of membership in this women's group whose formal event we were both attending.

He stood in front of a mirror in the changing area, handsome in his tux, as Dauphine pinned the hem of his pants.

"I'm glad I kept this one," she said. "It's too big for Mark. Though I have a feeling even getting that boy in a tux that fits him will be a lot harder than I expect."

A week later, the night of the event, after a clumsy attempt to assemble the damn bow tie, Will asked why I'd never mentioned I belonged to this charitable organization, especially one flush enough to give away fifteen million dollars.

"Because, it's a secret. It's sort of part of the whole schtick, the anonymity, the quiet servitude, that sort of thing. But you've seen me with Matilda a thousand times. I wasn't hiding anything."

Oh my god, was I becoming a liar? Or more comfortable with the truth? It was becoming difficult to tell the difference.

"But now this group wants the whole city to know it's giving away millions?"

It was a question I had put to Matilda too, but she said in her experience it was best to hide in plain sight. A donation that big, to that many organizations would hardly remain anonymous, so why not openly celebrate it? And

S.E.C.R.E.T., under its other name, desperately needed the tax deduction to keep afloat a little longer.

"If you don't want anyone to know about your underground group dedicated to female sexual fulfillment and exploration," she said, "house it in a mansion in the middle of the city. Why? Because no one would believe you even if you told them the truth."

Absently fastening my charm bracelet to my wrist, forgoing his assistance, I suddenly felt nervous to bring Will to such a strange event. But I trusted the women, especially Matilda, not to blow my secret. Also, it was the last bit of solidarity I could show, before leaving S.E.C.R.E.T., for these women who'd done so much for me and asked for so little in return. I even bought a beautiful black dress for the occasion, a long backless, strappy number, in luscious sateen.

I backed out of my bedroom wearing it, so Will could pull up the zipper—a bad idea. No sooner had he secured his fingers to the clasp than the damn thing was around my ankles and I was being carried, naked again, kicking and screaming to my bed. "Pick up the dress, don't leave it on the floor like that, Will! It'll wrinkle! That cost me a fortune!" I laughed as he collapsed on top of me, telling me, "Fuck that dress," while bunching his own beautifully tailored tuxedo pants down around his ankles, sheathing himself, then entering me sharply enough to stop the giggling altogether. God, the look in his eyes that night, burning and fierce while he drove into me again and again, my head cradled in his strong hands; I never wanted to lose that gaze.

Yet I was also looking forward to a time when just being alone with him *didn't* make me want to rip my clothes off. I actually longed in some strange way to be a little bored by all this, for a time when his skin brushing mine in the Café *wouldn't* make me damp with desire.

It was love, yes, but it was more than that. He was my deepest, closest friend. I felt like he was the only person on the planet (besides Matilda) who really, truly knew me. And now, moving on top of me with the grace of a man who understood my body as well as his own, searching my face, almost studying it, smoothing my hair back and thrusting, thrusting, my nails digging into his skin, his eyes closing, I couldn't imagine being with anyone else. I couldn't remember other men. He pressed my knees back and up, pushing both our limits, mine of exquisite pain, his of pleasure, his body clenched and straining, on the verge of another orgasm that *I* was giving him, while I tightened and writhed beneath him, finding my perfect spot, until, pleasure undulating through us and over us, we finally brought each other over the edge, calling each other's name, both our bodies a greedy blur, and we were left gasping and laughing—because that's what you do when you're utterly astonished by love.

"Holy hell, Cassie," he said, lying beside me, clasping my hand until his breathing steadied.

I rose to take a quick shower, but he held my hand down into the bed, rolling up on an elbow next to me.

"You know what? It's all been worth it."

"What's been worth it?"

"All the bullshit of the past year, all that stuff, the lies that kept us apart. It's been worth it. A few weeks ago I was so fucking angry. I said to myself *no more women.* I wanted nothing to do with love. I was going to take a good long break. And today, now . . . now I feel like I'm out of some long tunnel. I feel light. I feel brand-new. Like my faith's been restored."

"Me too," I said, pulling his face in for a kiss.

He fondled my bracelet. "I haven't seen this on you in a while."

"I wear it only on special occasions," I said, letting him examine it, knowing there was nothing to hide anymore.

"So let me get this straight—for every sort of good deed or challenge, or whatever, you get one of these charms?" he asked, reading some of the Steps under his breath, *Generosity, Bravery, Trust.* "Reminds me of Girl Scouts."

"Ha. Sort of," I said, sliding out of bed.

"What kind of charm do you get for having a restaurant named after you?"

"What do you mean?" I asked.

"I've decided to call the new place Cassie's. A sign's going to be delivered tomorrow—and here," he said, fishing a piece of paper from his jacket, which he'd retrieved from the floor where it was tossed with the rest of our clothes. He presented me with a folded-up prototype of the new menu, *Cassie's* printed on a pretty scroll across the top. I gasped, speechless.

"Are you serious?"

"Never more so," he said, kissing me.

"I don't . . . I can't . . . no one has ever . . ."

"Cassie, just say thank you. And let's get dressed and get this event over with."

"I'm not going to say thank you now. I'm going to say thank you later, when I get you back here alone."

"So I take it we're not staying late?"

"Hell no."

We showered, one after the other as my tub was too small for two, and later as he zipped me tenderly into my dress. I felt blessed, and, dare I say it . . . very loved. Had I known it would be the last time we'd be together, I would never have left that bed or that apartment, and I certainly wouldn't have washed him off my body so quickly, before slipping back into that beautiful, cursed dress.

Latrobe's was an intimate corner building, made of cream stucco, tucked in the heart of the French Quarter. With its curved Moorish ceilings and dim interiors, it was the perfect place to hold a private party or a small elegant wedding, something discreet and un-showy. So it was unusual to see a boisterous crowd of reporters lining the entrance. But fifteen million dollars was going to be donated to at least eight different local charities that worked to help women and children who were abused, hungry, neglected or who were in any other way disadvantaged. It was the kind of money that could change lives. So it was a big deal, deserving of big coverage.

Matilda was handling all the press, all the questions and all the follow-up. We were told to relax, mingle and eat. A Committee meeting was struck for the following day. That's when we'd find out how much money was left in the S.E.C.R.E.T. coffers. That's also when I planned to formally resign, but not before profusely thanking each and every one them for my good fortune and my lovely life.

We ducked past a throng with clacking cameras and into the narrow foyer that led to the main dining area. The room was filled with the highest echelons of New Orleans society, including, much to our shock, a very solo and newly re-elected District Attorney Carruthers Johnstone, mopping his brow and greeting guests in a too-snug tux, his PR person hovering close by, fielding questions.

"Are you going to be okay with him here?" I asked, pulling Will away from the greeting line, avoiding Carruthers. It had been almost a month, and while I'd been several times to see the sweet baby, and a very humbled Tracina, Will still felt like a chump. He still harbored some ill feelings I hoped would fade soon so Tracina could freely bring the baby to the café she was named after.

Eyeing Carruthers, Will said, "It's okay. Mostly I feel sorry for the poor bastard. He has to take on all that crying and screaming . . . *and* a new baby on top of it all."

News of Carruthers' dalliance had come too late to affect his re-election, but its consequences were trickling in. There were a lot of questions, of course, most of which he was avoiding while his wife moved his things out of their mansion in the Garden District and into a lovely cottage on Exposition Boulevard, facing Audubon, where he and Tracina could raise the baby in relative privacy until the worst of the scandal blew over.

City councilwoman Kay Ladoucer was also there. She had chaired last year's Revitalization Ball, and tonight she was behaving like a queen bee, greeting guests and posing for pictures, even though this was Matilda's event. Will made a point of saying hello to her, knowing his final building inspection was soon, after which, assuming he'd pass with flying colors, the only things stopping us from opening Cassie's (*Cassie's!*) were securing the liquor license and cutting the ribbon. Kay had blocked every attempt he'd made in the past to expand upstairs, citing too much growth on Frenchmen Street. So he was taking no chances now, and even went so far as to compliment her hair and her dress, feeling my elbow in his side when he started in on her shoes.

We gathered with Dauphine and Mark for a minute, she in a stunning jet blue off-the-shoulder cocktail dress, her hair a Veronica Lake tribute; he in a tux, with jeans, of course, both wearing dopey grins, a match made in heaven if there ever was one.

"Cassie! So fucking good to see you," Mark said, throwing his arms around me and lifting me off the ground. In my ear, he whispered, "I owe you big-time."

I had long reassured Will of my "friends only" status with the "skinny boy" who had stopped into the Café that day to invite me to hear him play. And I think he believed me. But Mark's enthusiastic greeting had Will instinctually putting a warm hand on my back.

"You look gorgeous, Cassie," said Dauphine, leaning towards me and out of Will's earshot. "And promise me you'll come by the store more often. This isn't goodbye. You changed my life."

"And you two better be regulars in *my* restaurant," I said, announcing its new name. Will looked as chuffed as I felt. "Congratulations," they both said. And after Mark promised to hold court in the corner with a guitar on opening night, they left to navigate the crowd back to the bar. I turned to slide my arms through Will's jacket, wending them behind his back in an embrace.

"You have nothing to worry about," I said, looking up at him, my chin on his chest.

"What? I know that," he said, moving a strand of stray hair behind my ear.

"I never thought you were the jealous type, Will."

"I'm not. I'm just . . . I guess I'm a little sensitive these days. I'll get over it. And soon, I'll start taking you completely for granted."

"I'm looking forward to that," I said, kind of meaning it.

The evening was unfolding so beautifully. Even after Angela Rejean strolled by in a criminally short silver mini-dress that tilted the attention of the entire room in her direction, including Will's. Her legs had me spellbound, so much so, I didn't notice the light hand on my shoulder. I assumed it was Will again, his touch becoming such a lovely constant, I almost noticed it more when he didn't have a hand on me.

"Cassie Robichaud, how nice it is to see you again. And looking ravishing in black satin."

I turned around and there he was, Pierre Castille, holding a glass of red wine, his frustratingly handsome face lighting up when I met his gaze. With his free hand he clasped an upper arm to kiss my two cheeks, my skin beneath his touch becoming goose-fleshed and chilled. He'd been drinking. Quite a bit. *Oh God, what is he doing here?*

"Hello, Pierre," I said, my voice faltering. I looked around for Dauphine, suddenly worried for her.

"And that dress. Oh, and if it isn't my old childhood pal, Will Foret. Seeing you in a tux—now that's worth the price of admission!"

"Pierre, I see you're still always happy to attend the opening of any old envelope," Will said, giving me a *what the fuck is he doing here?* kind of look.

I shrugged, looking around frantically for Matilda.

"I could hardly miss tonight, Will, my man. After all, it is—or rather *was* my fifteen million that this organization is giving away."

Will turned to me. "*His* money?"

"But what can you do?" Pierre continued, doing his best to camouflage a slight slur. "You try to support causes you care about and sometimes they just don't want your help. Women! Am I *right*? A man can only deal with so much bullshit from them . . . Speaking of which, here's our lovely Matilda Greene now."

Thank God, I thought, as Matilda stiffly approached us.

"Mr. Castille, what a *surprise* to see you here," she said. Her voice was steady, but I knew her; I could tell by the way she fussed with her charms that this was throwing her for a loop. Sweat broke out across my brow.

"I bet it is. I can only assume my invitation was lost in the mail. I don't think, considering my *passionate* patronage of S.E.C.R.E.T., that you'd have deliberately left my name off the guest list."

"You're kind to forgive the oversight," she said, wincing at the smell of his breath when he leaned close to kiss her cheek.

She turned to Will. "And it is so nice to see you again, Will. And Cassie . . . why I hope you don't mind my saying, but you do look a little flushed. Forgive me, but you might have the same thing Dauphine has. Poor thing just left. I hope it wasn't the shrimp."

Matilda's face was imploring, her words sounding as though she were pressing them into firm clay. She placed her hand on my forehead.

"In fact, you're quite clammy. I wouldn't blame you one bit if you wanted to duck out of this shindig a little early too, before all the boring speeches. I know how much you hate these things."

That's what she said instead of *Pierre's here to do damage, serious damage, not just to S.E.C.R.E.T., but to you. Leave now. Take Will.*

"Are you okay?" Will asked, picking up on Matilda's concern. "If you're not feeling well we can—"

"Yes, let's. I am a little—"

"Thirsty?" Pierre said, grabbing a glass of ice water from a passing waiter's tray and handing it to me. "If you leave now, you'll miss the best part, Cassie. And I know you," he said, poking Will in the chest, "*you* will be very interested in how the night unfolds. No more secrets. No more lies. They're so toxic, wouldn't you say, Will?"

"What the fuck are you talking about, Pierre?"

But before I had a chance to say, *Will, please take me home now before you hear something that might kill you, kill us,* Pierre drained his wineglass and deposited it on another passing tray.

"What am I *talking* about? I'm talking about the sexy little group these ladies belong to. Has Cassie told you how it's financed? They sell off paintings. Valuable ones. I bought one recently for fifteen million dollars. But turns out they don't want my money. And I'm not giving them the painting back. So they're donating all of it. So generous. So magnanimous. So *sanctimonious.*"

"Pierre, you've said enough," Matilda said, trying to signal Security. We were a small group, just Matilda, Will, Pierre and me, but ears around us were pricking up, and not those belonging to members of S.E.C.R.E.T.

"And they *need* the money. Sex fantasies are not cheap, Will. Especially when they come with little prizes in little boxes," he said, snatching my wrist and holding my bracelet up in front of Will's face. "Did Cassie ever tell you how she earned these charms? Or where? Wasn't this one with *me*, in the back of my limo?"

His fingers were roughly digging through my charms, trying to find the one he was talking about. I wrenched free of his grip.

"Get your fucking hands off her," Will hissed.

"Will, let's just get out of here," I said, my whole body now pressing him away from our little circle, this awful place. He must have felt it, me vibrating with anger and fear.

Matilda tried to calm Pierre, to shut him up, as though there was time to rescue the evening, as though the damage hadn't already been done. But Will's eyes were wild with confusion. Angela and Kit sidled over, using their bodies as shields to prevent onlookers from watching the drama, to keep more details from leaking beyond our group into the party at large.

"Sometimes at events like this, Pierre," Matilda said, grabbing his elbow, "when the drinks flow more freely than the food, we say things we don't mean, and we hurt people terribly, people who don't deserve it."

"And sometimes, Matilda, we tell the truth," he spat, releasing his arm. Turning to Will, he said, "I hear the truth's been in short supply in your life lately, buddy. Heard about old Carruthers and your little girlfriend, or rather, ex-girlfriend. Again my money backed the *wrong* candidate. Family values my ass. Not that you suffered for long. Must have been the happiest day of your life, Cassie, when you found out that his ex was a bigger slut than even *you*."

Wham came the punch, which sailed over my shoulder, landing hard, then sealed with a good kick to his ribs even before Pierre hit the ground. Will's arm was cocked, loaded, about to launch, or so I thought. But when I got over my shock, I realized I wasn't looking at the back of Will's tux standing over Pierre's writhing body, but rather chef whites belonging to Jesse Turnbull.

Time seemed to stop in that instant, allowing me to feel for a brief second like an observer, hovering eerily over the events, watching Angela and Kit holding Will back from completing the job that Jesse had started, seeing two burly bodyguards scoop up a bleeding Pierre, still yelling, despite the blood and the missing front tooth, "Just *ask* her, Will! Ask how she got those charms, how all of them did!" "Asked" sounded more like "asstht," something that would have been funny, might one day, in some faraway future, *still* be funny, to other people unaffected by his drunken tirade. Even after he shook his arms free of the security guards, Pierre wouldn't stop.

"Because they just use men, Will, they use them for their pleasure and then throw them away and she'll do that to you too, buddy! So goodbye, whores," he said, giving a flaccid salute, before getting hustled out the door and thrown into the back of his own waiting limo.

Everyone heard that, heard a drunken Pierre Castille sounding more like a jealous ex than a bitter man rejected by a group of women he now deeply resented. So beyond some whispers and stares, the party instantly recognized the sight, then healed over when the limo drove away and returned to their drinking and hors d'oeuvres. I silently thanked Jesse with teary eyes, then took hold of Will's lapels, pushing him gently away from the crowd, down a dim hallway leading to the washrooms. There I pressed him up against the wall, holding him upright with my forehead in the middle of his chest for a second, where I left a little prayer, something to help him better listen while I desperately tried to explain things.

He was breathless.

"I'm very confused, Cassie," he said, his voice up an octave. "I'm *confused* by some of the things that were just said by that asshole. Can you . . . enlighten me?"

"I don't know. I think, I guess . . . Pierre wants to ruin us."

"Ruin who?"

"Ruin S.E.C.R.E.T., our organization, me, us."

"Why? What does he fucking *care?*"

"Because . . . I rejected him. *We* rejected him."

Will laughed, genuinely laughed.

"Sorry. Let me get this straight. You rejected the richest man in the city, so he bought a *fifteen-million*-dollar painting from your . . . *group*. But you don't want the money because he's a bad man. So he's mad and called you sluts and whores—"

"I know it sounds like a ludicrous story."

"Not ludicrous, just *incomplete*," he said. "You know, Tracina once said Angela and Kit did some freaky-deaky things in some mansion in the Garden District. Those were her words—*freaky-deaky*. I never pressed her because we'd been out and she was drinking. And I never thought it was any of my business. But tonight I see that Kit and Angela and you all belong to this same little group, this S.E.C.R.E.T. thing. Is that what Tracina was talking about?"

Tears that felt like shame started streaming down my cheeks. Why? I had done nothing wrong. But there it was in Will's eyes: disgust.

"Will, don't look at me like that."

"Tell me, Cassie? Because I'm telling you this: one more fucking lie, one more secret, and I *will* snap directly in half. Yes or no. Do you belong to some kind of . . . sex group?"

Mortification set in, starting at my feet and inching up my body. I hadn't lied to him. I had only shaded away parts of the truth that weren't his to know, or that were beyond my ability to explain to him. In that moment I made a decision. If Will couldn't accept the whole of S.E.C.R.E.T., what it did for me, how it brought me back to me, then it was better I know that now. I opened and closed my fists, pulling in the courage to tell the truth. I grabbed his hand and looked into his dark blue eyes, now churning with bewilderment.

"Will you promise to listen?"

"All ears, baby. I'm all ears."

"Well . . . I have told you the truth. S.E.C.R.E.T. *is* a group that helps women. That part is true. But it helps them . . . sexually . . . by granting them a series of sexual fantasies, the kind that help them develop things like courage and trust and . . . confidence. Things I always lacked," I said. His face remained still, but I could tell his brain couldn't process the information fast enough.

"Throughout the year, I experienced several . . . scenarios. I felt terrified, I felt overjoyed. I was lost and I was found. And by the end of it, I was a different person, but the same too, just stronger, more myself. Even *you* said last year when we first slept together that I seemed different, yet very much the same. That was it exactly. That's what S.E.C.R.E.T. gave me."

I paused, waiting for him to chime in, waiting for him to say something, anything, but his face remained as implacable as an Easter Island statue.

"So after my fantasies, I was offered an opportunity to stay in the group and help other women, or I was free to leave if I wanted to pursue something else, something real. After I was with you, I chose to leave S.E.C.R.E.T. Until I found out about the baby and you returning to Tracina. I was bereft. Belonging to S.E.C.R.E.T. offered me solace, distraction, a sense of purpose. Then when the truth came out about the baby's father, I decided it was time to leave S.E.C.R.E.T. Because I could finally be with you."

I hoped my words would fill him with some measure of understanding, but they seemed to have taken the light right out of his eyes.

"So . . ." he said, blinking hard. "Let me get this straight. You joined a secret sex group. You had sex fantasies with . . . how many men last year?"

I took a deep breath. "Nine. Including you."

"Including me. And how many *this* year? Do you, like, try to double that number? Is that how it works?"

"No, there's so much more to it than that. It's not about numbers. You're making it sound—"

"How many men? Do you get a little charm for each guy? Is that how it works? *Collect all ten?*"

I slid my bracelet, my beautiful bracelet, behind my back, catching it on my black satin dress, which minutes ago had felt so sexy against my skin and now felt skimpy, wanton. I heard a voice down the hall, one tinged with kindness.

"Are you okay, Cassie?"

At the end of the dim hall, I made out Jesse's silhouette. He stepped closer to us and into the light.

"Oh hey!" said Will. "It's coffee guy with the excellent left hook! Which one was he, Cassie? Was he from this year's roster or was he last year's model? Did you two swing from chandeliers? Something tells me no. Ropes and chains, I bet."

"Will, *stop* it."

"Or maybe you're into having *him* spank you."

"Will!"

"Hey, listen, man," Jesse said, his hands raised in surrender. "I didn't mean to interrupt a personal discussion. I'm just a friend coming to see if she's all right."

"I bet you did. Cassie, you interested in going home with your fantasy friend here, or plain old me?" His voice cracked. "A guy who never fucking knows when he's being played for a complete chump."

He gave his head a vigorous shake and shoved his hair back in the way he does when words need his hands' help to come out.

"Will, I'm sorry you heard about it like this. And I know this is a lot to process, but here's the truth that matters most: I love you. And I'm sorry I never told you everything before, but I was worried you'd react like this," I said, realizing I was probably hurting Jesse in the process of trying to comfort Will.

"Know what? Before I say something I regret or that I don't mean, I'm out of here. Because this . . . *this* is all a bit too *freaky-deaky* for me. I'm just a regular guy, who likes sex with regular women, nothing too weird or out there. No big group thing. Sorry to disappoint, Cassie, but it's probably best I tell you now that I'd bore the shit out of you. So I'd prefer it if we keep things strictly professional between us from now on, okay? That way what you do after hours is your own fucking business. Because me? I have had *enough* bedroom drama to last me a fucking lifetime. So, enjoy yourselves. Enjoy each other, for all I care."

"Will!" I yelled as he walked away, Jesse gently holding me back from chasing him.

"It might not be the best time to reason with him, Cassie. Might wanna let him sleep on this."

I flung my back against the wall, unable to look Jesse in the eye.

"He'll see it differently after a few days, Cassie. Just give him a bit of time," he said.

"What are you doing here, anyway?" I asked.

"The event was last-minute. Matilda needed a caterer."

"I didn't mean . . . of course you're here. Thank *God* you were here. Way to give it to Pierre," I said. Then it came, a cascade of tears. "I'm so sorry, Jesse. I am so sorry."

"Hey, hey, hey. You don't need to say sorry to me, Cass. You've never lied to me," he said, pulling me in for a tight embrace while I briefly, quietly, cried into the front of his chef whites.

After I stopped shuddering, he handed me a cloth napkin that was dangling from his pocket.

"Here. Let's get you the fuck out of here."

And that's what he did. He carefully walked me through the main hall; the party was loud, in full effect. It was as though no lives had been ruined, no love lost, no secrets revealed. Matilda was in conversation with a local news anchor, her eyes locking on me as I passed. She reached out a hand, excused herself and came to me.

"Cassie," she said, gently tugging me by the forearm to speak directly into my ear. "It will be okay. I promise you."

"No, it won't, Matilda. I'll call you tomorrow," I said, my tone flat, my expression deadened.

She looked from me to Jesse. "Take good care of her."

He nodded, his hand at my back, my own arms wrapped around my body like I was one big wound. Jesse held the door open for me and we were both hit with the first fall chill of the year. Silently, we walked down Royal to Saint Louis, where his truck was parked halfway up the block.

My body, drained of all emotion, felt like flesh pressed against bone beneath a dress I couldn't wait to rip off and burn. *Will knew my secret and he didn't want me anymore.* I could hardly take the new job at the new restaurant named after me. How would we cope, him knowing what he knew, me feeling how I felt?

Jesse and I didn't say a word to each other as he drove the narrow streets of the French Quarter, drunk tourists tumbling in front of our slow-moving truck. We crossed Esplanade and Elysian Fields and pulled up next to the Spinster Hotel on the corner of Mandeville and Chartres, where the Delmonte sisters were still up, no doubt, watching and waiting for me to come home. Would they notice that the man dropping me off was different from the one with whom I had left? And indeed, what did this say about me? It said nothing, I decided. It said that I had accepted help when I needed it the most, and in doing so changed my life. I forged real bonds, including with men, and definitely with the one sitting next to me now, looking at me with soft eyes.

"Here you are. Want me to come up? Make you a cup of tea? Tuck you in? I promise that's all I'll do. I know where your head's at."

I wanted to say, *Yeah, it's where my heart is, with a very hurt man who left me feeling broken and dirty.* A man I loved who I thought loved me, unconditionally. But I was wrong. Of course there were conditions. There are always conditions when it comes to men and women and love and sex. But if for Will to love me like he once did, I'd have to be like the old me, then Will could keep his love. I would never again go back to being that tiny, chaste, timid woman. Never.

I looked at Jesse's face, his eyes mellow in the dark of the truck's cab.

"Well? What say you, Miss Robichaud?"

That's when I felt it; it started behind my belly button and worked its way up, settling around my heart: *defiance,* the necessary kind, the kind that pushed back on whatever judgment I'd seen in Will's eyes, a look that had made me feel undesirable, unworthy of love. That wasn't coming from him; that feeling was in me already, and it was time, time to let all of that go: *No more judgment, no more limits and no more shame, Cassie.* Starting now.

I turned to Jesse. I turned to face the man who knew my darkest parts, my fears and desires, and wasn't turning away.

"Actually, I would like it if you came up, Jesse. I've had a hell of a night . . . and I think I could really use a friend tonight."

He wet his thumb with his tongue and rubbed stray mascara off my cheek.

"Then use me, darlin'," he said. "Use me."

ACKNOWLEDGMENTS

I have several "Committees" to thank, both personal and professional, who've help carry my S.E.C.R.E.T.: Susan Gabriele, Lisa LaBorde, Jenn Goodwin, Julietta McGovern, Sarah Durning, Debra Thier, Charlene Donovan, Arlene Dickinson, Vanessa Campion, John Campion, Lee-Anne McAlear, Jim Harris, Meredith Oke, Arwen Humphreys, Joanne Morra, Katrina Onstad, Becki Rose, Steve Erwin, Natasha Stoynoff and the rest of my wonderful family.

Random House and Doubleday Canada: Kristin Cochrane, Brad Martin, Adria Iwasutiak, Cassandra Sadek, Zoë Maslow, the speedy, talented Scott Richardson, and especially Nita Pronovost, the brains behind this whole operation.

My gals at Gowlings: Susan Abramovitch and Shelagh Carnegie.

Random House US: Alexis Washam, Molly Stern, Dyana Messina, Danielle Crabtree, Julie Cepler, Sheila O'Shea and Gregg Sullivan.

Everyone at Fletcher and Company NYC: Melissa Chinchillo, Kevin Cotter, Mink Choi, Rachel Crawford, Grainne Fox, and of course, my marvelous agent Christy Fletcher.

Much love and thanks to all the publishers and readers around the world (what writer doesn't want to write that sentence?) for embracing S.E.C.R.E.T. and making it your own.

S·E·C·R·E·T
SHARED

ABOUT THE BOOK

One year ago, Cassie Robichaud joined S.E.C.R.E.T.—the sexual sisterhood dedicated to fulfilling erotic fantasies for one lucky woman at a time. Now that she has completed her ten steps, Cassie puts her newfound expertise to work as guide to Dauphine Mason, S.E.C.R.E.T.'s latest recruit. The two women come from different worlds, but both know the feeling of being shackled by old wounds: Northern-born Cassie, heartbroken from a failed marriage, endured a years-long sexual dry spell before she earned her S.E.C.R.E.T. charms; Southern girl Dauphine, still reeling from a painful betrayal eight years ago, dresses her customers beautifully and watches her favorite bands from the crowd, but lacks the confidence to join the party herself. Like Cassie a year before, Dauphine craves the courage to come out of her shell—and the women of S.E.C.R.E.T. are ready to show her the way. Sex and sensuality are at the heart of S.E.C.R.E.T.'s work, but as the fantasies are fulfilled, the women also see their whole lives changed. Dauphine is finally able to make strides she never thought possible as she begins to leave the past behind. But as Cassie is learning, the kick-start that S.E.C.R.E.T. provides is only the beginning: each woman now faces choices that only she can make as she learns to live fully in her body, mind and heart.

1. Cassie Robichaud and Dauphine Mason were both hurt by the men from their past. Both women isolate as a result. By partaking in S.E.C.R.E.T., how does Dauphine successfully leave those memories behind? How did Cassie? How does Dauphine's journey differ from Cassie's? How are they similar?

2. When Dauphine Mason is on the shore of the Abita River for her first fantasy, she is nervous, self-conscious and frozen, but she tells herself: *"Stop thinking. Act,"* and takes the plunge as she accepts her first Step. What are some other examples throughout the book where Dauphine stops thinking and acts? What results does she get? Have you ever had to "shake yourself free" this way?

3. If you were a member of S.E.C.R.E.T., would you want to be a guide, recruiter or fantasy facilitator? Cassie experiments with all three roles—which do you think suits her best?

4. "You did it. You gave up control." For Dauphine, her journey in S.E.C.R.E.T. is a path leading her from a life ruled by control to one where she is finally able to let go. With each Step, she lets go of the familiar, routine and isolated life to which she finds herself increasingly clinging. What kinds of things do you control that you could benefit from letting go of? What steps have you taken to give up that control? What would freedom from those habits look like?

5. What did you think of Matilda's recruiting methods? How was she able to spot a willing and able recruit in Dominic? Where would you go to spot a recruit? And what is the answer to Cassie's question: how did Matilda "get the hottest guy in the park" to come to her?

6. As Cassie reflects on her relationship with Will, she marvels at the notion that she had known him for so many years, yet never allowed herself to see him as a potential lover until she was transformed by S.E.C.R.E.T. What other unseen gifts does she uncover? What are the gifts in your life that you might not be noticing?

7. After Luke leaves Dauphine and writes his bestselling book, humiliating her, how does Dauphine continue to give him power? When Dauphine meets Mark, how is that relationship different from her relationship with Luke?

8. Cassie's experience with S.E.C.R.E.T. was successful in transforming her from someone withdrawn and timid to a confident, self-realized woman of action. But with Will, she feels stuck, unable to be with him. Matilda advises Cassie to get on with the business of life—not to let heartbreak get in the way of practical concerns. "Don't give men that much power, Cassie. Get on with the task of living." Do you agree with this advice?

9. "I always went with the most powerful force governing my life at the time," says Dauphine. What are the powerful forces governing Dauphine's life when we first meet her? How do they affect her life? By the end of the book, how have those forces shifted?

10. The first time Dauphine sees Cassie at Ignatius's, Cassie gets Mark Drury's phone number with an ease and confidence that impresses both of them. Have you ever seen a similar example in your life, when someone pulled something off that you couldn't dream of doing? When Cassie then visits Dauphine at the Funky Monkey, how does she establish trust?

11. Before Dauphine decides to tell Cassie that she is interested in pursuing S.E.C.R.E.T., she asks her why she thinks fulfilling wild sex fantasies will fix everything. Cassie explains that it won't fix everything but that it will create a "cascade effect" in her life. Do you agree that this is how change can occur? Is there any one thing you would like to change that might create a similar effect in your own life?

12. When Dauphine meets the S.E.C.R.E.T. committee at the Mansion, she makes a list of rules for herself from which she won't budge: no flying, no lights on, nothing to do with beaches and no water. She breaks every one of her rules. What rules would you have if you were to take the S.E.C.R.E.T. Steps? Which ones might you consider breaking under the right circumstances?

13. What surprised you about Dauphine handing her completely empty fantasy folder over to the Committee, telling them, "surprise me"?

14. Cassie has Mark's phone number yet she hesitates to call him. What holds her back? Do you think there remains a general perception that women shouldn't call men? Why? Or why not?

15. Both Cassie and Dauphine hesitate before joining S.E.C.R.E.T. But Mark's reaction to being recruited into S.E.C.R.E.T. is different. According to Cassie it "required no preamble . . . no psychic obstacles, [or] social conditioning to fight against; [it] didn't cause him to question everything he was taught about his role in society or his sexuality." Do you think when it comes to men, women and sex, that there is still a double standard?

16. During Mark's training with Angela, Matilda explains that making a woman feel desirable is the greatest aphrodisiac. Is that true for you? Angela instructs Mark to smolder, not smile, to take his time but not to be too deliberate and to maintain eye contact. Would you find this sexy? Are there are behaviors you would like a partner to exhibit to make you feel desirable? What do you make of Mark's training session? What would you have done differently? What did you agree with?

17. In Buenos Aires, Dauphine trusts her instincts when she meets Pierre Castille and refuses to take the Step with him. What was it about him or that situation that made her feel unsafe? Do you have a reflex that allows you to protect yourself when you feel unsafe?

18. The theme of sexual rebirth is prevalent throughout the book. In addition to her fantasies, particularly the first one where she is submerged in a river, what are some other firsts in the book for Dauphine? What about Cassie?

19. Matilda says to Cassie: "The word 'slut,' unless employed by iron-clad feminists or ironically, by irony *experts*, has no business coming out of a woman's mouth." Talk about that word and its ramifications. Why do you think Matilda is so passionate about the word "slut"? Do you agree with her?

20. Beside hair color, age and general shape, L. Marie Adeline does not describe Cassie or Dauphine's physical appearances in very much detail, leaving much of what they look like up to the readers' imaginations. She also refrains from referring to them as beautiful or sexy though the men they're with often flatter them. Why do you think this is the case? How do you picture Cassie and Dauphine?

21. Dauphine and Cassie encounter many different men in the course of their S.E.C.R.E.T. journeys, including a police officer, a pilot, an athlete and a musician. Which one of these male archetypes would appeal to you the most, and why? Who is the sexiest character in the book? Why do you feel that way?

22. In the end, Will abandons Cassie after the revelations about her involvement in S.E.C.R.E.T. Do you understand why he felt he had to do this? Or do you think he was overwhelmed by this news so soon after Tracina's betrayal? What do you think they'll have to overcome to be together again?

23. At least for a while it looks like Cassie might pair up with Jesse again. Do they make a good pair? Do you think they reignite their passion at the end of the book? What are their chances for the long haul?

24. *No Judgments. No Limits. No Shame.* Over the course of the book, each tenet of S.E.C.R.E.T.'s motto is put to the test. Talk about the challenges the S.E.C.R.E.T. members face in upholding these values, and whether there are any times they fail to do so. What do you make of this motto in your life?